Matt Sikes Stared at the Spotted Baldness in the Mirror . . .

He had imagined it a hundred times. Seeing it, however, placed him on a new plane of reality. This was no disguise. It was him.

His eyebrows were gone. He touched them with the fingers of his right hand. They had been shaved and covered with a thin film of artificial skin. Then he ran his fingers across the top of his spots.

Looking at the front of his left thigh, he smacked it with his open hand and watched where his fingers had struck. No redness appeared, only a plain anemic pink.

Looking into the mirror again, he didn't feel he was a human disguised as a Newcomer. Instead, he felt like a Newcomer with some rather eccentric memories of being a human.

Alien Nation Titles

#1: The Day of Descent
#2: Dark Horizon
#3: Body and Soul
#4: The Change
#5: Slag Like Me

Published by POCKET BOOKS

#5 ALIEN NATION™

SLAG LIKE ME

A NOVEL BY BARRY B. LONGYEAR

POCKET BOOKS

New York   London   Toronto   Sydney   Tokyo   Singapore

This book is a work of fiction. Names, characters, places, and incidents are products of the author's imagination or are used fictitiously. Any resemblance to actual events or locales or persons, living or dead, is entirely coincidental.

An *Original* Publication of POCKET BOOKS

POCKET BOOKS, a division of Simon & Schuster Inc.
1230 Avenue of the Americas, New York, NY 10020

ISBN: 0-671-79514-7

First Pocket Books printing July 1994

10 9 8 7 6 5 4 3 2 1

POCKET BOOKS and colophon are registered trademarks of Simon & Schuster Inc.

Cover art by Dru Blair

Printed in the U.S.A.

A dira ih urvek den
In honor of the truly blind

—Ivo Lass, *Saverna nas Ria*

The real story is the universal one of men who destroy the souls and bodies of other men (and in the process destroy themselves) for reasons neither really understands. It is the story of the persecuted, the defrauded, the feared and detested. I could have been a Jew in Germany, a Mexican in a number of states, or a member of any "inferior" group. Only the details would have differed. The story would be the same.

—John Howard Griffin, *Black Like Me*

SLAG LIKE ME

The Invitation

As my next-door neighbor would be pleased to tell you, I'm not a very nice guy. Habitually I do things different from the norm simply because the norm is the norm. I'm the only one in step; I'm the one wearing sweats at the black-tie affair; I clap at the end of the first movement whether I like it or not. Telling me "It just isn't done," whatever it is, more often than not will compel me to do it.

To bring light into a dark room, for example, some folks unlock doors. Others want to clean windows. Still others simply choose to get used to the darkness. Me? I never did like the dark. Of course, sometimes I can't find the key for the lock, and I don't do windows. Accordingly, if a dirty window obscures my view, I throw a rock through it. When a locked door keeps things dark, I use a chain saw. If nothing else works, I drive a bulldozer through the wall.

"Why on earth," you might ask, "is this attitude in print throwing words at me?"

Why I'm here is very simple. I was asked. It went like this:

Your editor in chief, Martin Fell, and I were at a party in West Hollywood a few months ago. It was an incredibly dull affair (the same young alcoholics slurring the same old words), and Marty and I got to strolling down amnesia lane as he tried to set me up for a pitch (no one invites me to a party without an ulterior motive). Recalling the electric impact four decades ago of John Howard Griffin's book, Black Like Me, Martin wondered aloud if it would be possible to do a similar exposé on modern human racism against the Tencts (Tenctonese, Newcomers, or slags, depending on your ilk).

"What would it be like," Martin mulled, "for a human to go undercover as a Tenctonese? Blend into Newcomer society, become one of 'them'? How do 'they' really look at 'us'? How do 'we' really treat 'them'?"

"Tell me," I said to Martin, "when you go fishing, is it really true that you throw hand grenades into the water to concuss the fish to the surface?"

"I lack subtlety?" he asked.

"You are as graceful as an ostrich with a greased wastebasket on each foot attempting to carry a watermelon down a crowded-up escalator."

"No interest in it at all?" he whined.

"Incorrect. In fact it's something I've thought about for a long time. I've even accumulated a considerable body of research on it. In fact, I even went so far as to discuss my idea with a certain blabbermouth administrative assistant of yours named Julia Winslow. I think it's a fascinating idea originated by a brilliant intellect of towering proportions."

2

"Will you do it?"

"I'll do it, Marty, but there are three conditions."

"Oh?" His eyebrows arched.

"Don't pop your hair plugs. None of the conditions has anything to do with how much I get paid." The eyebrows lowered a notch. "We'll talk money later." The eyebrows went back up.

"What are the conditions?" he asked.

"First, I'll try it and see what it's like. I'm no superhero. If I want to quit, I back out, you pay for everything, and nothing goes into print. Is it a deal?"

He nodded. "Very well."

"When I said you pay for everything, it could be a high pile in exchange for squat."

"I understand. It's my risk, and unless we're talking over six figures, I'm willing to take it."

"That high it shouldn't get."

"We're in agreement so far." His eyebrows climbed a little higher. "The second condition?"

"No personal data about me is to appear in any bios. Not my age, sex, sexual preference, skin color, hair possession, shape, or color, eye shape, date or place of birth, diseases, previous publications, nationality, religious afflictions, or marital status. All the readers will know about me is that I am human and undercover as a Tenct. My byline will be a pseudonym. Agreed?"

The eyebrows plunged into a frown. "Part of what we're paying for is your name. With a pseudonym, our readers won't know you at all. And what about your readers? They won't be able to find you."

"You aren't paying me anything yet." I searched for a way to turn up a very dim bulb. "Look at it like this, Marty. If the readers knew what pigeonhole to stuff me in, in a flash I'd have half a dozen agendas I don't

3

ascribe to tacked on my ass. See, that's the point. You want me to cover human-Tenct relations and report it as it is, correct?"

"Mmmm."

"See, there's no point in giving peeks at racism through some kind of ethnic prism, real or imagined; the Latvian black gay midget biker's view of the Newcomer situation. My job is to bust windows, and the most successful window-busters are always anonymous."

"Tell it to Norman Schwarzkopf," he grumped. Then he fixed me with a gimlet eye and asked, "If you use a pseudonym, what will draw the readers?"

"You know how I write, Marty. Your readers will be trampling each other to read my column and call me names. After the third column appears, you can depend on a mob of torch-bearing villagers surrounding the Times, storming the walls, demanding my capture and incineration."

"This is a selling point?"

"I thought you were the one who was selling, Marty."

Grudgingly he nodded. "Okay. I understand." He looked glum for about fifteen seconds more, then said, "I'm not tranquil about it, but okay. The third condition?"

"If we decide to go ahead with the series, we go all the way. I mean all the way. We don't edit, cut, or slant copy to avoid offending city hall or some big advertiser, and we don't pull our punches to avoid offending the readers. If that crowd of lawyers the paper has on retainer gets nervous, that's tough. If the Times gets whittled down to only four readers and a half-inch ad for recycled condoms, I want those four readers still to be able to read my column the way I wrote it."

He gagged on that one. He squirmed, whined, promised, cried, cajoled, bribed, begged, and threatened the way editors do (it's an ethnic thing). Finally, after making a telephone call and communing with his other Higher Power, Martin Fell agreed. Whatever happens, short of death or the *Times* going out of business, the column "Slag Like Me" runs as it was written, warts, split infinitives, naughty words, and all.

I was a hungry piranha and "Slag Like Me" was my very own literary dead cow. I was impatient to arrange my passage into Newcomer society. I had no illusions that my experiment held a candle to Griffin's impersonation of a Negro in the segregated south of the late fifties. What he did took courage. What I planned to do only took an attitude.

The laws have changed since the fifties, and most visible racists have had to change their spots. From the accepted respectable majority of the past, overt "white" racists of today are considered part of the nut fringe. It is not fashionable. Overt "black" racists, as well as other ethnic militants, are declining in their acceptability, but covert racists of all stripes are where they've always been—in the majority and in charge.

It's very simple: the ideal of the American melting pot has broken down. Many so-called ethnic groups blended together and became "Americans." The "Anglos" are made up of persons of English, German, Irish, French, Basque, Spanish, Italian, and Middle East origins. If revisionist anthropology is to be believed, this mix includes an indigenous population (Indians, to you) made up of Phoenician, Egyptian, and Celtic, as well as native antecedents. But the pot never was hot enough to melt in the descendants of the slaves from Africa, the railroad workers from China, and others who simply looked different. The promise was always there, however. But then the pot cooled even further. The gravy became very lumpy, and each lump had a grievance against every other lump.

Into this hostile hypocrisy, hundreds of thousands of real live aliens from outer space crash in, and long before they're released from the quarantine camps, the wonder and novelty of this first contact wears off and "they" simply become another "them." The magical beings from other worlds we've dreamed about for generations turn out to be just another lump in the pot. And how does this particular soup smell? I was eager to take a sniff.

It took a couple of days before I was ready to try on my spots. The day began in Hollywood with a friend of mine in the business. My friend took about six hours and made me up with about twenty pounds of latex and paint. When I first looked into a mirror, a stranger looked back. There was a bizarre feeling in my chest, and when I pulled it into the light and looked at it, I felt my face grow warm.

I was afraid of that image in the mirror. It wasn't an alien. It wasn't a Tenct. It was me! Yet the shape, the color, the large head, the startling baldness, the spots, the image was on some level something I was tuned to fear, to regard as less than clean, not okay, inferior. It was right there in the pit of my being, this hard nut of racism.

Life is a series of self-discoveries. Once in a while we like what we find. Most times, however, the discovery points to something that needs work: cleaning, repair, or replacement. Too often we opt not to see what we have seen. The mental roof continues to leak, the psychological garbage ripens, and life takes on all of the ambience of a summer cesspool. If this was something that needed to be addressed within me, then let's do it, I told myself. I took another look into the mirror, decided I looked terrific, and took to the streets to try out my new appearance. The day ended in humiliation.

I have a knowledge of Tenctonese, as well as several other tongues. Because of my previous work, I knew quite a bit about Tenct customs, manners, history, and beliefs. To me my disguise was perfect, and it appeared to work very well among humans. Yet, not five minutes after I began strolling down Hollywood Boulevard, a rather striking Tenct prostitute stared at me for a moment, wrinkled her nose, and commented to her sister of the mattress, ["Nugah. Mea te've esk?"]

This translates, roughly, "A pervert. Sad, isn't he?"

Nugah, however, is a new kind of pervert; so new, in fact, that the word nugah came into being only within the past few years. It refers to a human who finds sexual gratification in impersonating a Tenct (sort of a slagvestite).

That wrapped it up for my first try. If I wanted to continue, it would be necessary to get some special help to eliminate whatever it was that marked me as human. My overwhelming curiosity to find out just what that thing was, was one of the things that caused me to continue with the project.

I did some research and picked the brains of several close friends. One of those friends has very special talents. My friend agreed to help me not impersonate a Tenct but to emerge as one. She also had a few ideas and she introduced me to those who could do the sculpting. It took a new kind of bloodless surgery, some high-tech gadgetry (close to half a million of Marty Fell's money), and about eleven weeks of training. At the end of the process I emerged a different being. The image in the mirror no longer frightened me because it was me. I took that walk on Hollywood Boulevard again and passed well enough to be roughed up by a couple of thugs and admitted to Mt. Andarko's Hospital, after a thorough examination, as a Tenct by a Tenctonese doctor. I was given Tenct hospital cuisine, and the crap they served was almost as bad as the meals at Beverly Glen on West Pico. Did you know it's possible to make a custard out of earthworms? It tastes sort of like curd of cream of mushroom soup. Not bad if you're into mortified insect flesh. In any event, the police arrived, and then came the real beginning of my education.

The police officer who took my statement, a human named Davenport (badge 12114), twice made references to "you slags" (no offense intended, of course) and pointed out there wasn't much that could be done about the muggers. They fade into the night, long gone, evidence all shucked, that's the way it goes. Anyway, what'd you expect on Hollywood Boulevard at that hour? Besides, with unemployment being what it is, broken homes, child abuse, unsatisfactory potty training, I really should try to be more understanding.

The upshot of the whole thing was that getting mugged was my fault and I probably shouldn't bother wasting everyone's time by filing a report. Strangely enough, Officer Davenport changed his mind once I told him that the muggers were Newcomers. Immediately he took a detailed statement and had a police artist at my bedside within two hours.

Listen up, Goober. I am your worst nightmare in bleeding Technicolor: a victim who refuses to be a victim armed with a poison pen, a compulsion to name names, and a statewide forum. Be careful how you treat that next rubberhead that walks into your office, your store, your squad room, or down your street. It might be someone whose job, and pleasure, it is to fight back. The only way to make the melting pot work, I am convinced, is more heat. That's what this column is, Goob. Heat.

CHAPTER  1

IT WAS THE kind of hot that drove normally well-balanced and serene persons to look for reasons to fight. On the sizzling streets of L.A. that morning, however, no one needed the assistance of the weather. Everyone was arguing about the newest editorial column in the *Times,* "Slag Like Me" by a mysterious columnist who wrote under the name Ellison Robb.

He was either devil or saint, enlightener or hell-raiser, peace-bringer or rabble-rouser, moral icon or pervert, depending on who was talking. No one was neutral. All those who had ever managed to hide for years from social conflict within cocoons of denial or indifference had been rather rudely yanked into the burning light of the discussion, thanks to the Robb column. They were fighting in the city council, the county board of supervisors, in the churches, the businesses, the homes, on the streets, and in the unit being driven by Detective Sergeant Matt Sikes.

"Matt," said his Tenctonese partner, George Francisco, "I see no reason for you to become so defensive about this Robb character!"

"If you attack, what else am I supposed to do? Roll over and say, 'Well, George, I guess I just made a foolish error'? Don't hold your breath waiting for that, partner."

"Damn it, Matt, I'm simply saying that 'Slag Like Me' is increasing problems for Newcomers, not lessening them. The anger level against Tencts is towering, thanks to the *Times*'s sensationalistic circulation-building ploy."

"Ploy? Ploy?"

"Yes. Ploy. Your hearing is excellent, every so often."

"Robb is out there risking his damned life to expose anti-Tenct racism, George, and all you can do is to call it a ploy?"

"What? You want gratitude? Matt, with his column he's set back human-Tenct relations twenty years."

"Give it a rest, George. Twenty years ago there weren't any human-Tenct relations."

"Exactly my point! Do you think there are any relations now? All Ellison Robb is doing is increasing the problems, and we have more than enough right now, thank you very much!"

"Increasing the problems? He's increasing the problems? Don't you mean calling a racist a racist? Jesus, George, what's the Tenct equivalent of an Uncle Tom or a Tio Taco? Don't make waves, don't confront racism, just grin and bear it and maybe someday it'll all just go away."

"You don't clear up muddy water by stirring it, Matt."

"Welcome to Fantasyland, George! What about

those slaghunts, buddy? They drive on by and just blow someone out of his socks because he's a Newcomer. How's that for muddy water? What about that little boy who was gunned down on Third? What about that woman who died at Grace emergency yesterday because she was Tenct and the physician on duty decided that the Hippocratic oath didn't cover her? Think maybe those puddles need a little stirring? What about that, George?"

"*Ubi Dugi.*"

"What?"

"*Ubi Dugi,*" George repeated. "The Tenct equivalent of an Uncle Tom—*Ubi Dugi.*"

"Aaargh!" Sikes bellowed and pounded his fist on the steering wheel.

"That is not an argument!" George countered.

"Then maybe *this* is an argument!" Sikes punched the roof of the car and bellowed more loudly. When he was finished, he grabbed the steering wheel and glared at the jammed traffic.

Punching the roof, thought Matt as he felt the ache in his knuckles. *Punching the roof is stupid.* He hadn't connected with the center of a panel. Instead he had hit a welded seam bent on right angles. The cheap upholstery covering the interior of the roof was nothing but one thin layer of cloth. He glanced at his knuckles and saw that they all had been scraped white. The skin had not been broken, but they hurt like root canal with a hangover.

Stupid. Hitting things to express anger at a person. Not as stupid as hitting the person, perhaps, but stupid all the same. But what else do you do with anger—rage? The pressure of maddening frustration that left no option save exploding at something. As a child he had taken to punching walls, trees, and dirt as an alternative to punching an abusive alcoholic father or a judgmental mother flying through life on pounds of prescription drugs.

At that Adult Children of Alcoholics meeting he had attended there had been a man called Benny. Benny had said something about praying for a hero when he was a child. Someone who would swoop in, punish those who had made him suffer, and then take him away. Matt Sikes had never prayed for a hero. He had never prayed for anything. He had always figured that a god who could allow the horror of his life to happen would not make a very reliable repairman. Not exactly Maytag.

There had been television and movies, however. Heroes who came onto the scene and did what needed to be done, laid waste to houses, buildings, cities, entire planets, to make wrong right. Red tape, custom, manners, the opinions of others, the law, rules and regulations, thoughts of personal safety, none of these could bound a Ripley, or the second Terminator, Connagher, Quigley . . .

He grimaced as a phrase from an old song drifted through the tangle of his mind, "someone to watch over me." Maybe that's what Ellison Robb was: the Anonymous Avenger, a nameless masked knight in newsprint seeking out evildoers and kicking ass big time. There was plenty of ass out there that needed kicking, too.

Matt glanced at his partner. A big piece of that ass was in the passenger seat. If the victims of abuse defend and shield the abusers, what hope can a little child have? What chance does anyone have? "George?"

"What?"

"Let me try this just one more time. You can't argue

with the fact that Ellison Robb is saying some things that need to be said."

George shrugged and turned his head to look out the window. "There are ways and there are ways."

"What's that supposed to mean?"

Francisco faced his partner. "You don't use a cannon to kill flies."

"If dead flies is what you're after, George, a cannon will do one hell of a job!"

George Francisco growled out a strangled bellow and pounded on the dashboard with his fists. "Look at what this Robb has driven me to!"

"At least we're communicating on the same level, George!"

Francisco strained against his seat belt as he turned toward his partner. "Is now when you call me slag, Matt? It's right on your tongue! I can see it!"

Matt heard a scream from outside the car and faced forward in time to see that he was headed directly toward two children, a man in a suit, and a bag lady crossing the street with the light. He jumped on the brake, stalled the unit, and felt his head slam into the backrest as the car following them slammed into the unit's rear bumper. Matt roared and punched the steering wheel.

CHAPTER 2

AFTER REACHING HOMICIDE, the division rather than the criminal condition, Matt and George maintained a mutual smoldering silence as they stormed to their desks. Sergeant Dobbs, seated at his desk, barked into his telephone, "Look, Kelly, I don't give a damn what you do with the old roofing, downspouts and rain gutters! Just get all that junk off my lawn! I want it done today, understand?" He listened for a moment, pulled the handset away from his head and stared into it as though the machine had lied to him. Again he shouted into the handset, "Kelly? You heard anything I've said? I'm a police officer, you understand? Maybe your business license is something that needs a little review—Hello? Hello?" He glowered and slammed down the handset. "Stupid lazy ignorant son of a bitch." Dobbs glanced up at Sikes and Francisco, caught one look at their faces, and leaned back in his chair. "I see our float for national brotherhood week is going to be late this year."

Francisco glared at him. "Stick it up your ass, Dobbs," said George, causing Dobbs's jaw to drop to his chest. The most even-tempered, least profane person on Earth had just told him to stick it up his ass. It was equivalent to Mr. Rogers grabbing his crotch and growling "Eat me!"

When Dobbs recovered sufficiently, he pointed toward Captain Grazer's office. "The man wants you both about twenty minutes ago."

George glanced at his watch and raised his gaze to glare at Matt. "I told you that shortcut of yours would make us late."

"How was I supposed to know that truck was blocking the alley?"

"One lane wide? In the middle of how many stores and markets? At morning rush hour? How many humans *does* it take to screw in a light bulb?"

Sikes turned on his heel and stormed toward Captain Grazer's office. Dobbs looked up at George and asked, "How many?"

"What?"

"How many humans does it take to screw in a light bulb?"

"Six billion and one." He shrugged and allowed a touch of embarrassment to lower his voice. "You know, one to hold the bulb and six billion to twist the planet." George grimaced. "Tenctonese humor, don'tcha know."

Dobbs pointed toward Grazer's office. "Watch your back in there, George. I don't know what's going on, but the cap's got a fed with him." He pointed toward his wrist and made a jagged motion with his finger. "Your old Overseer buddy?"

Francisco frowned, turned, and followed Sikes. By the time George finally entered the captain's office, he took up a position on the opposite side of the room from Sikes. Grazer, struggling through his fourth day without a cigar, was a lump of glower behind his desk. In a chair facing him was a slender human male in his late fifties, financially fashionable in muted charcoal stripes, wine-colored tie and vest. The suit, the tie, and the vest were wrinkled, and the man had a thin brush of white whiskers on his face. Sitting next to him was a face that George Francisco recognized from the Maanka Dak affair the year before. It was Paul Iniko, the Overseer who had become an agent for the FBI.

"You worked with Agent Iniko before," Grazer stated. Nodding toward the man in the rumpled suit, the captain said, "This is Martin Fell, editor in chief of the *Times.*" The captain glanced at Sikes and returned his gaze to George. "Do you two know about this columnist Ellison Robb?"

"Who doesn't?" George answered, his tone quite acid.

"Some of us better than others," added Sikes, his tone equally caustic.

"You two want to knock it off," snapped Grazer.

Martin Fell shook his head and held his hand up, the palm facing Grazer. "My own office is the same way, captain. In fact, I would venture to guess that every office within fifty miles of here is the same way. Ellison Robb was something of a social catalyst."

"A shitstorm at a white sale," muttered George.

"Was?" Matt asked Fell, ignoring his partner's comment. "You said he *was* something of a whatever. What's this about? What's happened?"

Fell nodded, his expression grave. "Perhaps my

17

verb tense is premature, but he's missed his last two delivery drops."

"Delivery drops?"

"We had a prearranged series of different locations where I could go unobserved to pick up his copy and leave messages during those periods when he wouldn't or couldn't come into his office. We haven't seen him for almost two weeks and he's missed his last two drops, yesterday's and today's. Perhaps I'm only projecting, but he told me that if he missed a drop, it's only because he's either dead, critically wounded, or under restraint."

Grazer dropped an expired piece of chewing gum into his wastebasket and said, "Possible kidnapping." He nodded toward Iniko. "That's why the fed."

"If he missed his drop yesterday," said Matt, "how come you waited until he missed another before you came to us?"

Fell raised his hands and then dropped them to his lap. "I needed to be sure. Mick walks in constant drama. He's given, if you prefer, to casting things in the most theatrical way possible."

George spoke first, "and you had to be certain this wasn't some kind of stunt Cass pulled to get a rise out of everybody."

"There were other reasons for my reluctance, as well." Fell seemed to stare into space for a moment, then continued. "I was concerned after he missed the first drop, but after the second was missed my concern moved to panic."

George thrust his hands into his pockets and leaned his back against a filing cabinet. "Forgive me, Mr. Fell, but couldn't this be just another little piece of sensationalism designed to get Cass a bit of publicity?"

Martin Fell's face flushed bright red. "The person we're talking about, officer, is the same person who once called Yassir Arafat a schmuck to his face. He doesn't need to stage a kidnapping to create interest."

"Micky Cass?" asked George, his eyebrow arched. "Do you mean that Ellison Robb is *that* Micky Cass?"

"Yes. You've read some of Mick's work?"

George nodded, folded his arms and held out a hand as though the revelation of Micky Cass's name explained everything. Cocking his head to one side, George said, "If something has happened, I'm not surprised. Something was bound to. The thing you mentioned just underscores my point. I mean the man went out of his way to anger as many persons per word as possible. The anger was mostly justified, and it was frequently entertaining, but having Cass write about racism is like sending in Rambo to conduct crisis control."

Paul Iniko studied George Francisco's face for a beat and then said, "Nevertheless, he or she is entitled to the same legal protection as any other citizen."

"He or she?" George repeated. Facing Fell he stated, "Micky Cass is male."

The editor in chief of the *Times* held up his hands in an eloquent shrug. "Probably. Possibly. I'm not sure."

"What do you mean, you're not sure?" demanded Grazer. "Didn't you hire him?"

Martin Fell lowered his hands to his lap and chuckled sadly as he shook his head. "I hired him and I don't know. Not for certain. He's probably male . . . maybe." He shook his head in frustration. "I know how this sounds, but the only other thing I know is that Ellison Robb is novelist Micky Cass. I don't know Micky Cass's sex." His shoulders issued an additional tiny shrug. "I guess I don't know his name, either. Micky Cass is a pseudonym, too. At least that's what he told me."

"Or she," said George as he folded his arms across his chest. "I know he's had this bit in his column about refusing to identify himself, but I've read a number of his books. He's obviously . . ." George shook his head. "The stories were very strong."

"What do you mean 'strong,' George?" asked Sikes, his eyebrows upraised.

George frowned as he recalled the image of a square-cut jaw, a gleaming white grin coming out of a dark face. "There were pictures on the dust jackets of his books. I've seen pictures of Micky Cass. He's a man. He looks like a man, writes like a man." Francisco looked at Matt and then faced Martin Fell.

"I cannot believe I just said that." He took a deep breath and let it escape slowly from his lungs as he sorted his thoughts. "Mr. Fell, how long have you known him—her—Cass?"

"Almost fifteen years."

"You know this person for fifteen years and you don't know the person's sex?"

Fell nodded, sadness creeping into his eyes. "I didn't know a great deal of unimportant detail about Mick."

"Sex isn't exactly unimportant," said Matt.

"It is at my house," muttered Grazer to no one in particular. Noticing that everyone was looking at him, his face flushed and he said, "Go on."

Fell shrugged and looked thoughtful. "As far as Micky was concerned, one's sex was only important to a physician or to someone with whom he was sexually involved. He wasn't sexually involved with me, and I'm no doctor. As for everyone else, it's none of their business, as far as Mick was concerned. Sex, sexual identity or preference, race, name, religion, favorite sport, hobbies, politics—nobody's business."

Grazer shook his head. "I can't believe you knew him for all those years and didn't know his sex."

"Not for lack of trying, captain. Mick once told me if I needed to make an issue of it, the friendship would end. Hence, if I valued his friendship more than the satisfaction of my curiosity, I'd best get onto some other subject."

"I don't get it. There must be a million forms he had to fill out that asked his sex and so on."

"You're right, captain. I have his social security number and some other forms that list race or sex. Where he had to fill these things out, for sex he'd enter 'NA' for not available, or he'd simply answer 'yes.' For race he'd either enter 'human' or 'IL.'"

"IL?" asked George.

"Intelligent life," said Matt quietly.

Fell looked at Sikes and nodded. "Yes. Intelligent life." He nodded again "That's right. Mick mentioned that in the cards and letters piece." He faced Grazer. "What's really amusing about that IL thing was the response of the paper wizards who would process Mick's forms. Every time they ran across that IL, all they saw was the I and proceeded on the assumption that Micky Cass was a Native American, an Indian. He might be, too. God, I would've hated to have been the census taker on his block."

"What about that?" asked Iniko.

"You mean the census?"

"Yes."

"Forget it. Before coming here I scraped together

every scrap of information I could get on Mick, including checking with the Census Bureau. There is no record of Micky Cass under any name that I know appearing in any census in U.S. history. None of their business."

"You have a home address on Cass?" asked Matt.

"He has a place in Coldwater Canyon. And before you ask, the property is not in Mick's name."

"In one of the columns I read," said Matt, "the one set in Chayville, Ellison Robb told someone, the sister of the gang leader, that he was married. Was Cass married?"

"Yes. He's married."

Matt raised his eyebrows and held out his hands. "Okay, are we talking a man or a woman?"

"A woman," said Fell. "Tian Apehna."

"She has a Tenctonese name," stated George.

"She's Tenctonese."

"Funny how that worked out," cracked Sikes. Matt held out his hands. "Let's get back to her being a woman. If Micky Cass is married to a woman, by a process of elimination doesn't that make him a man?"

Everyone found somewhere else to look while the silence in the office stretched into eternity and Matt Sikes's face acquired a rosy hue. "So what are we talking here? Lesbian? Gay?"

"All kinds of irrelevant detail," said Fell, looking up at Matt. "What I do know about Mick was that he swung his honesty like a war club, and that his mortal enemies were stupidity, injustice, and cruelty."

"So why do you call him he?" asked Grazer. "You use the male pronoun."

"So did Mick. It didn't offend him."

"Probably because he's a man," muttered George.

"You're still talking in the past tense, Mr. Fell," said Matt.

Martin Fell's face flushed again. "Look, detective, I'm the one who came in here to report this." His frown deepened. "I suppose I'm taking Mick at his word. He's missed two drops in a row and something's happened."

Matt shifted his weight from one foot to the other. "About the irrelevant details you mentioned, Mr. Fell—sex, race, religion, and so on. A lot of people around the world kill and die over those irrelevant details every day. If we don't know those things, we might never find out why this Micky Cass was either nabbed or killed. If we don't know why, we're never going to find out who, and we don't even know his real name or even if he is a he."

"I think there are already plenty of suspects to keep you occupied," said Grazer. "I'm guessing there are only about ten people in the state that 'Slag Like Me' didn't offend, and they're all doing solitary out at China Lake Federal Pen." He nodded toward the editor of the *Times*. "Now, Mr. Fell here has agreed to turn over all of Ellison Robb's notes, correspondence, hate mail, schedules, office and home phone logs, and so on. Until we know for certain that it's a kidnapping, the FBI is leaving it in LAPD hands, although every bureau resource will be made available, including more agents on an unofficial basis should we ask for them. Right now, I'm organizing the task force on this case. It'll become a federal task force once the bureau makes its investigation official."

"Task force?" asked George.

"You have a problem with that, Francisco?"

"You're running a task force on the suspicion that

something that may or may not have been a crime might have happened to someone, we're not really certain who?"

"It was ordered by the chief himself. If you have any complaints, I suggest you take them to his office." He nodded toward the FBI agent. "I'm bringing in missing persons, the gang units, homicide, department intelligence, and the sheriff. While we're setting up, you and Iniko will wade through the records, chase down and interrogate the suspects mentioned in the column, with particular attention to all of the police officers he mentioned. The last thing I want is for there to be even a hint that we're running some kind of department cover-up. If there's some rotten blue out there, you rat him out. You have zero tolerance, sympathy, and understanding. Understood?"

"Understood," said George, his expression troubled.

"What about me?" asked Matt.

"Yeah, Sikes. About you." Captain Grazer unwrapped another stick of chewing gum and folded it into his mouth. "There's an end of this investigation that's just hanging in the breeze right now. I'd sort of like to have you take it on."

"Hanging? What do you mean, hanging?"

"How would you like to go undercover as a newspaper reporter? Go through the same procedures with the same people that this Robb went through? Trace his footsteps?"

"Under cover? How would I *like* it?" Sikes frowned and cocked his head to one side. "Let me get this straight, cap. You want me to go through all that surgery that Robb went through, using the same facilities, and conduct an investigation as a Newcomer?"

"A human disguised as a Tenct," Grazer corrected. "The Newcomers have their own racial purity nuts, such as the *Ahvin Rivak*, and there might be a Tenct or two somewhere who freaked about this Micky Cass being married to a Tenctonese woman."

"Or," added Iniko, "someone might have taken offense at Cass impersonating a Tenctonese."

"Such as?" asked Matt.

"Such as me." Iniko's gaze shifted from Matt to George. "And others."

George nodded. "Yes, it offends me. The whole experiment offends me, but it doesn't have anything to do with racial purity."

Matt snorted out a laugh. "So, what is it?"

"What it has to do with, Matt, is getting along." George faced the captain. "There are problems, and no one knows that better than a Newcomer. However, I never saw anyone change his opinions by having a finger stuck in his eye. That's all 'Slag Like Me' does. It sticks fingers in people's eyes. It tries to put out brush fires by throwing gasoline into the flames." He took a deep breath and let it escape from his lungs, his voice quieter. "I'm not up on any barricades waving a flag, cap. As with most Tenctonese, I'm just trying to do my job and raise a family. I'm not out to change the world."

"Micky Cass *was* out to change the world," said Fell to George. "He knew it was impossible, yet all he ever asked for was a fist and room in which to swing. That's what his column was to him."

"Anyway," said the captain in an attempt at regaining control of the conversation, "disguising himself as a Tenct or being married to one might be the 'why' we're looking for, Sikes, and we might not draw out the perp without the right kind of bait."

"Bait." Matt gave George a nervous look, then faced the captain. "The budget crunch is still on, right?"

"Yeah. What's your point?"

"As I understand it, that surgery and stuff cost a heap of change."

"Close to five hundred thousand dollars," said Martin Fell. "Nevertheless, the *Times* will pay for your disguise. We're anxious to get Micky Cass back safely, and if that's not possible, to see Micky's abductors punished."

"Anything else?" asked the captain.

"Yeah," said Matt. "There's something else." He moistened his lips and thrust his hands into his pockets. "What about wiring me?"

"No wire. A number of the suspects you might run into know as much about that kind of gadgetry as we do. They'd pick it up in a second. If one of them is it, that might be the end of little Rico. What you will have is a tiny video recorder implanted in your head the same as Cass's. It's shielded and its emission level is very low. We can't use anything they can detect."

"Then how are you going to work my backup?"

"Budget safe and simple, Sikes." Grazer began unwrapping another piece of gum. "There won't be any direct backup. We'll have you under observation as much as possible, but some of the time you'll be on your own. Anything else?"

Matt's face flushed red. "Yeah, I think I got something else. This is asking a hell of a lot, cap. You hand over my partner to the feds and stick me with trick or treat? How did I draw this one?"

Grazer nodded. "Fair question." He popped in the fresh piece of gum and chewed as he asked, "You know some Tenctonese, right?"

"A bit," answered Matt. "I'm told I speak with a Deck Twenty-seven twang." He glanced at his partner.

Captain Grazer shrugged and leaned back in his chair as he said to Matt, "You speak a little Tenct, you know a lot about Tencts because of your partner and, er, others."

"You mean Cathy?"

"Unh huh. You going with a Tenct is almost as good as being married to one for what I've got in mind. You're perfect."

"I can't speak Tenctonese well enough to pass myself off as anything more than a mute."

Grazer rubbed his chin and raised his eyebrows. "When you come right down to it, Matt, your job won't be to pass yourself off as a Newcomer. Your job will be to flush out whoever it is who doesn't want humans climbing into spot suits."

Matt's eyes narrowed as he scratched at his chin. He held up a hand and cocked it toward Grazer. "There's something else here, cap. Something rotten, and the smell is pointing right at you. It's beginning to make my eyes water."

Grazer raised his eyebrows and shrugged again. "Yeah, I guess you could say there's something else. It's not real important to the investigation though."

"Not real important?"

The captain took the wad of chewing gum out of his mouth and tossed it into the wastebasket. Turning back to Sikes he said, "This Robb, or Cass, has done just about everything possible to put the department's feet in the fire. Every other cop out in that squad room hates Ellison Robb's guts. You make some noises like you admire the guy."

"He's saying some things that need to be said." Sikes's eyebrows went up as understanding flooded his features. "What you mean is, no one else'll do it. No one else'll go undercover as a Tenct to help Robb."

"Yeah. That's right, Sikes. Nobody else'll do it. Most of them don't give a crap about Ellison Robb. None of them, though, wants to become a Tenct. How about it?"

"Ellison Robb gave the department a boo-boo, and now the blue frat wants to see him dead for it?" Matt faced George and said, "See? Isn't this exactly what Robb was writing about?"

"Give me an answer," Grazer demanded.

"You can't order me to do something like this."

"That's right. I can't." He raised an eyebrow and aimed the eye beneath it at Matt. "But if you don't do it, it's not going to be done. What about it?"

Martin Fell reached into a leather folder. "The surgery is completely reversible, sergeant." He pulled a sheaf of papers out of the folder and held it out toward Sikes. "Here are copies of Mick's notes on the surgery and training. You're free to examine them. I'm having the remainder of his materials brought over, as well."

Matt took the notes, glanced through them, and looked at his partner. George Francisco's features were crowded with terminal smirk. Sikes nodded toward Grazer. "I'll give you my decision once I've seen the notes." Looking back at Francisco, he said, "I wouldn't be too smug if I were you, George. If I agree to do this, I only become a Tenctonese. Compared to what you're going to be, I'm going to be way up there on the social scale."

"What do you mean?"

Sikes smirked and polished an imaginary smudge off his fingernail. "I've read all of Robb's columns. A bunch of the suspects in this case are L.A. cops. Maybe I'll become a Newcomer. It might not be so bad. A lot of good people I know are Tencts. Whatever else happens, though, you and the fed there go down as shoo-flies, which is four steps down the social scale from worm shit."

CHAPTER

"DON'T YOU FIND the concept of 'shoo-fly' interesting?" asked Agent Iniko.

George Francisco, his back leaning against the interrogation room table in the new Franklin Avenue substation, put aside his concerns about Matt's assignment and snapped, "What's so interesting about it?"

"It's the ultimate absurdity of 'us' and 'them' thinking, Francisco. The number one complaint among police officers is that no one likes them. Everybody hates cops. Yet the police officers hate their own police officers, internal affairs. They call the IA officers shoo-flies and make them social outcasts."

"Everyone hates authority, Iniko."

"Not everyone, certainly. I don't."

"You've never been a slave."

Iniko laughed. "Overseers were slaves, too."

"Slaves in charge."

"Slaves all the same, which is neither here nor there. Most police officers haven't been slaves, yet every single one of them hates IA."

The door opened and a tower of constipated anger put in its head. "Francisco and Iniko?"

"Yes?" said George.

"Aw, Jeez," said the intruder as the expression on his face soured. He opened the door all the way. He was a tall uniformed officer in his late forties, raw-boned and blond, his thinning hair cut close to his scalp. "Leave it to IA to hire a couple of rubberheads." He shrugged his lanky frame. "Hell, maybe it makes sense to slip slags into Internal Affairs. You don't lose anything important by going shoo-fly. Everybody already hates your guts."

"You must be Officer Davenport," said George. "I'm Sergeant Francisco from homicide, and this is Special Agent Paul Iniko of the FBI. Please come in."

"Homicide?" Davenport's scowl dissolved into a look of utter confusion. "FBI? If you two aren't IA, then what's up? What do you want me for?"

"Come on in and close the door," said Iniko.

"Should I have a lawyer?"

"Do you need one?" asked George.

"No. I don't need any damned lawyer." Davenport entered the room, left the door open, and remained standing as he tossed his cap on the table. Placing his hands on his hips, he kept both Tencts in view at the same time. "Okay. What's this about?"

George closed the door and turned to face the officer. "We're investigating the disappearance of Ellison Robb, the column—"

"Ellison Robb?" Davenport's face blossomed into smiles. "Kidnapped? Killed? No kidding? Something happen to that smart-mouthed son of a bitch?" He pulled out a chair, sat in it, and clasped his hands behind his head as he leaned back. "Tell me more; tell me more. You can call me Rudy."

"We're asking the questions, Rudy," said Iniko.

"I guess I'm a suspect, huh? What happened to him, the rotten-mouthed little bastard? Something painful and lingering, I hope."

"Why would you be a suspect, Davenport?"

"Shit." The officer lowered his hands, and pointed at George. "You telling me you don't know what that bad-mouthing little bastard did to me?"

"You mean mentioning you in his column?"

"Mention me in his column? Oh, yeah. That's what I mean. Let me tell you what life for Rudy Davenport has been like since that first 'Slag Like Me' appeared in the paper. First thing that happened was that my captain and me were trotted into the chief's office. The chief of police? Downtown? I never thought I'd live long enough to meet the chief of police, and there I was, right in the middle of the man's carpet, having him ream me a brand new asshole with a post hole digger." He leaned his elbows on the table and pointed at George. "Maybe this is something you rubberheads just can't understand. I got a family—a wife and four kids. We only got the one income. Because of that column, I was suspended without pay for a month and had a turd slipped into my jacket down in personnel. In this age of kiss the ass of your local alien, you want to know what my chances of promotion are? How in the hell am I supposed to pay for my little girl's braces? I'm not worried about paying for my kids' college education. I'm busy trying to get goddamned food on the table!"

Iniko pulled out the chair opposite Davenport's and sat in it. "You make it sound as though it's Ellison

Robb's fault that you called him a slag and tried to slough off his complaint until you found out the perps were Tencts."

"You believe everything you read in the papers?"

"In his column," asked George, "did Robb describe what transpired at the hospital accurately?"

Davenport took a deep breath and let it sigh out as he slumped back in his chair and gave a reluctant shrug. "As far as he went."

"What was missing?"

"What he didn't write about was what an irritating little son of a bitch he was." The officer glanced up at Francisco. "Look, it was the end of a long day, I had more on my plate than I really needed, and that bastard's really got a mouth on him. He really got under my skin."

Iniko smiled. "What you didn't know, though, was what was under his skin."

"Look, J. Edgar Rubberhead, I don't care what Robb was under all that plastic. He was a bad-mouthing little bastard and he pissed me off. Besides, the whole thing was out at Mount Andarko's, the slag hospital? The place gives me the creeps. Nothing in it looks the same as a real hospital."

George bent over and leaned his hands on the edge of the table. "Where've you been for the last few days, Davenport?"

"What d'you mean?"

"Your record shows you took three sick days ending yesterday."

"What about it?"

"So, where were you?"

"You don't have to be a rocket scientist to figure that out. I was sick. I was at home except when I was at the doctor's office."

"Is there anyone who can verify that?"

Davenport nodded. "Yeah. My wife, my kids, four hundred salesmen and religious nuts, and the doctor."

"What was wrong?" asked Iniko.

"Wrong?"

"Yes. Your illness. What was it?"

Davenport glared at Iniko for a moment then turned away. "None of your business."

"Was it a police physician?"

"It would have to be," answered George. "Sick day notes from outside doctors don't count."

"They still can't give out information like that," insisted Davenport. "Not legally, they can't."

"What's the doctor's name?

Davenport pointed a shaking finger at George. "Look, spottop, you go check with my lieutenant. What I was told was that everything about me seeing my doctor was confidential, including the doctor's name."

Iniko pressed his fingertips together and looked over them at Davenport. "So, what are we talking about here, officer? Addiction? AIDS? The clap? Nervous breakdown? Wife battering? Child molesting?"

Rudy Davenport's face became like stone as he placed his hands on the edge of the table and pushed himself to his feet. "I got nothing more to say." He looked from Iniko to Francisco. "You have anything more you want to know, you speak to my lieutenant."

"There is just one more question," said Iniko. "The muggers who attacked Robb."

"What about them?"

"Were they ever arrested?"

A genuine shrug crossed the man's shoulders. "I don't know. I only filed the report. Chances are, unless

34

they got heads packed with pine, they haven't been brought in. In this town you got to be unlucky as hell or real dumb to get nailed for mugging, even a rubberhead. Anything else?"

Iniko looked at Francisco. "I don't have anything."

George faced Davenport. "That's all. Thank you for your cooperation."

"Go fuck yourself, slag," said Officer Davenport, "Don't get me wrong, now. I mean that in the nicest possible way." He stormed out of the room leaving the door open behind him.

Iniko glanced at Francisco as he rose to his feet. "Well?"

"A rather disagreeable fellow." George folded his arms across his chest and studied the empty doorway. "We've got the juice from the chief's office. You go and question Davenport's superiors and check out the doctor. I'll follow up on the muggers. If they haven't been apprehended, I'll start on the two LAPD officers Cass wrote about who beat him up and dumped him in Chayville."

"Do you think Hong and Kent will be as hostile as brother Davenport?"

"Probably more so. They were both fired."

Iniko stood and pushed in his chair. "As I said, interesting concept, shoo-fly."

CHAPTER 4

MATT SIKES NIBBLED at the inside of his lower lip as he sat at his desk leafing through Micky Cass's notes. It was all there, scribbled in Cass's free and open handwriting: steps for becoming a genuine alien from outer space. The columnist obviously entrusted nothing to memory. Every note, every reference, was carefully entered and cross-referenced. Phone logs showed where, when, and with whom he talked. He had made extensive notes and had done quite competent drawings of the plastic surgery and modeling done with Realskin, a vat-grown biofilm that looked and acted like real skin used primarily for treating burn victims.

By backing Realskin with the proper liquid implants, it could be made to bleed like a Tenct when cut, providing the cut was not too deep. Human skin could even breathe through it. It was attached by "welding" it to the original skin, a cellular bonding that could be dissolved by applying the proper enzyme.

The head, of course, had to be made larger, which allowed a tiny transceiver recorder to be implanted beneath the skin. The video feed was provided by two miniaturized cameras, one peering through a button in his jacket or shirt, the other fixed into the jewel of his ring. The cameras were not wired in the usual sense. Instead they transmitted their signals to the recorder through the skin.

Providing all of the expensive technical gadgetry worked the way it was supposed to, everything that had happened within Cass's sight and hearing must have been recorded. If all they could do was to recover the recorder intact, some perp's cakes were on the griddle. Matt turned to the notes on the *vo*, the school where Tenctonese and humans alike learned to see things for what they are and to accept that it is so.

The training there had been brutal, in a psychological sense. The brutality was necessary to overcome that thing that marked a human to a Tenct: ego. Matt's gaze flew over the notes as he read that Tencts and humans both were telepathic to a degree. Only a rare few could actually transmit and receive coherent thoughts, but everyone was sending and everyone was receiving on some level. That's why if you stare at the back of someone's neck for a period, the owner of the neck will feel uneasy and turn around to see who is looking at him.

To a Newcomer, a human "felt" obviously different from a Tenct. It wasn't a difference between the thinking mechanisms; it was a difference between the thoughts. Most Newcomers, both Overseers and their former charges, were oriented around a "we" identity. Most humans were oriented around an "I" identity. It made for different vibes.

"The Tenct is trained from birth," wrote Cass, "to regard himself as part of a greater machine: the Tencts. How do I fit in? How am I affecting the whole? How are the others regarding me? Humans, if trained at all, think in smaller units: sex, color, religion, party, nation, region, city, neighborhood, industry, guild, army, club, gang, family, status, our 'circle,' and the smallest unit of all: I, me, my. Each Tenctonese is taught to be an indistinguishable droplet in a smooth-flowing communal stream. When I took my walk on Hollywood Boulevard I went and took the boulder of Micky Cass's ego, dropped it into the water, and wondered why the Tencts saw ripples."

Matt pushed the notes aside, put his feet on his desk, and tore the wrapper off a Milky Way. He paused and studied the candy bar. For the same reason that alcohol had no effect on Tenctonese, neither did sugar. After all, sugar is alcohol's granular form. A Newcomer who continually stuffed candy bars into his face would stick out like an oompah band at a rock concert. Actually, he'd stick out like a human popping rancid cheese cubes or tossing back a six-pack of Coor's carbonated sour milk. If Matt was to disguise himself as a Tenct, that would be the end of candy bars for a while. He'd pass on the sour milk, though. He knew Newcomers who abstained and no one appeared to be bothered by them.

He frowned as something occurred to him. To go undercover as a Newcomer, would he have to eat that crap? Weasel jerky, beaver burgers, squirrel nuggets, Roach Toasties, rotten cheese doodles? Some of the stuff Cathy ate was really gross. Broccoli. Cream of

Wheat. Lipton Tea. Moxie. Squash. Mounds. Although there was no appeal in sugar, most Tenctonese loved coconut. Matt Sikes would just as soon suck on a dead rat as eat a Mounds.

Looking around the squad room, Matt studied the Tenctonese officers, staffers, and the two Tenct suspects who had been brought in on the sweep to find the Soto Street Slag Slasher. All of them—cops, custodians, clerks, and crooks—had enough thinking in common that most of them could recognize an impostor, unless the impostor had plastic surgery and special mental training.

He turned his head and looked over at Dobbs. Sgt. Dobbs was manning his desk by himself again, his new partner, Jerry Kirk, once more having found an excuse to be elsewhere. Matt knew the purpose of that perpetual "elsewhere." It said to the fraternity, "Hey, it's not my fault my partner's black. I'm changing as soon as I can. The papers are already in."

Matt nodded to himself. The rule was still there: isolate the newcomers, and the newcomers in question weren't only Tencts. They were "non-whites" and female officers, as well, even though the "whites" were no longer a majority. He remembered how he had been ostracized for volunteering to partner up with the first Tenctonese detective in the department. He hadn't paid any attention to that. Pairing up with Francisco had been his best chance to be assigned to hunt down and kill the slag bastards who had slain his old partner, Tugg.

Sikes frowned as he thought back to when he and Bill Tuggle had been paired up a thousand years ago. Tugg was blue all the way through, but to the fraternity he was "black." Okay, useful in certain neighborhoods, necessary to keep the equal opportunity pogues in line, but not to be taken into the inner circle, not to be trusted. Those were the days when it was still necessary for a "white" probationer to pound the shit out of an occasional "black" suspect or perp just to prove to his training officer and the frat at large that he was not afraid of "them" and was, therefore, eligible to become a part of the thin blue "us."

Matt had been paired with a "black," and they worked the job together, ate at each other's homes, went to ball games, treated each other like humans. Hence, Matt Sikes was not trustworthy either.

The '92 riots, the Christopher Commission, Willie Williams, and a heavy influx of female, Tenctonese, and other minority recruits notwithstanding, the frat was still running things. You could still hear the pause and shift in conversation in the locker rooms when a "non-frat" officer of any stripe entered. Female, other colored, other named, other religioned, especially Newcomer. It was an issue from the past that had never left. Matt wondered if it ever could.

Dobbs's new partner wanted to belong. Not a terrible thing in itself. Belonging always seemed to have an artificially high price, though. Jerry Kirk seemed to think the price was worth it. Matt had belonged with Bill Tuggle. Tugg was dead, his chest blown all over the street. Matt now belonged with George Francisco. George was off shoo-flying with the fed. Matt looked again at Dobbs. He was seated with a uniformed officer and a gang banger.

There was a wealth of body language going on over at Dobbs's desk. The gang banger appeared quite relaxed between Dobbs and the uniformed officer. Dobbs was in a serene groove, too. The uniform, on the other hand, looked just a little uncomfortable.

Us and them, thought Matt. There were color divisions, occupational divisions, and divisions by age, status, and dress over at Dobbs's desk. At that moment the division by perceived color seemed to be stronger than that by occupation. The uniformed officer, second generation Irish-American, was the odd man out until another uniformed officer arrived. The second uniform, an umpteenth generation Afro-American, slapped the other uniform on the back, and suddenly the bonds dissolved and reformed along occupational lines.

In the space of half a second it went from two "blacks" against a "white" to three "blues" against a banger; three "goods" against a "bad." Loyalties, manners, objectives, all changed and none of the officers or their suspect seemed to have noticed. They were all still arguing about why the gang banger was where he had been when he had been there. Matt turned back to the notes.

"How does one crush an ego?" Cass had written. "Even social, political, and ethnic groups who traditionally place nation, family, or church before self have too much 'I' to fit in among the Tencts undetected. A human individual who defers to his family in a family-oriented culture does so for reasons of self-interest. The 'I' is still uppermost. The 'I': what does it take to submerge it? For some humans, though, it is already submerged—crippled—sufficiently that on a level of feelings the human is indistinguishable from the Tenctonese. Years ago I had been like that myself. It was the only way I managed to survive."

"Your head is smoking."

Matt looked up and saw George standing before his side of the desk looking back. "Hi. Where's the FBI?"

"He's checking out Davenport's alibi. Are you still coming over for dinner this evening?"

"Sure," he said as he smacked his lips and patted his belly. "Mmmm mmm! Badger Wellington, parsnip chips, and snail dip."

George laughed and pointed at Cass's notes. "Make up your mind yet?"

Matt shrugged as his face grew serious. "I'm three quarters of the way there. What've you been up to?"

Rubbing the back of his neck, George shook his head as he answered. "I just finished interviewing two very hostile former police officers."

"The thumpers? Kent and Hong?"

"Yes."

Matt placed his feet on the floor and sat forward. "I thought they were just on suspension."

"They were. After the 'Slag Like Me' column concerning them appeared, the chief ordered both officers put on suspension. The investigation showed Ellison Robb's column to have been accurate and the chief pulled both their badges. It should be in the morning papers."

"Ouch."

"Ouch indeed." George sighed and nodded. "Kent had eleven years and Hong was three years short of his twenty. They're both married and both have children."

"What about the Robb disappearance? They both have alibis?"

George pulled out his chair and dropped into it, shrugging slightly as he did so. "They can't account for every minute of the past three days with witnesses, but neither can I." George closed his eyes. "Between those two—Hong and Kent—they have seven citations for bravery. They are—were—two very valuable police officers."

Matt shook his head. "What they did put them on

the other side of the line, buddy. It's tough. I understand why they did what they did better than you
could, in fact. But the line is there for a reason. It's
broken, thin, and faded here and there, but without it
you can't tell the good guys from the bad guys. When
you can't see anything but bad guys, this town has a
tendency to go up in flames."

"In the words of a partner of mine, sometimes this
job sucks."

"George, I take it you're not exactly ready to
transfer to Internal Affairs."

"The job would be a lot easier if the bad guys were
bad all the way through all of the time." George faced
Matt. "Call it a hunch or a gut feeling, but I don't
think Davenport, Hong, or Kent had anything to do
with Micky Cass's disappearance."

Matt tossed the notes onto his desk and held out his
hands. "They have possible opportunity and are soak-
ing wet with motive. Check it out, partner. That gut
you're measuring everything against just might be
true blue."

George shrugged. "You're right about one thing,
though. They have plenty of motive. Too much motive. You should've seen Davenport when we told him
something might have happened to Ellison Robb. He
did everything but clap his hands, swing from the light
fixture, and squeal with glee. Come to think of it, he
did squeal with glee. Kent did the same thing. When I
told Mike Hong, I thought he was going to give me a
hug."

"You figure the real perp would be less free with his
feelings?"

"Wouldn't you?"

"Yeah, unless I was a cop and knew it would throw
you off. Anyway, you have to check every corner. The

front office is real touchy about looking like it's covering up for suspect cops. Them you have to prove innocent." Sikes nodded toward Interrogation Room One. "They brought over Micky Cass's notes and all his mail a couple hours ago. Grazer's already got a team sorting the letters." Matt glanced around the room and lowered his voice as he continued. "There are some leads in there pointing to an FBI connection."

"Oh?"

Matt nodded. "Some kind of link between the bureau and the *Ahvin Rivak*. You've heard of them?"

"Those Who Would Return," translated George. "Do you know that most of the membership of the *Rivak* aren't even Overseers? It's hard to believe that there is an organization that devotes its time and money attempting to plunge its membership back into slavery. What connection would it have with the bureau?"

"I'm not sure it even amounts to anything, George. It was just something Grazer said. The only reason I said something was so you can watch your back."

"Watch my back?"

"Iniko. The FBI man? Former Overseer? Your new partner? You usually aren't this slow, buddy."

George frowned as he rubbed his chin. "The FBI," he muttered. "Who *isn't* a suspect?"

"I'm not," answered Matt, "but I'm not so sure about you. You've had some rather rough things to say about our possible victim, whoever he or she might be."

Francisco reached across the desk and pointed at the papers on Sikes's desk. "What about this be-the-first-kid-on-your-block-to-be-an-alien-space-freak kit? Are you going to do it?"

Matt thought a second and nodded. "I'm going to do it."

"Have you talked to Cathy about it?"

"No." Matt's eyebrows raised. "Why would I? This is a police matter."

"I'd talk to Cathy about it."

"George, it doesn't have anything to do with her. I'll still be me. It's just going undercover."

"I'd talk to Cathy about it."

Matt's eyebrows came down. "She doesn't consult with me about every new research project her lab's assigned."

"I'd talk to Cathy about it."

"Okay." Matt shrugged and folded his arms across his chest. "I'll talk to Cathy about it."

"Well, I see we have achieved peace in our time," said Dobbs as he ambled over to the pair. The two uniformed officers were leading the gang banger toward the stairs. Dobbs cocked his head toward the three and added, "it doesn't look like either Jimmy Do or the Black Rain is going anywhere. I guess we can count on the Soto Street Slag Slasher getting another one tonight."

Matt saw Francisco's eyebrows drop slightly into a frown. "What is it, George? Did you think of something?"

Francisco looked up at Dobbs and nodded. "Yes. I did. You know that case out of Newton Street Division?"

"The Snatch?"

George nodded. "Yes. That's the one." He faced Matt, his eyes black with anger. "Some sicko over at Newton Street has been kidnapping, sexually molesting, and killing homeless women."

"I looked into it," said Dobbs, "and I don't think

there's any connection. The Snatch only goes after blacks. There's a population of Newcomers in the same area, so if he wanted to cut 'em up, he could do it on Newton. Why do you think there's a connection?"

George slowly shook his head. "I don't think there's any connection at all."

Dobbs held out his hands. "Then, I don't get it, George. Why'd you bring it up?"

Matt could see that George was surface super-calm, which was the warning sign for a major eruption in the making. "Dobbs, you know how your group dubbed the knife artist on Soto who kills Tencts the Soto Street Slag Slasher?"

Dobbs lowered his hands, frowned, and shrugged. "Yeah. What about it?"

George folded his arms and leaned back in his chair. "I was just wondering why they called the perp on Newton the Snatch instead of something more catchy, such as the Newton Street Nigger Nicker."

Matt saw Dobbs's jaw drop at the same time as he felt his own hit his chest.

Dobbs, his face locked between confusion and rage, held up his hand toward Matt. "Look, Francisco, you've been here long enough to know what a fighting word is. And what a fighting word *that* fighting word is."

George shrugged and raised his eyebrows. "I see my suggestion has not been enthusiastically received. Well, it doesn't have the same alliterative quality that Soto Street Slag Slasher or Newton Nigger Nicker, but I'd be perfectly willing to settle for Jigaboo Jumper or Coon Croaker—"

Dobbs took a step forward, his fists raised, and George stood to face him. "It's not the same thing!" Dobbs growled through clenched teeth.

"It *is* the same thing!" George growled back. "And *I've* been here long enough for *you* to know *that!*"

The two detectives glared at each other for a moment, then Dobbs pivoted and stormed back to his desk as George turned and headed toward the stairs. Matt looked at the notes on his desk, confused because he felt as if he wanted to cry very old tears.

Matt Sikes was going to do it—go undercover as a Tenct. He knew that. He had just realized, though, that he had no clue as to what he was getting into. Whatever it was, he suspected it was much bigger, more vicious, and a hundred times more senseless than anything he had ever experienced before.

A Policeman's Lot

She isn't the villain, so let's just call her Suzie. It was at the newly remodeled and dedicated Bradley Elementary School on Seventh Street in L.A. I was passing by, and Suzie was curled up inside the fence, crying. She was wearing a bright yellow cotton dress that was covered with grass stains and pale pink blots I recognized as Tenct blood. She had a bloody nose and a bad scrape on her elbow. In Tenctonese I asked her, "What's wrong? What happened?"

She turned her head, looked up at me, and shook her head. She didn't understand Tenctonese. (Ah, the old ways pass so quickly.) I repeated my questions in English. She answered, and the answer was predictable. She was one of sixteen Tenctonese children in the school, and the only Tenctonese in her class. Three of her schoolmates, in a step toward racial purity and to urge her to help improve the grade point curve (Suzie is a 4.0 student), beat her up during recess and left her there. Again. They do this to her on an average of three times per week. Since they are the products of their homes, peers, and upbringings rather than villains, let's call her classmates Biff, Rosco, and Lola.

You could tell that Suzie had been warned by her parents against talking to strangers, and that's sound advice for children in the weirdo-sicko capital of the world. However, when the teachers are too busy doing paperwork or taking their breaks, and her classmates are punching the snot out of her, and her parents can't do anything but tell her to try harder to "fit in," to whom is little Suzie supposed to talk? Is it any wonder that a kid eventually breaks down and talks to the next kind voice he or she hears? Do you really want to know why so many children are missing, or why addiction, suicide, and murder among preteens keeps climbing?

There is a whole universe of ignorance, pain, suffering, and humiliation behind those schoolhouse walls, and behind the walls of every school in the city and across the face of the planet. I had neither the time nor the ability to lift up the edge on this particular scab. Modern cosmetic surgery notwithstanding, I am considerably past the time when I can impersonate a sixth-grader. Moreover, just about that time an LAPD black-and-white pulled up behind me (you remember: "To serve and protect") and two officers got out, slipping their batons into their belts.

Does anyone know why everyone else in the world calls them nightsticks, cudgels, billy clubs, bludgeons, truncheons, yea, even war clubs, but the LAPD insists on calling them batons? I suppose it's an attempt at evoking the image of a sixteen-year-old twirler leading the Pimple Park Flag Corps during a high school halftime show. An object is not what it is; it's what we call it.

Anyway, the cops told Suzie to scat back to class, they upped me against the fence, and while Harry ground my face into the chain link, Waldo cuffed my hands behind me. In a second I was in the back of the black-and-white while Waldo climbed in next to me to explain some of the burdens of the judicial system in the city and county of Los Angeles.

L.A. and its environs are awash with perverts, dealers, gang bangers, killers, and scum of every stripe and description. For every one that is arrested, the system can't even see fifteen. Of those who are arrested, maybe one out of eight actually goes to trial. Of those who go to trial, maybe one out of four is actually found guilty of something. And of those found guilty, maybe one out of seven actually gets to serve some time. There's not much time to serve, in addition, because the penalties are too light and the jails too crowded.

The officer would've had my wholehearted agreement, except for him punctuating his allocution every clause by thrusting the end of his baton into my gut and thwacking my underarms. It took my entire concentration to produce the appropriate reactions. The thwack under the arm is the Tenct answer to getting kicked in the groin, you see. Curious, isn't it? That is the only fact about Tencts that every human seems to know.

When I had been beaten almost senseless, the unit rolled for a while, then the black-and-white pulled over. I was dumped out of the cruiser into a gutter and advised to go forth and sin no more. Waldo reclaimed the passenger seat, and the black-and-white drove off, carrying its pair of blue knights forth to do battle once more with the powers of multicolored darkness and evil.

Two members of the Nightshade, a Chayville Tenct

gang, picked me out of the gutter and took me to the home of a gang member's mother where I was cleaned up and a doctor called. Under normal circumstances, a member of the Nightshade would as soon kill you or rob you as notice your existence. Perhaps that is what Waldo and Harry were counting on by dumping me on Eagle Street. Tencts killing Tencts and who cares?

Curiously enough, they couldn't have picked a better place or mode of transportation. By punching the poo out of me and jettisoning me in L.A. on Nightshade turf, Waldo and Harry ("them") made me part of the Nightshade "us." Better credentials simply were not to be had.

I called the officers Harry and Waldo because they aren't villains, either. They didn't see a constitutionally protected being exercising his right to free speech on a public right-of-way. In the midst of riots, murders, gang rapes, arsons, kidnappings, robberies, spouse batterings, child molestings, and a city rotting to death from addiction (and that's right, Goober, alcohol is a drug), Harry and Waldo simply couldn't take the time out from all their paperwork, court appearances, riding the streets, stakeouts, union meetings, and risking their lives to dispose of a suspected Tenct child molester by the book.

No villains.

People, that was the lesson of the '92 riots: dozens dead and there are no villains, only victims. And, Goober, if you buy that, I've got a trunk full of "Daryl Gates for Mayor" bumper stickers you won't be able to pass up.

As part of my training for this project, I spent some time learning what I was able in a school called a *rama vo,* which is Tenctonese for garden of wisdom. The *vo* is an association of men and women, mostly elderly, who meet to pass on their wisdom to those who are teachable. The Elders, both human and Tenct, have a view of the world forged by understanding that wisdom is seeing things for what they are and accepting that it is so. I picked up a few things there. Such as:

Rule #1. Acts have consequences.

Rule #2. Those who act are responsible for the consequences of their acts (either that, or they should be locked up and put away in a high-security institution until such time as they are responsible).

Rule #3. No one's tale of prestige, power, influence, legal exemption, poverty, injury, or woe invalidates either Rule #1 or Rule #2.

Hence, despite disadvantaged upbringings, alcoholic homes, fears of the strange and unknown, and mostly because it serves some universal sick need to torture the odd person out, here are the names of the gang members who beat up little Suzie almost every school day: Bradley sixth-graders Ricky Gallegos and Anita Wicker, and seventh grader Randy Cook.

In addition, despite disadvantaged upbringings, alcoholic homes, fears of the strange and unknown, and a really lousy slice of life's occupational pie, here are the names of the gang members who beat me up and dumped me in the gutter like a bag of garbage: Officer Michael Hong, Badge 27127, and Officer Jason Kent, Badge 26871, LAPD.

(Notice to lawyers: pant though you will at the possible libel litigation this column might represent, be advised that everything described herein is on videotape and has been thoroughly documented and witnessed. Ta ta.)

CHAPTER 5

THAT NIGHT MATT looked into his bathroom mirror and studied the features one local news broadcaster had once referred to as "early world-weary infant." Maybe the cheeks were too chubby, the eyes too open, the effect a little too cute. Perhaps there were crow's-feet and a semipermanent scowl. A little scar here and there; keepsakes of a dozen years chasing down the bad guys while trying to stay out from under bureaucrats, pogues, and paper wizards. It was his face, though, and although he didn't particularly like it, he was used to it. He touched his brow and drew the fingers of his right hand down the line of his chin.

What would that face look like as a Tenctonese? His eyebrows went up. "The question is," he said to the image in the looking glass, "what will everyone else's face look like once this face looks like a Tenctonese?"

That was the question. Every gaze that touched

him, whether Newcomer or human, would convey to
the one doing the gazing, certain things—certain false
things—simply because of how Matt looked. If the
observer were human, it would be assumed that Matt
Sikes was gullible, although unfairly intelligent and
physically strong. Sexually he would be regarded as
being equipped with a dream machine and no idea
how to use it. Of course he would also have to have a
stupid, degrading immigration name.

Dick Short.

Jay Byrd.

Cookie Baker.

Tim Barr.

Cole Frost.

Tipper Kanu.

Peter Jerkmeov.

If the observer were Tenct, however, what?

Matt frowned as he admitted to himself that he had
absolutely no idea how a Tenct would look upon
another Tenct. Fellow former slave? The Tencts could
all count on having certain things in common. A
certain humility. A certain camaraderie, like soldiers
who have shared combat. Cons who have done the
same bad time in the same bad place. A common rage.
To impersonate a Tenct would take a world of gall to
keep from feeling like the worst kind of fraud. Matt's
time paired up with George had convinced him that,
except for a few bizarre interludes, Tencts think the
same way humans think. But even humans don't all
think alike. He seemed insane to himself at times.
How could he judge the mental machinery of another
human, much less a Tenct?

He thought back to the scene in the squad room that
afternoon between Dobbs, the gang banger, and the
uniformed cop. Matt had an idea how "whites"

generalized about "blacks," but how do "blacks" generalize about other "blacks"? He smiled as he realized that even in his thoughts he placed quotes around certain racial labels indicating that they really don't refer to anything real. That had to do with Buck Francisco and his experiences attending a *ruma vo* for the past year. Buck was smart, frighteningly so, to Matt. It was as though life were an insane game Matt had been born into and no one had been issued a rule book. Somehow young Buck seemed to have acquired a copy.

There was something George's son, Buck, had said that evening when Matt was at his partner's home for dinner. As around most dinner tables in southern California that night, there was a fight over Ellison Robb and his column. The Francisco's daughter, Emily, had been complaining angrily about related racist incidents that had happened to her at school, Emily's mother, Susan Francisco, was attempting to "understand" them all away, and George was staunchly deploring both racism *and* Ellison Robb's methods. The youngest Francisco, Vessna, had been crying loudly in reaction to the tension around the table, yet Buck was calmly eating his dinner.

"Buck," said his father, attempting to enlist support for his side, "don't you agree that Robb's childish refusal to reveal anything about himself is at the least provocative if not inflammatory? Not only that, it borders on being fraudulent. Isn't he denying what he is by keeping this information from the readers?"

"No, Dad. I disagree."

"What?" The look on George's face at that moment reminded Matt of his own father's face the day he told the brutal alcoholic he intended to become a police officer. Although many years later he had gone on to join the LAPD, the ten-year-old Matt had been cowed into silence by his father's wrath. Buck, however, seemed to believe that he could disagree with his parents without betraying them or starting a world war. Radical stuff.

Buck put down his fork, wiped his mouth with his napkin, and gathered a thought or two. "I disagree, Dad. Ellison Robb isn't denying what he is. He's attempting to prevent what he is from being sabotaged and submerged by what some others might choose him to be if he revealed these things about himself."

That brought silence to the table. George leaned back in his chair, a frown on his face, a defensive edge in his voice. "I'm not choosing him to be anything. In fact I want to know who he is. At least if he's a he. Is that unreasonable?"

Buck smiled as he shrugged. "I don't know what 'reasonable' or 'unreasonable' mean, Dad. What I do know is male or female is just sex; some plumbing and hormones along with some arbitrarily assigned roles and assumed attitudes. Male or female isn't who or what Ellison Robb is. Robb doesn't want to reveal his sex because then his column would forever after be regarded as having either a female or male slant."

"Isn't that valid?" asked Susan.

"I don't think Ellison Robb thinks so. The only slant he wants his column to be perceived as having is an Ellison Robb slant. It's the thing that's at the core of why he's doing what he's doing in 'Slag Like Me'."

Matt frowned as he leaned across the table. "This is the stuff they've been teaching you at the *rama vo?*"

"All they teach at the *vo*, Matt, is how to see things for what they are and accept that it is so. It's what things are perceived as being that Robb is shaking up." He looked at his father. "Some Christians, for example, wear their emblems in full view because they wish to be identified with that belief. It's a uniform that says 'This is what I am,' although the real meaning of it is 'This is what I believe,' or perhaps 'This is what I want you to believe that I believe.' Perhaps it just means 'I belong.' It's the same with any political, religious, or cultural uniform. In most cases, as with a cross, a yarmulke, a turban, colors, a swastika, long hair, a badge, or a suit and tie, they're things with which the individual chooses to adorn himself to identify with a particular group, idea, obligation, or belief."

"I don't get it," said Matt. "It's not like you can see him wearing a cross in his column."

"You could if he revealed the information," said Susan. "Would that change how you read the column?"

"I don't think so," Matt answered. He frowned and pondered for a moment. Then he nodded. "Okay, it would if I found out he was a shove-it-down-your-throat Jesus jammer or a Moonie."

"Or a Celinist," quipped Emily.

He thought for a long moment and then nodded slowly. "Yeah. Okay. It would color how I read his words."

Buck leaned back in his chair and frowned as he searched for some phrases. "Matt, there are other things, things that are taken as outside emblems, that are not generally considered matters of choice."

"Such as?"

"Well, except for the application of some fairly extreme measures, there is little choice regarding one's species, sex, height, eye shape, skin color, nose shape, and so on. Yet most persons, when they see a bald spotted head, a large pair of mammary glands, almond-shaped eyes, or a dark brown skin color, accredit to the individual reams of prefabricated beliefs, values, intentions, capabilities, and deficiencies that may or may not have anything whatever to do with that individual. Remember the Latvian black gay midget bikers Robb wrote about as a tongue-in-cheek example of a narrow agenda? The point is that there are many who believe that if they are not Latvian, black, gay, midget, or a biker, they can legitimately pass off as weird, strange, different, slanted, or generally untrue whatever uncomfortable thing that might be said by a Latvian black gay midget biker."

Susan nodded and faced George. "It's true, dear. If Ellison Robb revealed herself to be female, many men and many women would pass off what she said as fuzzy-headed, impractical, unrealistic, rabid, or foolish; the wacko feminist slant; PMS with a vote. A good many of them would, too."

"If he's a grown-up," interjected Emily, "the kids wouldn't have to pay any attention because he's petrified and from yesterday. And if he's a kid, none of the grown-ups would listen because they think he's stupid."

"You're a kid," said Matt. "I don't think you're stupid."

Emily's eyes yellowed slightly from embarrassment. "Oh, okay. But you know a lot of grown-ups wouldn't pay any attention to anything a kid says, and that's the truth." She looked at her mother. "How many times have you said to me, 'You'll grow out of that,' when you don't want to take what I feel seriously. You say it to Dad, too. 'She's young. She'll outgrow that.' 'She's going through a phase.'" She faced her father. "I bet if you learned that Ellison Robb is twelve or fifteen years old, you'd be saying the same thing about him. I think it's a way of throwing away what he has to say without dealing with it."

"I think she's right," said Buck.

George looked from Buck to his daughter and studied her for a moment. He closed his eyes and nodded. "You're right, Emily. You're absolutely right."

In his room later that night, Matt tugged at the problem:

Who *is* a person?

What *is* an individual?

What *is* true courage?

George had once told Matt about the *Krakor*, the mythological Tenctonese Godzilla, half devil, half dragon, the eternal monster. Somehow, in a past no one could remember, the legend began among slave mothers to frighten their children away from the ship's power decks, which were thought to be dangerous. The *Krakor* walks, the beast flies, there's no stopping it if you set foot in its forbidden land. Somehow Matt Sikes felt as though he were entering the beast's lair.

Matt pulled his mind back to the present and frowned as he heard a key rattling in the lock. The sound was followed by Cathy's voice. "Matt? I'm home."

He turned away from the mirror and stood in the bedroom's doorway. Cathy was closing the door to the apartment, and for just a moment her spotted baldness—her alienness—jarred him. He knew a great deal about the person beyond the physical form or once thought he did. But all one ever knows about another is from what the person says and does, and everyone, Tenct and human both, can lie and trick, and from the best of motives. At the top of the list of noble motives was true love, despite the truth that true love cannot survive a lie, which means I'm in big trouble, thought Matt. He hardly ever let anyone know how he really felt about anything.

Cathy turned from the door and saw Matt. Her full lips broke immediately into a smile that immediately faded as she caught the expression on his face. "Are you all right?"

"Fine," Matt answered.

"Fine," she repeated. "Does fine still stand for 'Frustrated, Insane, Neurotic, and Emotional'?"

"What're you talking about?"

"That time you came back from that Adult Children of Alcoholics meeting. You heard someone there say that 'fine' in response to the question 'How are you?' means 'Frustrated, Insane, Neurotic, and Emotional.' In other words, 'I don't want to talk about it.'"

"Look, Cath, all it means to me is that I'm doing fine; okay, marvy, hunky-dory."

"Maybe you should tell your face."

Matt's face crashed into a glower. "What're you talking about?"

She dropped her purse on the couch and crossed the living room floor. When she was in front of Matt, she put one arm around his neck and touched his face with her other hand. "You look as if you've just lost your best friend."

"My best friend?"

She placed a tiny kiss on his lips and smiled. "Tell me what's bothering you, Matt. I can't fix it 'til I know what's broken."

He placed his hands on her waist and drew her toward him as he looked into her eyes. The skin of her face was very smooth and pale, her ear folds little more than bumps on the sides of her head. But what was that thing that made her "feel" different to him? What was the thing in him that would make him "feel" different to a Tenct? Her eyes were captivating. Strange eyes. Were they a touch Asian? Or were they just a touch alien?

"Well, now I know," she stated.

"Know? Know what?"

"Now I know what it feels like to be a bug under a microscope."

"Sorry, Cath. It's this new undercover assignment. It looks as though something might have happened to Ellison Robb."

Cathy's eyebrows went up as her mouth fell open in shock. "The columnist? 'Slag Like Me'?"

Matt nodded. "That's the one, except Ellison Robb is a pseudonym. His name's Micky Cass. About something happening to him, remember I just said might. Nothing's for sure yet. He seems to have missed a couple of appointments and that's all we know right now. We're taking every precaution, though, just in case."

She held him at arm's length and looked into his eyes. "In case? Just in case of what? What does this have to do with you? What kind of undercover assignment?" He couldn't meet her gaze. "This must really be good," she cracked.

Matt shrugged his shoulders slightly. "Oh, it's good. Grazer wants me to follow Cass's footsteps through the entire process of becoming a Tenct in case some Tenct purist wacko out there took offense—"

"Bait," she said, her voice flat, her expression angry.

"Yeah," Matt answered, nodding his head. "Now that you put it that way, that's a good way to put it."

He elevated his gaze until he was looking into her eyes. "I don't think it's anything to worry about. Micky Cass is famous enough to have enemies. I'm Elmer Q. Cop Nobody from Craphead, CA."

"For not having anything to worry about, you certainly look worried to me."

Matt scratched the back of his neck, still unable to meet her gaze. "Well, it's going to involve a little bit of plastic surgery."

"A little bit?" One of Cathy's eyebrows went up. "To turn a human into a Tenctonese? A *little* bit?"

"Okay. Quite a bit. But it's all reversible. I'll still be the same jerk everybody ignores and hates when the job's done."

"Then what's the problem?"

Again he found it unbearable to look into her eyes. He focused instead on a cobweb in the corner of the ceiling that neither of them had found the time to remove. "I may be that way for a number of days."

"That way?"

"Looking like a Newcomer. Here at home. Together, you and me, in bed, in the shower. It's not like a Halloween costume. I've got to wear it until the doctors take it off. Is that going to change things? I mean, between us? If I look worried, I think that's what I'm worried about."

"Mmmm," she hummed, "kinky. It just *might* change things. Kind of like the time you wanted me to wear that lace postage stamp from Victoria's Secret." She grabbed him around the buttocks and squeezed. "I don't care what they do to the rest, but they'd best keep their hands off your cute little tush. That's mine."

"I'm serious, Cathy. Is me changing going to change things between us?"

For a moment a look of pity crossed Cathy's face to be replaced immediately by one of compassion as she put her arms around his neck and drew him close to her. "I know you don't believe this, Matt, but you aren't what you look like or what others think about you. You are you."

"That's what I was afraid of," said Matt. "So the undercover assignment doesn't bother you?"

She pulled her head back and looked into his eyes. "Police work bothers me, Matt." She buried her face into his neck. "But this isn't any worse than half a dozen other undercover jobs you've been given. You'll have backup, others there to help."

"Yes," he lied as he glanced up at the cobweb, his mind's eye imagining a tiny fleck of protoplasm climbing into the *Krakor's* mouth. "Someone to watch over me."

CHAPTER

DOBBS LEANED AGAINST the sink and closed his eyes. Words, regrets, and a curse on a planet's science that could not come up with a practical time machine to aid the verbally impulsive to take back what they had said. The past is the past, however, and living in it and in the land of "what if" is the core of the sickness. Hence, empty the head. Wipe that slate; focus on the present moment.

Taking out the mental garbage. That was always the first task of any day if it was to be a bearable day. Lesson one from the cop shrink. Detective Sergeant Richard Dobbs was still on lesson one.

Many days weren't bearable. Dobbs could always trace the cause of the disaster to failing to take out the head trash. He never would have listened to the police shrink if that's all the guy had been. But the therapist had once carried the tin, and so Dobbs had listened.

He looked at his half-shaved image in the bathroom

mirror. His eyes were hooded, the jaw set, the face a wall built to hide himself from the world. "Rick," he said to himself, "your head is full of shit."

He closed his eyes as he whispered the words the cop shrink had put on him after his partner had been killed the year before. "You can't function, you can't even survive, if you live in a constant state of rage, guilt, and shame. The consequence of cutting yourself off from those feelings, however, is you wind up being unfeeling and insensitive."

He felt the heat fill his face. He couldn't make up his mind where the heat came from: his rage over Francisco's Newton Street Nigger Nicker or his own guilt and embarrassment over his use of the term Soto Street Slag Slasher. "Both," he whispered to himself, "Both."

There was more.

It wasn't so much that using the label had angered George. It was that Dobbs couldn't see that it would hurt him. It had never crossed his mind. As he picked up his razor and scraped at his face, he remembered something his father had told him. It had been about the utter astonishment of some of the "white" people in his hometown of Waynesboro, Virginia, to learn back in the sixties that the "coloreds" in the town objected to the term "nigger."

When he had first heard the story, little Ricky had been eight years old. He hadn't believed his father because he couldn't bring himself to accept that any human could be so deadened in his feelings and perceptions not to know how that word landed on certain ears. As he rinsed and dried his face he mentally whipped himself with the fact that he had done the same thing with the Tencts.

He had never called anyone a slag except when

telling a joke to a non-Tenctonese. That he had done. Like any member of the blue frat in the locker room telling old Rastus jokes, that he had done. Some of the jokes *were* funny.

"Just like some of the nigger, Hebe, and Polack jokes are *really* funny," he muttered. "Yeah. How many humans *does* it take to screw in a light bulb?"

What was it the cop shrink had said? Flogging yourself never was part of the recovery process. That's easy for him to say. He didn't believe that there were certain mistakes he just couldn't make.

Slag.

The term had come easily to Rick's lips. Too easily. That was the mistake he couldn't make: to do to another what had been done to him.

Slag.

Why not? "Slag" didn't have anything to do with him. The word "slag" didn't touch him any more than the word "nigger" touched the "whites."

How *did* the name "whitey" land on certain ears? What about Redskin? Chink? Spic? He didn't really know. Why should he develop a case of nerves over it? Why, indeed?

"Damned idiot," he muttered to himself as he wiped up the sink and tossed the dirty towel into the laundry hamper and slammed the lid shut.

"What was that, Rick?" came a sleepy voice from the bedroom.

"Nothing."

There was a pause followed by the sleepy face of Kit Dobbs appearing in the door. "Nothing? You sure you don't have a fork stuck in your garbage disposal?"

Slowly he faced his wife, his eyebrows raised. "Say I'm tossing out my melon mush in a noisy bucket?"

Her face grew serious. "What's the matter, Rick?"

"Honest. It's nothing."

"Honest?" Her very fair skin reddened as her brown eyes grew darker. "Honest? Don't you let that word out of your lying mouth, baby. You know what the therapist said. You keep stacking it up inside, sooner or later it'll come out the top of your head. Let me be honest, too. There isn't anything that makes me happier than sending my man out the front door with a gun full of hot loads and a heart full of murder."

"I'm not going to murder anyone."

"So, Rick, you going to tell me what it is?"

He glanced down, sighed, and folded his arms. "It's George. You know, Matt Sikes's partner?"

"Sure. I remember George. Beaver burger raw, mushrooms and Swiss, hold the mayo." She grinned, "At the cookout year before last."

"Yeah. Well, I said something to him. Something not very nice, he figured. I didn't think much about it—hell, I didn't think about it at all."

"And then George said something, and you said something more, and George said—"

"You got the picture. I had to get out of there before I *did* kill someone."

Kit Dobbs came all of the way into the room, her delicate fingers pushing her auburn hair back from her eyes. She wrapped her hands around his arm, reached up, and kissed his cheek. "You've had fights before and gotten over them. What is it this time?"

He turned his head and looked down into her eyes. "Kit, am I a racist?"

Her eyebrows went up as her jaw dropped. "A racist? Rick, don't you think marrying me is a pretty weird thing to do for a racist?"

He shook his head. "I don't mean it like that. I don't think of you being 'white' anyway."

"Neither do I. Have you suddenly gone 'black' on me?"

Dobbs burst out with an involuntary laugh. "I don't know, but I sure had a black attack yesterday. I know because George Francisco had me smokin'."

A tiny frown creased her forehead. "Now, why would he do a thing like that, Rick?"

"I guess I pushed a button of his."

"You guess?"

Dobbs pursed his lips and arched an eyebrow at her. "Are you sure you're not sneaking out nights to go to law school?"

"All I do is teach piano, baby. Teach piano and love you."

"You'd make a great prosecutor."

"I still haven't forgotten my question."

Dobbs shook himself free from her grip, took his fresh shirt from the hanger on the back of the door, and began putting it on. "Like I said. You'd make a great prosecutor." He buttoned it up, turned up his collar, and took his tie from the hanger. "Okay. I pushed a button. I used the S word around him and he took offense."

She looked at her husband's reflection in the mirror. "And he came back with the big N?"

"Sort of. He was trying to show me that what I was saying was basically the same thing that he was saying."

"And?" She turned him around and began straightening his necktie.

"And he was right. It was. It was, and I needed to be told that. But, damn, I don't like it. I don't like being told, and I especially don't like the fact that I needed to be told." He turned and looked down at her. "So, am I a racist? Am I just as bad as those *New Republic* liberals in the 'burbs, carrying their equality signs on prime time and telling watermelon jokes after hours?"

She searched his eyes for a moment, then sat on the edge of the tub. "On a talk show once I heard a person—she was Tenctonese—I heard her say that anyone who uses racial labels and believes that they're actually talking about something is a racist."

"Racial labels?"

"The usual invectives, in addition to 'black,' 'white,' 'Asian,' 'native American,' and so on."

"Hell, that makes pretty near everybody a racist. Everybody in the world."

"Almost everybody. The show I was watching was about persons, both human and Tenctonese, who reject the usual labels and refuse to use them."

"Well, what do they call us?"

She shrugged and held out her hands. "Rick and Kit Dobbs."

"You know what I'm talking about, baby. What do they call *us?* You know, the brothers and sisters? African-Americans? Blacks? Negroes?"

Kit smiled as she stared into space for a moment. "It was a very interesting program. They would take someone's definition of a racial label, such as 'black,' and then they would search through the audience until they found one or more exceptions, invalidating the definition. Just for example, there was melanin. Anyone who has melanin in their skin is 'black.' They showed that all of the so-called 'whites' in the audience had melanin in their skin, and some of them had more melanin than some of the so-called 'blacks' in the audience. There was one person in the audience who had no melanin in his skin at all, and he was an albino who called himself 'black.'" She grinned. "They did the same thing with nose shape, hair, eyes, ancestral origins, and everything else. The point they were making was that none of the labels refer to anything real. According to current science, every American, with the exception of the Tencts, are African-Americans."

"You can't define racism away."

"No. Racism is very real. It's only races that are fictions . . . according to the show." She held out her hands and shrugged. "It was just another talk show."

"What do you think about it? What they said. Do you believe it?"

"They were very convincing and I haven't heard anything since that disproves what they were saying."

"Kit, if you go along with that stuff, that makes me a racist."

"It makes me a racist, too, baby. Everybody's got a heap of head trash to toss out, including me." She stood up and placed her hand against his cheek. "That trash is some damned sticky stuff, too."

After breakfast, Dobbs's partner, Jerry Kirk, drove over to the edge of Monterey Park and pulled up in front of Dobbs's house. As his partner stood on the stoop with his wife, Kirk turned his head and looked away. "Damn!" he swore beneath his breath. It just didn't go. It didn't go at all. Dobbs, blacker than the proverbial ace, married to a white woman. They didn't have to do that stuff in public view—all that kissing and ass-patting. Why can't they at least keep it indoors? It's wrong! It's flat damned wrong!

He looked to his left at the house across the street from Dobbs's. Some Chicano guy in a suit was walking from his front door across his tiny lawn to the curb where he got into his bright red Mazda sports coupe. The woman at the door looked Korean. Maybe

Japanese or Chinese. Maybe Indian or Chicano. A lot of them looked Asian. Sometimes it was hard to tell.

"Man, what in the hell is eating you?"

Kirk turned his head and saw Dobbs's face looking at him through the passenger-side window. His face flushed as he looked to the front. "Nothing. Get in, we're late."

Dobbs pulled open the door, dropped into the passenger seat, and shut the door. As he pulled the seat belt across his body, he kept looking at his new partner. "Give, son. If you've got a problem, I need to know."

He started the car, put it in gear, and pulled away from the curb. "You don't need to know anything about my personal life."

"If it affects your performance, I do. I know we haven't hit it off together, Kirk, but we have to work together. When we get jammed, my life is going to depend on you, and if you're worried about your leather bar date dumping you—"

"I am not gay!"

"I didn't say you were. But you better tell me what's eating your ass, man. If you don't, you can forget about checking out Trassler, Rantu, the makeup man, and the slaghunters because we're going straight to the command center where I am going to have Grazer send you to the shrinker. You got me?"

They drove in silence for a long time. As Kirk turned the car south onto Atlantic, he said, "Okay, Dobbs. I'll tell you what's bothering me, and you're not going to like it, okay?"

"Get it off your chest."

Jerry Kirk nodded in silence for a moment, and then said, "Okay. Understand I got nothing against blacks. I grew up around them, worked with them in the army, and went through the academy with them. I even had one for a training officer when I was assigned to University division. I think I could've even worked with you. We wouldn't be taking showers together, but we could've been okay. Understand?"

"Is it my deodorant?"

"No! It's not your damned deodorant! Now if we're going to be serious about this, let's get to it. Otherwise, let's just drop it."

"Sorry. Go on."

Jerry Kirk moistened his lips and nodded again as if to give himself permission to proceed. "Okay. I'll just say it. It got me the first time I picked you up."

"I thought you might want to use the car. Would you rather I picked you up?"

"No, it's not that. It's not picking you up. I'm glad to do it, and you're right, I needed the car. Thanks." He glanced at Dobbs, frowned, and returned his gaze to the street ahead. "It's—you know—your wife."

Dobbs's eyebrows went up. "Kit? What about her?"

"Not her exactly. It's her and you. You know what I mean?"

"No. What do you mean?"

"I'll say it plain, okay?"

"That'd be a new wrinkle."

Kirk's eyes narrowed as he said, "It's this race mixing: blacks and whites together. I don't go for it. I don't go for it at all. It makes me real uncomfortable."

"I can see that."

"Well, that's the problem, Dobbs. Blacks should stay with blacks and whites with whites. That's just the way I see it."

"You think my wife's white?" asked Dobbs. "Is that what's chewing on you?"

"Isn't she?"

72

Dobbs chuckled as he shook his head. "Man, let me help you put down that burden. Kit isn't white."

"You could have fooled me."

"I guess she already did. So don't worry about it. Kit's not white."

Jerry Kirk grinned as yards of knotted tension dropped from him. "Man, am I ever sorry."

"No sweat."

"No, Dobbs. I've been a real jerk this past couple of weeks. Thinking your wife was white. I feel like a real jerk."

"Don't worry about it."

"I sure thought she was white. I guess it shouldn't, but it really bothered me. Know what I mean?"

"Yeah. I think I do. The fact is, though, she's not white." Dobbs turned his face toward Kirk, pursed his lips, and put his elbow up on the backrest. "I think I can ease your mind about something else, too."

"Oh?"

"You aren't white, either." Jerry Kirk frowned as Dobbs laughed and slapped the dashboard with his hand. "C'mon, pilgrim. Let's get out to Toon Town and see Rantu, the makeup man."

CHAPTER 7

At the same time that morning, George Francisco drove in silence as Paul Iniko sat in the passenger seat looking at the graffiti sprayed on the fences, buildings, and houses along Whittier. He looked up and the sky was crowded with blacks and grays, the rare threat of rain imminent. Iniko turned to the open file on his lap and leafed through the tear sheets of "Slag Like Me." As he read he said, "I thought we had taken care of these little problems last year when we worked together on the Maanka Dak case."

George glanced to his right, then returned his gaze to the road. "What little problems?"

"Me being a former Overseer and you being a current asshole."

"Asshole?"

Iniko nodded and said in Tenctonese, *"Tirivi."*

"I *know* what 'asshole' means!"

"I imagine such knowledge would be difficult for you to avoid."

George shook his head and continued looking through the windshield for the street he wanted. "What are you talking about, Iniko?"

The FBI man closed the file and faced Francisco. "Well, George, the way my superior in the bureau puts it, 'We was in the trenches together, boy, on the same team, fightin' the same bad guys, bleedin' the same goddamned blood.'" Iniko grinned. "My superior, Nate Crook, is a very colorful character."

"No doubt."

Paul Iniko looked back at the street. "What I'm trying to say, George, is that a year ago we were approaching the brink of a rather substantial friendship. Then, nothing. Right now you're as cold as an iceberg in suspended animation."

"What do you want from me, Paul? A hug?"

George was astonished as the former Overseer burst out in laughter. When he had calmed himself, Iniko nodded and said, "A hug would be just fine, George. It would be just fine."

"Some other time. I don't think I'm quite ready yet to hug an Overseer."

"Former Overseer," Paul corrected.

"Yeah, right."

They rode in silence for a half block, then Iniko said calmly, "I talked to my superior about you, George."

"Oh?"

"About five months ago. I tried since we had worked together to stay in touch, and although I developed a curiously friendly relationship with just about everyone else in your family, you I couldn't reach. When I did get you on the phone, there was always one excuse or another why we couldn't get together."

"You know how things are."

"Yes," said Paul. "I think I do." There was a pause, then Paul continued. "Nate Crook is a very wise man. When things bother me, I go and have a talk with him and he often has an insight that's helped. Do you have anyone like that, George?"

"Perhaps. Do you remember Malcolm Bone?"

"The human *hila* at the East L.A. *Rama Vo?*"

George nodded. "Yes. Sometimes I talk to him." George frowned as he thought. "It's been awhile though. What about it?"

"There was a story Nate Crook told me. The short version began quite awhile before our ship crashed here. Nate was in the army stationed on Okinawa during the Vietnam War. He didn't do much in the war except swing a club as an MP, but it was the friends he made on Okinawa while he was there that were important. During his training in South Carolina, you see, all the whites sat at those tables, all the blacks sat at those other tables, and everyone else divided up pretty much the same. There was no law that required this segregation. That's just what seemed to cause the least friction. On Okinawa, though, these lines seemed to melt. They were all American soldiers and the 'thems' were the Okinawans. He made what he thought to be some very good friends on Okinawa. When his military police company was brought back to South Carolina, however, everyone was sitting at separate tables again. When he tried to sit with his best friend, the others at the table told him to sit with the whites. He sat across from his friend and waited to hear what he had to say. The man nodded and said, 'Go on. Sit over there.' It was all black and white again. Us and them. Nate says it broke his heart."

"I bet this story even has a point," said George, the sarcasm suspended from his syllables.

"Yes, George. It has a point, a rather important one." Iniko's voice grew very quiet. "Back when we were working together to take down Maanka Dak, Dr. Norcross and the MDQ, back when we were trying to protect your family, save your partner's life, and protect each other's asses, we weren't Overseer and slave, master and servant, torturer and victim. We were two cops against the bad guys. If not friends, I thought we had at least achieved a degree of mutual respect."

George rode in silence for a long while, the horrors of a year ago flashing through his mind. "It was a confusing time for me, Paul. I was going through *riana,* Matt was dying, and the craziest bastard on earth was after me and my family. That tattoo around your wrist didn't seem so big against all that."

"Look at this, George."

Francisco faced Iniko and the former Overseer had his sleeve pulled up, exposing his left wrist. There was no sign remaining of the jagged tattooed cuff of the Overseers. "It's gone," remarked George.

"It took a doctor about half an hour with a special laser pen. Then it was a few weeks more for my body to absorb the bruises and the remains of the dye. I had it done eight months ago."

"Why? Aren't you proud to be an Overseer?"

Iniko pulled his sleeve back down. "No more proud than you are to have been a slave. I've said it to you before, George, neither one of us had choices as to what we were to become back on the ship. We do have choices now, however."

"That's our street," said George as he swung the car right onto Marietta. Soon after the turn, he found the address he was looking for and pulled the car over to the curb. He put the car in park, shut off the engine, and looked at Iniko. "Let me tell you a little story, Paul. Not long after we were released from the quarantine camp, my children were going out to celebrate their first Halloween. My daughter Emily surprised me by dressing up as an Overseer, complete with washable tattoo." George averted his glance and grimaced. "No. Let me be perfectly honest about it. She didn't surprise me; she frightened me half to death." He shifted his gaze to the former Overseer. "For just a moment my instinctual reaction was to kill her, my own daughter." He looked at Iniko, his face a mask. "The memories are too sharp, Paul; the scars run too deep. We can work together, as it appears we must for the time being, but being friends is out of the question. Can you see us going fishing together, playing cards, our families having a picnic together?" George frowned as a question presented itself. "Do you even have a family?"

"In a manner of speaking, but not the kind of family you mean." Paul turned to the file on his lap, a resigned expression on his face. "So, shall we go call upon the family of young Randy Cook and see how 'Slag Like Me' has touched their lives?"

CHAPTER 8

"IT'S ALL BULLSHIT," declared Gil Cook from his kitchen table, his balding jowled countenance perched on a tank of a body clad in sweatpants and a T-shirt sporting the stars and stripes. The writing on the T-shirt urged the reader to "Try and burn this one." Old Glory had several holes in it and appeared to have a much better chance of rotting to pieces than being set aflame. Randy Cook's father had a florid face that was kept that way by frequent ingestion of Coors Lite. Iniko picked up an empty can and read the printing. According to the label, each can contained a considerable number of calories less than the same size can of regular Coors, and by the look of Gil Cook's gut and the bulging bags of empty beer cans in the kitchen, Gil was saving thousands of calories every day.

"In southern California," cracked Mrs. Cook to Paul, "everybody's a health nut." Linda Cook looked to be about half her husband's age, although the file showed her to be only a year younger.

"What're you swingin' your ass at them for?" Gil said to his wife. "You think a couple of slags're interested in a dried-up old bitch like you?"

"If we could get back to the subject," urged George.

"I already said it was all bullshit," said the man with the beer can. "Randy never beat up on no little girl. I don't care what that damned Jew said in his column."

"Jew?"

Mr. Cook nodded. "Sure. That name—Robb. Short for Rabinowitz, right? Everybody knows that, 'cept maybe a couple of slags. Not that I got anything against the Jews, y'unnerstand."

"Of course," said Iniko.

"Yeah, right," said Mrs. Cook.

Ignoring her, the elder Cook stabbed at the air with his finger. "Hittin' a girl, even a slag kid. I'd punch the shit outta Randy he do anything like that. He knows it, too. What kinda kid you think I raised? He didn't beat up no little slag bitch. He didn't beat up nobody at all, 'less they asked for it." He held his beer can up and nodded at Francisco and Iniko. "Don't mean no offense there, officers. About the slag thing, I mean. No offense, there. I don't have no rotten milk or I'd offer you somethin'."

"I don't care for the stuff, myself," said Paul. Iniko placed the empty beer can next to the sink as George pulled several photographs from the file.

"Mr. Cook, these are prints of photographs taken by the security cameras at the playground of your son's school." He tossed them on the table in front of Gil Cook. "Do you see the two boys and the girl beating up on a smaller Tenctonese girl? Isn't that larger boy your son?"

Randy Cook's father leaned forward and cast a bleary gaze toward the photos. He shook his head and looked up at George. "Shit, that's not Randy. The boy don't own a shirt like that."

"Why don't you try looking at his face?"

The man shrugged. "He's so cruddy, how can you tell? All that hair down in his face."

"That's Randy all right," Mrs. Cook declared. George looked at her as she looked up from the photo and nodded. "Randy takes after his father."

Gil Cook renewed his purchase on his beer can and slumped back in his chair. "My lawyer says I shouldn't answer no questions about what happened there. We're takin' the paper to court, see? Snotty-assed damned *Times*. Lie about my kid." He shifted his weight from one hip to the other, finished off the can in his hand, and pointed the empty at Iniko and Francisco. "Look, you two. The child protective laws in this state. The paper and that Ellison Rabinowitz can't take a twelve-year-old kid and smear his name all over the papers like that. It ain't legal. I got a lawyer who says so."

"Thirteen," said Mrs. Cook, her voice flat.

"What're you talkin' about?" asked her husband, his face screwed up in confusion.

"Thirteen," she repeated. "Your son Randy is thirteen years old."

"Thirteen?" He waved a hand, dismissing the minor point of his son's age. "The point is that they can't do that to my boy. It's not legal."

"Tell him what you and that lawyer are claiming for damages," said his wife.

"Seven million dollars. That'll teach that Hebe paper to drag my name through the mud. Goddamned rich snots. Seven million. They'll think twice before they go after some other innocent sweet kid, you can bet your ass on that."

"If I might interrupt this homage to truth, justice, and the American way," said Iniko, "can you account for your whereabouts for the past seventy-two hours?"

"My what? Whereabouts?"

"Yes."

"Nobody says whereabouts anymore."

"I just did."

"You mean where I was, not whereabouts." Gil Cook's expression of righteous certitude collapsed into confusion. "For seventy-two hours?"

"That's three days," offered George.

"Three days?" repeated Cook, his expression even more confused. "I know how long three days is. Sure. I know where I was. I guess so." He moistened his lips and looked at his wife, an edge of panic in his eyes.

"Gil couldn't account for the past fifteen minutes," said Mrs. Cook, "but I can account for the past three days for him." Her gaze moved slowly from George's face until it settled upon her husband's form. "Sergeant, I can tell you where Gil has been for the past three months, the past three years. He's either been in here, in the living room in front of the TV, or in bed, making empty cans out of full ones. I think I can safely say that he hasn't left the house once since he was released from the hospital seven months ago, except to go to the supermarket." Her eyes hazed over for a second, then grew clear and hard as she said, "He was in the hospital for a drug overdose."

"Alcohol poisoning," corrected her husband.

"A drug is a drug," she answered.

Gil Cook pushed himself to his feet, went to the refrigerator, took a fresh six-pack from it, and stumbled off to the living room. In a moment the sounds of a beer company commercial extolling the virtues of responsible drinking came booming from the living room television.

The mother of Randy Cook looked at Iniko and said, "Are you looking into the lawsuit that ambulance-chasing leech got my husband to file?"

"No. We're investigating the disappearance of Ellison Robb."

Her face was stiff, and suddenly she looked very old. "It would be a shame if anything happened to Ellison Robb. She's very brave. She's saying some really important things."

"Why would you say that?" asked George.

"Why would I say what?"

"Why did you call Ellison Robb she? Is Ellison Robb a woman?"

"Of course." Mrs. Cook shook her head and smiled. "I guess I just assumed it. I don't know anything for certain, except Robb has a heart. If a little girl cries, Ellison Robb feels it and does what's right, even if it's against the law."

"Against the law?" repeated Paul Iniko.

"Mentioning a minor's name in the paper like that is illegal. Gil was right about that."

"Well, then," said George. "Doesn't that mean a big settlement for your family?"

Her eyes narrowed as they glared at George. "My family couldn't survive any kind of a settlement. Right now Gil's drinking is limited by the amount of his disability pension and whatever Randy can steal. If Gil can buy and drink all the booze he wants, he won't last a week."

When it was time to leave, Iniko stayed behind for a moment as George went to the car and reported in. After Iniko came out of the house and climbed into the passenger seat, George pulled into traffic and said, "I was just thinking how unreasonably restrictive the laws governing justifiable homicide are."

"Still have that asshole problem, don't you, George?"

"You want to clarify that, Overseer?"

"Gil Cook isn't a fugitive from a horror movie. He's a very sick man. His whole family's sick." Surprised, George faced him. The FBI man was looking back, his gaze steady. "You may be right after all, George."

"Right about what?"

"The friendship thing between us." Paul Iniko faced the street. "It just might be impossible."

CHAPTER 9

"TIAN APEHNA?" MATT Sikes looked at the sad-eyed Tenctonese woman holding the front door of Micky Cass's Coldwater Canyon home. The skin of her face was smooth and very pale, the lips full and touched with warm blush. Her eyes were hidden by sunglasses. She carried her expression like a mask, allowing no entrance into or observation of her secret heart. That, too, was the purpose of the sunglasses. Any Tenctonese answering the door on a cloudy day only wore sunglasses to hide the color of the eyes. Her eyes would be tinged with green, the color of pain. Or perhaps that was what she would have an observing detective believe.

"Sergeant Sikes?" She left the door open and turned to lead the way. They entered a rustic, pine-paneled living room. Everything else about the house was the typical stucco, red tile, late Hollywood mongrel Spanish ranch. The living room, however, was a jarring throwback to downeast wood stoves and black-fly infested summers in Maine. Tian held out her hand toward a corner of the room. It was filled with an old wooden desk, a high-backed leather office chair and a word processor sitting amidst a litter of papers, books, and models of everything from fighter planes to human skulls. "Not exactly West Coast, is it?"

Matt felt his face flush. "Sorry. This room all of a sudden reminded me of my grandparents' house in Maine."

"Mick never took me to Maine. Do you miss it, sergeant?"

His eyebrows went up. "Do I miss Maine? Are you kidding? Ice, mud, bugs, and more ice? The only state with a picture of a dead animal on its license plate? Black flies and mosquitoes that use Raid for gargle? Home of the pink plastic flamingo? Acid rain toilet of America? Principal imports: government regulations and bureaucrats; principal exports: alcoholics and people looking for work?" Matt closed his mouth and shook his head. The anger in his words surprised him. Because he had thought Maine and a couple of alcoholic grandparents were behind him, another feeling surprised him, as well. He shrugged as he nibbled at the inside of his lower lip. "I'm sorry, Mrs. Cass. Yeah, sometimes I miss Maine. I guess it's one of those love-hate things. Is Mr. Cass from Maine?"

"Let's get something straight, sergeant. First, I am not Mrs. Cass. My name is Tian Apehna. Next, Micky Cass's full name is Micky Cass. Mick allowed no titles such as Mr., Miss, Mrs., or Ms. to be attached to his name. And, lastly, I don't know where he came from. He used to live in the Northeast, but there's hardly a place on the planet he hasn't been. He used to tell me he was from another planet until I made it clear to him I didn't find his humor amusing."

Matt stopped next to the desk and pushed around a couple of papers. "What should I call you?"

"Tian would be fine."

"Okay, Tian. I'm Matt." He turned his head and let his gaze settle on her eyes. The glasses were off and her eyes were green. She was looking at his hand where it rested on Micky Cass's desk. "Tian, I know your . . . mate, spouse, partner, or whatever—"

"Micky."

"Yes, Micky. I know Micky has this thing about keeping certain things secret, but it makes this investigation ten times more difficult. For example, is he a man?"

"Micky Cass is one hell of a man, Matt."

"Thank y—"

"She's also one hell of a woman."

Matt folded his arms across his chest, tilted his head forward, and looked at Tian from beneath his eyebrows. "This isn't a joke."

"Do you see me laughing?"

"Do you mind telling me, then, why Cass, his editor, and you—all three—refer to Cass as 'he'? Why not 'it' or one of those 'he or she' or 's/he' things?"

"This is all quite meaningless." She looked at the expression on his face, then shrugged and sat down on the varnished pine and plaid canvas upholstered couch. "It's a habit one gets into, saying 'he.' Mick referred to himself that way because, as far as he was concerned, 'it' sounds like something from a black and white science fiction film, constant repetitions of 'he or she' makes for very clumsy sentences, and 'shehe' sounds and looks stupid. I wouldn't read anymore into it than that."

Shaking his head and holding out his hands in disbelief, Matt said, "What is so damned important about keeping this person's sex a secret?"

"It's not important," answered Tian. "It's not important at all. That's what's so important about it."

"You're not going to tell me?"

"No."

"Not even if it would save Micky Cass's life?"

Tears came to her eyes as she looked up at Matt. "That's something else where Mick's priorities are different from everyone else's. Life isn't as important to him as what he is." She pointed toward Cass's desk. "He wants you to read those words by Micky Cass. Not a woman's words, not a man's words, not a hermaphrodite's words or the words of a gay, straight, atheist, religionist." The corners of her mouth tugged into a sad smile. "Not even a Latvian black gay midget biker." The tears streaked her cheeks and she reached to the coffee table for a tissue. "You want to know what Mick's big regret is?"

"What?"

" 'Slag Like Me' doesn't work at all unless it's written by a human undercover as a Tenct, and so that's what he had to do. Mick would've loved keeping his humanity a secret, too. He doesn't want the readers to get a 'human' view of racism. He wants them to see the creature itself. He wants them to witness racism."

"Isn't this speciesism instead of racism?"

She gave a sad smile and said, "Drugs and alcohol."

"What's that?"

She glanced away. "The difference between drugs

and alcohol—it's like changing seats on the *Titanic*. It's something Mick said to me once." She faced Matt. "Actually, it's us-and-themism. That's Mick's dragon, us-and-themism." She looked away. "Is Mick dead?"

"I don't know." He sat down in a wing-backed chair opposite the couch. "It's way too early to start throwing dirt on him." He glanced at her guiltily. "So to speak. Hell, we don't even know if we have a crime yet, and we already have a list of suspects that could fill the L.A. white pages. I just don't know."

She smiled, the sadness filling her face. "Matt, I understand that everyone is a suspect right now, including me."

Sikes leaned his elbows on his knees, clasped his hands, and shrugged. "That's really somebody else's department. I'm just here in preparation for going undercover. The powers that be figure somebody might've gotten a particular kind of bent nose by Micky Cass disguising himself as a Tenctonese, over and above everyone else whose noses were knocked out of joint by him, that is." He paused and looked at the woman. She was looking back, her gaze steady. "But as long as I'm here, is there some reason why you should be a suspect?"

"What a clever segue," Tian Apehna said coyly as she cocked her head to one side. At last she smiled warmly and nodded. "No one has a more profitable motive. Mick's will leaves everything to me."

"You've seen his will?"

Her smile faded and she looked down and unconsciously smoothed a wrinkle from her smock. "I'm his business manager. I collect the spoils, count the gold, hand out the favors, and keep Mick straight with Internal Revenue." She looked up at Matt. "The estate comes to just under two million dollars, not including Mick's copyrights and future royalties. The total could be well over five million."

"I didn't ask."

Her gaze was fixed on his eyes. "You wouldn't have been much of a detective if you hadn't asked. In some circles five million is a heap of motive."

"Yeah," said Matt, nodding. "That's a heap of motive in just about every circle I've ever seen, experienced, or heard about."

"Don't you want to know where I've been the past few days?"

Matt slumped back in his chair, crossed his legs, and held out his arms. "Look, Tian, other officers are handling this part of the investigation. The only reason I'm here . . . I don't really know why I'm here. Maybe I'm scared. Maybe I wanted to find out if Micky Cass was ever scared." He looked up at her. "Did he have any enemies?"

"That was a damned silly question."

Matt nodded as his face grew warm. "Yeah, I guess it was. Stock question in detective kindergarten. Was he scared, though?"

"He is always scared. This world, the peoples on it, how they think, what they do, and why they do it scares him. His reaction to fear, however, is to beat it to death with his words."

Matt nodded. "Okay, I'll bite. Where were you for the past three days?"

"I have absolutely no alibi at all. I was here working in my studio, out taking rides or walks, and here sleeping at night. I called no one, met no one, saw no one, except for Marty Fell and a pair of very rude police officers. Terrible, isn't it?"

"I don't know," he answered with a slight shrug.

"I'd figure a perp would be prepared to come across with a better story than that."

"Unless the perp knew that and said it to throw you off," Tian responded, the hint of a smile on her lips.

"Okay, lady. I'll bite again. Why did the chicken cross the road?"

She laughed out loud, the outburst ending as quickly as it began. She took another tissue, stood, and faced a large array of windows looking out upon the hills above. "Matt, I'm going to tell you one of Micky Cass's most closely guarded secrets. Have you ever read any of the Nance Damas police routine novels?"

"Sure. The sister in the San Francisco Police Department. The mysteries by Damita Real. They even made a couple of movies out of them. I'm reading one right now, *The Seventh Dragon.*"

She wiped her nose and nodded as she continued looking at the hills. "Mick and I have been doing the Damita Real novels for almost three years."

"Micky Cass is Damita Real?"

She faced Matt and raised her eyebrows in a display of mock offense. "Mick and *I* are Damita Real. He once said that I was Damita, which means little lady, and he was Real, which means real. I plot, outline, we both do research, and Mick writes and rewrites. Let me ask you something."

"Sure."

"As a police officer, what do you think of the Damas novels?"

"Looking for a testimonial?"

"Please," she urged.

Matt thought for a moment and sat back in his chair. "Gritty," he said. "Real. I can smell the streets. I know the same cops that fictional character knows. I've chased the same perps, been mulched by the same paper wizards, sweated the same sweat. In fact, I didn't think she was fictional. I was convinced the author was a policewoman on the SFPD. The pair of you certainly got into some cop's head to write that stuff."

"Thank you. Thank you very much. Mick will take that as a very big compliment." She faced Matt and fixed him with her gaze, her eyes brimming with tears. "Matt, Micky Cass is no ivory-tower word mechanic. He gets into the middle of it, rolls up his sleeves, and gets good and dirty. He doesn't write about it until he knows all about it, whatever it is. When he says the only reasons he might miss a manuscript drop are death, injury, or abduction, take it seriously. He knows the territory."

Matt nodded as he got to his feet, three things gnawing at the back of his head, two of them business, one personal. "I guess I shouldn't be bothering you. I really only have one reason for seeing you. It was something I wanted to ask."

"Go ahead. The worst I can do is tell you it's none of your business."

Matt raised his eyebrows and averted his gaze. "You just might do that." He looked at her eyes. "Tian, after Micky Cass had the plastic surgery done, you know, after he looked like a Tenct, did he spend any time here with you at home?"

"Almost every night."

"The disguise—did it affect things?"

"Affect things?" She burst out with a laugh. "Affect things? It bent how everyone on the street saw him."

His face reddening, Matt put his hands in his pockets and shrugged. "That's not the kind of things I meant."

"What things, then?"

"Did it affect how you saw him? Did it affect things between Mick and you? How did you feel about him showing up as a Tenctonese? You know—living together, seeing each other—"

"Sex," she completed.

"Well . . . yeah."

Tian Apehna's eyes seemed to mist over as she looked thoughtful for a second. She glanced up at Matt and asked, "Do you have a girl, Matt?"

"Yes."

"A Tenctonese girl?"

"Yeah. Sort of."

"Do you mean she's sort of Tenct or do you mean she's sort of a girl?"

"Tian, you're getting to be a real pain in the ass."

"It comes naturally to anyone who spends a great deal of time dealing with pricks." Her eyebrows raised. "Are you very much in love?"

He looked away for a moment. "Yeah. I am with her, anyway. She's one of the few good things that've ever happened to me. I don't want to screw it up. I don't want this job to screw it up."

Tian's lips parted in a smile as she touched Matt's face with her hands. "Matt, you aren't a patch of hair or a couple of ear flaps. That's what Mick's been writing about his whole life. You aren't a color, or a sex, or a life-style, an occupation, a background, or a name. You are a creature—an entity—unique to the universe, worthy to exist."

"What's that got to do with things between you and Mick?"

"Not a thing. It only concerns you and your worst enemy, you."

"That's what Cathy's been trying to tell me." Matt thought for a moment and then asked, "Those nights after the plastic surgery, while he was here at home, did he have any contact with anyone besides you?"

"No. Not at the house. He talked to a few persons on the telephone."

"Who?"

"I'm not certain. There was Martin Fell at the *Times,* that Tenct street gang leader he wrote about in 'The Color Pink,'—"

"Danny Mikubeh," Matt completed.

"Yes. There were a few others. I didn't overhear them all, but I saw his phone logs. The police have them."

"I know. What else?"

"Not much, except on the last night he was here he didn't stay. He had been writing hard all afternoon and he took a break for a few minutes. I remember because I took him some iced tea up on his balcony. I spent some time with him," she said, a catch in her voice. "Then there was a telephone call. He answered it, and after talking to whoever it was for four or five minutes, he told me he had to leave on an important matter. Shortly after dark he left, and that was the last I ever saw or heard of him."

"You have no idea who the call was from?"

She slowly shook her head. "There was nothing on any of Mick's phone pads and nothing revealing about the impressions left by previous messages. I know. I checked. So did your lab trolls. Nick had a terrible memory, so wherever he went, it was to a place he knew."

Matt turned toward the door and paused as he remembered one of the business items that chewed at his serenity. "Tian, there was one other thing I wanted to ask you."

"Oh?"

"In the first 'Slag Like Me' column, Mick started it off by making a crack about his neighbor."

"'As my next-door neighbor would be pleased to tell you,'" she quoted, "'I'm not a nice guy.'"

"Yeah. That's right. What's he mean? Who's the neighbor, and what's the problem?"

"The neighbor's name is Duke Jessup. His house is just above and behind ours. Believe it or not, when Mick bought this house, Jessup ran a petition campaign to drive us out of the neighborhood."

"Because you're a Newcomer?"

She laughed and held out her hands in a gesture of absolute bewilderment. "Not that exclusively. There are a number of Tenctonese in the canyon." She grinned sadly. "I guess you could say it was a color thing."

"Mick's color?"

"I'm guessing it was the color of the house. All of the houses around here are painted in pastels, and Mick Cass is not a pastel sort of person. Before we moved in, he had it painted its current color."

"When I drove up I noticed the house kind of jumped out at me. What's the name of the color?"

"Fire Island Red." She nodded toward the east and continued. "Duke Jessup even took Mick to court over it citing protective covenants, ordinances, and so on, but the court found in Mick's favor."

Matt held out his hands. "Then, what's the beef?"

"When he took Mick to court, Jessup committed the big sin. Mick hates lawyers, hates the lawyer game, as he calls litigation, and would prefer spending the remainder of his life having root canal to enduring a minute in court."

Matt nodded. "I can relate. I take it Mick retaliated in some way?"

"*Some* way. A perfectly legal way, if not terribly mature." She went to Mick's desk, picked up a slip of paper covered in cling wrap, and held her hand out toward a side door. "Take a walk with me, Matt."

She led Sikes through the door onto a shaded patio that led to stairs that climbed up toward the rear of the house. Behind the house was a small rose garden. Above the garden, high on the hill overlooking its own much grander garden, was a pale pink ranch dug into the hillside. The side facing downhill had an enormous deck with a panoramic view of Micky Cass's home. "I don't get it," said Matt.

"Turn around."

Matt turned, looked at the back of Mick's house, and had to take a step back from the sheer impact of what he saw. It was as though Salvador Dali, Stephen King, Isaac Asimov, and Elton John tripped out on acid to collaborate on a house-painting job, calling in Cher, Picasso, and Charlie Manson for art direction. Writhing bodies in hot pinks, black flies, snakes in electric greens, a spectacular nova in eye-shattering yellows, pinks, whites, and oranges, three neon blue dolphins killing and feasting upon a neon red tuna, turquoise stripes, bits of mirror, reflectors off bicycles, thousands upon thousands of rhinestones, and at the bottom, stuck into the ground, was a row of genuine pink plastic flamingos. There was a bank of floodlights aimed at the display, coolly awaiting the night's grotesque work.

"Holy shit—Excuse me, please. It—"

"No apologies necessary, Matt. When I first saw it,

those were my very words." She pointed toward the sky. "It continues up on the roof, as well."

"Jesus," said Matt.

"And Celine, too. You should see it at night with the strobe lights on."

"You're kidding."

"Come back here after sunset and see if I'm kidding. It's still on a timer."

Matt shook his head. "That can't be legal."

"Oh, it's legal. To make it illegal, the ordinance would have to exclude Christmas lighting, as well. When it comes to digging up pain-in-the-ass lawyers, no one can equal Mick. The local ordinances weren't up to him." She smiled. "Also, the way it's arranged, the only person the lights really bother is Jessup. The sightseers are another matter, however." She pointed up at the Jessup house. "Every day there's a steady parade of rubberneckers at the turn-off by Jessup's place to get a peek down here. Day and night. If anyone has a relative visiting from out of town, they'll take the visitor by Jessup's to see the freak house." She turned and pointed at a small balcony set into the top floor of Micky Cass's house. "When he was finished writing for the day, Mick used to get a glass of apple juice and a pair of binoculars and lounge around up there, watching and waving at the tourists, as well as at Jessup glaring at him."

"What do you mean?"

"Sometimes, depending on the light, we could see Duke Jessup sitting in his den up there, staring down at this house. Staring and drinking." She turned and faced Matt. "Actually, before you go back, you ought to roll by Jessup's place and take a look down here. It's really quite startling."

"How do you stand living in it?"

"Actually, you can't see any of this from inside or from the front or sides of the house. I just don't come back here."

"I take it you didn't exactly support Mick in this effort."

"Occasionally, Matt, Mick Cass thoroughly enjoys reveling in his character flaws. I'm not much into revenge myself." Her eyebrows went up. "Speaking of revenge," she said as she handed him the slip of paper she had taken from Micky Cass's desk. "This was thrust beneath the front door sometime last night."

Matt took the paper, noted the wrapping, and said "Fingerprints," as he nodded approvingly. He read the paper.

I was much distressed by next door people who had twin babies and played the violin; but one of the twins died, and the other has eaten the fiddle—so all is peace.

"What is it?"

"It's a quote from Edward Lear," said Tian.

"Who?"

"The author of 'The Owl and the Pussycat,' among other things."

Matt frowned. "Have you called this in?"

"Yes. Your Captain Grazer said for me to hold it for the detectives who're coming out here later today to question me."

As he handed it back to her, Matt asked, "What do you make of it?"

She looked down at the note, her fingers trembling. "I'm no authority, but I'd say it's a literary killer's way of wrapping a victim's overcoat around a dead fish and leaving it on his family's doorstep." There were tears in her eyes as she looked up at Matt. "Duke Jessup is the superintendent of Saint George's Academy. His background is English literature."

Before he left the canyon, Matt did as Tian Apehna had suggested. He drove his car up the hill and pulled into the turn-off next to the lush garden of the Jessup residence. Parked there were six passenger cars and an ancient pickup truck. The truck sported a fading Perot bumper sticker that partly covered another bumper sticker that began One day . . . leaving the resulting sentiment to read One Day Perot. The truck sported neon green mud flaps that urged all those behind the truck to Recycle for Tomorrow.

The cars carried plates from Nevada, Ontario, New Jersey, California (2), and Utah. The bumper stickers proclaimed everything politically incorrect and unaware from four time zones. The *turistas* were lined up along the masonry wall observing the freak house below and taking pictures to bring home to show Bud and Elmer. Matt shouldered his way to the wall and looked down.

After taking a glimpse down at the huge psychedelic eyeball painted on Micky Cass's roof, Matt felt a vague kinship with the writer. The business with the house was the kind of twisted sweet revenge he used to tease his idle moments with, and then forget. It was a way of venting frustration without actually dealing with it. Thinking about it was one thing, though. Acting out such bizarre little scenarios would be childish, perhaps sick, or even criminal. But in this case Cass had gone ahead and acted on his resentment.

Not very mature. Not very smart, especially if it had prompted Duke Jessup to react in a terminal way. But fun all the same. *Actually,* thought Matt, *if Jessup were mature, freaking up the back of Mick's house wouldn't have worked. Everybody knows how to stop playing Ping-Pong: you simply put down your paddle.* Except for Jessup's constantly quite entertaining reactions to Mick's provocations, there would be no point in either the freak house or Mick's afternoon gloatings on his balcony. Of course, if Jessup himself had been mature, he wouldn't have acted on his original resentment and taken Cass into court.

Matt pushed away from the wall and looked to his left at the proud home of Duke Jessup perched above its immaculate gardens like a luxury cruiser sailing upon billows of blossoms. Two gardeners were working among the shrubs and flower beds. Would Jessup's brand of resentment be enough to drive him to either murder or to kidnapping? And then leave a note? The gardens were beautiful, the object of an obsessive person. Was Jessup's gardening mania sufficient to drive him to kill the author of the freak house below? Matt remembered his father. If his dad had created such a garden, he would've killed Micky Cass in a second. Alcoholics tend to be doers if what needs doing is particularly inappropriate, immature, or sick.

Matt turned toward his car and shook off the questions. George and his FBI buddy would do the follow-up on Jessup. It was time to get on with the surgery.

CHAPTER 10

"RANDY, GET ON down here!" shouted the construction foreman. Dobbs and Kirk stood in the construction litter and looked up at the spruce skeleton of the two-story dwelling, the sky growing darker. A man in a white hard hat came to a rough opening that would one day, economy permitting, contain a window. The young man eyed the trio, took his unwrapped sandwich, dropped it in his lunch pail, and turned away. After a long moment, he exited from the not yet hung front door and shuffled over to them. He glanced at Dobbs, looked at Kirk for a moment, then fixed his gaze on his foreman.

"What's up, Toby?"

"These two cops've got some questions. Lunch break's over in twenty minutes." He faced Dobbs and Kirk and raised his eyebrows. "Twenty minutes, understand?"

"I think we can figure it out, sport," answered Kirk.

The foreman spat on the ground, walked off to his pickup, and resumed eating his lunch. Randy faced the two plainclothes officers and appeared to swallow against a very dry tongue.

"Yeah?"

"This is Sergeant Dobbs and I'm Detective Kirk. Is your name Randy Giandra?"

"Yeah. What about it?"

"Your crew looks a little shorthanded."

"So, good help is hard to find. What's it to you two?"

"So," said Kirk, "you want to tell me about Frank Chadburn, Tony Sarzana, Nick Panek, Archie Cash, and Billy Knapp?"

The suspect's gaze moved to Jerry Kirk's face. He seemed to be hovering somewhere between flight and resignation. "What do you want me to tell you about them? People get sick, some people move on. They don't have to check in with me."

"Uh huh. We know during the night out you boys had a few weeks ago, you were all stoned. Booze, pot. Tony Sarzana was shot dead in the Chay and fell out of the bed of Nick Panek's pickup truck." Kirk reached to his inside coat pocket and pulled out a small notebook. He didn't need to consult his notes. It was for effect. He flipped a few pages, allowed his gaze to play among the scribbles for a moment, and continued. "See, Randy, your boy Archie Cash is still in County Hospital getting glass cut out of his face and eyes. They don't have much hope he'll ever see again. Too bad it took you people so long to get him to a hospital. Billy Knapp was treated at County for gunshot wounds in his shoulder and left thigh. He was released a week ago and has vanished. No one has seen hide nor hair of either Frank Chadburn or Nick Panek since Tony was shot dead."

The carpenter shrugged his shoulders. "So, why ask me?"

"Randy," began Kirk, "everyone who's physically able has gone to ground. How come you're still here smacking your thumb with a hammer?"

"I got a family to support, bills to pay. I call it being responsible. What do you call it?"

A wry smile came over Kirk's face. "Stupid. That's what I call it. Real stupid. What're they charging you potheads and drunks with—premedicated murder?"

"You know, cop, they've already asked me about this. More'n once. Homicide officers."

"Then you already know it won't make your hair fall out." Kirk replaced his notebook. "So, we have a couple of questions, too."

"My lawyer told me he has to be in on any questioning. This whole mess is going to trial in four months."

"No, no, no," answered Kirk. "We don't want to ask about the slaghunt you and your stupid friends were on in Chayville. You and your pals kill and cripple a few rubberheads and what's that to us? What we want to know has nothing to do with that."

"What's it got to do with then?"

Kirk's eyebrows went up. "What can you tell us about Micky Cass?"

"Micky Cass?" Randy frowned and slowly shook his head. "Who?"

"Micky Cass. You had to have heard of him. He's a very famous writer. Up until recently he was doing a column for the *Times* under the name Ellison Robb. Any of this ringing a bell?"

"I don't get the *Times*. I got a TV."

"You had to hear about his column, even on the TV.

'Slag Like Me'? It was the topic on C-Span and a couple other big talk shows."

"I don't watch jabbervid. I turn to sports mostly. 'Major Dad,' Rush Limbaugh, though the guy's a little far out for me."

Kirk shook his head in disbelief. "People in this town have been arguing about 'Slag Like Me' for months."

"I must've had other things on my mind." The carpenter frowned. "Why? Did he write something about me?"

"Oh, baby, did he ever write something about you; about you and all your boozed-up little buddies."

"What did he write?"

"Well, Goober, he was an eyewitness to that night when you and your crew went and shot up The Place, killed that little boy, crippled an old man, and then got the shit shot out of you when you went after five slags standing on the sidewalk. They shot back, didn't they?"

"I can't talk about it."

"Micky Cass was one of those five slags. He gave you quite a write-up in his column."

"You didn't say this Cass was a slag. You got a copy of that column?"

"No, I don't have a copy."

Randy Giandra shrugged and looked down as he stuck his hands in the back pockets of his jeans. "If he saw something, the DA would know more about that than me."

"We already know what he saw. What we want to know is what do you know about Micky Cass's disappearance?"

"Disappearance?" Randy Giandra pulled a hand from his back pocket and held it out to his side. "Man,

I never heard of Micky Cass. What in the hell am I going to be able to tell you about someone I never heard of?" He sighed and held out his hands. "Look, I know I'm in trouble. I don't know what to do about it, and I can't help you at all."

Jerry Kirk nodded once. "I believe you." He looked at Dobbs and said, "We got squat. Anything you wanted to say?"

Rick Dobbs nodded and reached into his pocket. He pulled out a dollar and stuffed it into Randy Giandra's shirt pocket. "Here."

"What's that for?"

"Save the universe," said Dobbs. "Buy a condom. Don't reproduce."

CHAPTER 11

"Where's that 'Cards and Letters' column of Ellison Robb's?" asked Iniko.

George pushed around the papers until he found it. "I've got it here." He leaned across and dropped it on Matt's side of the desk where the FBI man was peering through one of several stacks of Ellison Robb's reader mail. The command center was quiet, a few disinterested clerks having coffee next to quiet keyboards and blank screens.

"Thank you," said Paul. He picked up the tear sheet and began scanning it.

"You look as though you've discovered something," said George.

The former Overseer shrugged his shoulders. "It's surprising how many of Ellison Robb's readers knew he was Micky Cass, even though I see little similarity between the column and his writing as Micky Cass."

He glanced up and pointed toward a stack of letters. "All of those correspondents, over three hundred of them, made some comment that made it clear they knew who was writing the column."

"There's an even bigger stack of letters from persons who believe that Ellison Robb is anyone from Jimmy Hoffa to an incarnation of Elvis. What about the lead?"

Paul Iniko looked up from his reading and frowned for a moment, followed by a grin. "Now, isn't that odd?"

"What odd?"

"The thing you asked about."

"The lead you're working on?"

"Yes. It just occurred to me, George, if it turns out to be nothing, there would be no point in telling you. If I'm right, however, I can't tell you."

"Can't tell me?"

"I apologize for how this sounds, but I can't even tell you why I can't tell you because telling you why I can't tell you would tell you."

"Paul, are you on some kind of medication?"

"There is a universe of possibilities, George. However, that is not one of them."

George Francisco steamed for a moment and then leaned forward to emphasize his point. "Look, if it might be important to the investigation, I need to know. More than that, I have a right to know."

Iniko's eyebrows went up. "I'm sorry, George. Look, I don't know if it's important. I don't even know for certain if what I suspect is true. It might be nothing. Let's not make an issue out of it until I have the facts."

George clasped his hands across his belly and

leaned back in his chair. "And once you know for certain you'll tell me?"

"If what I suspect is false."

"But it's only important if it's true, right? You just made a point out of telling me that there wouldn't be any point in telling me if what I wanted you to tell me . . ." George waved his hands in the air as a puzzled expression crowded his features.

Paul Iniko nodded. "That's right."

"Hell, now I'm talking like you." He let his hands fall to his lap. "I don't understand. Why can't you tell me why you can't tell me?" George held up his hands, palms facing Iniko. "No, wait. I remember now. Telling me why you can't tell me would be telling me."

The FBI man nodded. "You've got it."

"You know, Paul, this isn't exactly the kind of thing that inspires trust."

"It can't be helped. Perhaps you can trust that I have a good reason."

"You're asking me to have faith in an Overseer?"

"Former Overseer."

George folded his arms across his chest and frowned. "There's some talk, Paul, that the bureau has you in here in an attempt at managing the investigation to keep the FBI's skirts clean."

"There's talk that Elvis still stalks the streets of Las Vegas," responded Iniko.

"Well, some talk is more talky than other talk."

"You're gibbering, George."

"Then let me clear things up a bit. There's some evidence to support that the *Ahvin Rivak* and the bureau have a connection."

Paul's eyebrows went up. "You think there's a government conspiracy to send the Tenctonese off planet and back into slavery? In a very real sense, we don't even know where we are. Earth science doesn't even have the ability to manufacture the components to communicate at supra-light speeds and won't have the ability within the foreseeable future. Even if there were a conspiracy, what would be the point?"

"I didn't say it was intelligent. The point just might be to cover up how stupid it is. The last time we worked together, your job was to help cover up the bureau's role in MDQ and the Maanka Dak business."

Paul Iniko smiled. "I didn't do a very good job, did I?"

"Very well. I'm aware you eventually did the right thing, Paul."

"I thought you might have forgotten. You were a little confused, as I recall."

"I'm not confused now, and I want to know why the FBI is in on this, and of all the agents available, why you?"

"There's nothing to cover up this time, at least not as far as I'm aware. The high-ups are very concerned about the disappearance of Micky Cass and they wanted to get on it right away with everything possible. The way my superior explained it to me, there is a very real fear in the mayor's office and in the attorney general's office that if something happened to Micky Cass, it might precipitate a disturbance in L.A. that would make the last riot look like a marshmallow roast. It's believed that such a disturbance could spread well outside the limits of L.A. The director is bending the rules a bit by assigning agents and facilities to an investigation that hasn't officially begun yet, but that's how important Washington sees it."

"What about the connection with the *Ahvin Rivak?* Cass had several notes in his files concerning it."

Iniko held out his hands and shrugged. "Perhaps there is a connection. The bureau might be conducting an investigation of the *rivakah* or something or someone related to the returners. What if, as you suspect, the director lost his mind and engaged in a conspiracy with the *Ahvin Rivak* to sell us all back into slavery, which, of course, would include all the humans on earth, as well. Even so, I'm not in the loop, as they say."

"What about Cass's notes?"

"I haven't seen those particular notes. Nevertheless, my best guess is that whatever connection that exists has more to do with the bureau infiltrating the *Rivak* as a possible threat to national security than it has with a desire to send everyone into slavery."

George stared at the former Overseer for a full five seconds and then said, "You're really not going to tell me what it is you're working on, are you?"

"That's right." Paul held out his hands and raised his eyebrows. "If the information comes out some other way, fine. It's just that I can't tell you. Sorry."

George drummed his fingers on the armrests of his chair, took a deep breath, and let it out. "Okay. For the moment, Paul, okay. What about Davenport's alibi? Did you get the name of his doctor?"

Iniko nodded and looked down at the top of the desk as his eyes yellowed in embarrassment. "Yes. I got the name of his doctor."

"And?"

Iniko pushed his chair back and stood. "And Rudy Davenport was right."

"Right? What do you mean, right?"

"I mean, he was right."

"Right about what?"

"His doctor's name is none of our business." The FBI man turned and walked from the squad room, his hands thrust into his trouser pockets, a frown perched upon his brow.

CHAPTER 12

"I DON'T GET it," said Matt Sikes hours later at Mt. Andarko's Hospital. He frowned at how thick and fuzzy his tongue was. "If you're not goin' to do any cuttin', why I gotta be doped up?"

The nurse, a Tenctonese named Lisa Kerr, looked down upon Sikes with a cold face. She was garbed in pale yellow scrubs. "It's really very simple, Mr. Cross."

Cross, thought Matt. *My name is Matt Cross, big-time writer. Fulla Dope Cross, one* really *mild-mannered reporter for the* Daily Plan—Times.

Part of a question with an absent answer floated before his eyes and he noticed that Nurse Kerr was moving her lips. Her hips. Her lips *and* her hips. She was very lovely. Not as lovely as Cathy, but very lovely indeed. It was all on the outside, though. Inside she was all business, or worse. Angry. Maybe bitter. What about?

The thoughts in his head were mired in pine tar. Nurse Kerr had a mean streak a yard wide inside. Cathy was beautiful all the way through. Did Nurse Kerr's anger take Micky Cass out of the picture?

Anger about what?

And she did have a terrific alibi. Part of a group vacationing in Germany, sixteen days, never left sight of her friends for more than seven hours at a stretch.

Seven hours. The connections just weren't there.

Matt felt himself frown. "You said somethin' 'bout simple, simp—simp—"

"Yes, Mr. Cross. Simple. I explained all of this to you in detail before. Don't you remember? There won't be any cutting of *your* skin, but you need to be anesthetized for two reasons. First, the operation will take several hours, during which time it is imperative that you do not move. Second, shortly after the Realskin begins bonding with your skin, it will begin forming nerve tissue and integrating it with your own nervous system. Midway through the operation, therefore, when we cut and suture the Realskin—"

"It'll hurt," he completed.

"It would be uncomfortable if you weren't anesthetized. In fact, when the anesthetic wears off and you awaken, you'll experience a little discomfort because the healing Realskin will be your own. Relax and we'll be by in a few minutes to take you down to surgery."

"Discomfort," Matt muttered beneath his breath. "Every time a doctor or nurse says 'discomfort' you can count on whatever it is feeling like shitting five pounds of rusty fishhooks."

Matt closed his eyes and vaguely thought he heard the door to his room open and close. After a moment he thought he heard it open and close again. Who was it? Was it anyone? Or was it the drugs playing tricks on his ears. Maybe it was Lisa Kerr coming to kill him. Lisa Kerr. Why didn't she change her name? It'd perk up her whole outlook.

He tried to open his eyes, but his sight was met by a mush of shapes and a swirl of colors.

"Relax," he muttered to himself, feeling something strange in his mouth. Big wet and fuzzy. It was his tongue.

Relax.

Relax, hell.

To relax you have to trust, and Matt Sikes doesn't trust. He's not stupid. If every time you trust you get betrayed, you don't trust. If you don't trust, you can't relax. If you can't relax, you walk through life as a big knot.

"'Sides," he muttered, "I'm onna undercover investigation. Oops!" *Mustn't let little things like that slip. Loose ships think slips. Something like that.*

He tried to open his eyes to check the room and his sight was greeted by a shower of strange lights and smears.

Can't trust eyes. Can't trust anyone.

"Matt?"

Cathy hadn't betrayed him. Yet.

"Matt?"

And there was George, his partner. They had argued, disagreed, and fought. But George had never betrayed him. If he ever would trust anyone, it would be Cathy or George. It certainly wouldn't be someone with a knife and a resentment about him disguising himself as a Tenct.

"Matt? It's George."

"George?" He opened his eyes and squinted in an attempt at wrestling the images before him into some sort of sense. There was a figure in the doorway. It moved forward, its face coming into the light. "George, it's you."

George Francisco took a chair, pulled it up next to the bed, and sat in it. "How are you doing, Matt?"

"Fine." He giggled as he thought of something. "Yeah, fine. Frustrated, insane, neurotic, and emotional." He wondered if his words had come out the way he'd said them. He tried to shrug and couldn't tell whether he'd actually accomplished the gesture or simply thought about it. As his eyes closed, he said, "I guess what I mean, partner, is I'm jus' plain scared. How's the investigation going?"

"Iniko's playing 'I've Got a Secret' and I'm going over the people around Jessup again."

"Why?"

"Oh, you don't know. A couple of hours ago we heard from the lab. They turned up a partial print on that Edward Lear quote. It was Jessup's. The lab trolls are rounding up typewriters as we speak."

"Didn't the Boston cops give Jessup an alibi?"

"Airtight," answered George. "But the note was on stationery Jessup has at his home office and at the academy. It could've been someone who had access to the paper. There's his wife, of course, as well as the housekeeper, Gloria Salcines, and the gardeners, Jimmy and Harry Lee. Those are the only regulars at home. At the school it looks as though the only ones with regular access to his stationery are his secretary, Nathan Lopez, and two file clerks, Alice Yuan and Roger Stanton. Stanton is a Newcomer. Lopez's wife gives him a shaky alibi, and neither Yuan nor Stanton has an alibi. All three of them are a bit short in the motive department, however."

"Wha—What. Sorry. Tongue's dry. The house-keeper and the gardener?"

"Alibis full of holes, just like everyone else's except Jessup. Gloria Salcines has two sisters that come out on a regular basis to help do the cleaning at his home. I gather the place is a whiteout nightmare and Mrs. Jessup is a clean freak. One of them, Felicia, was in the hospital having some cosmetic surgery, and the other, Marta, can only account for a few hours during the three days. Again, short of motives. The gardener, Jimmy Lee, is covered pretty solidly by his different customers, but there are gaps. His brother, Harry, works part time for his brother and part time for the Sierra Environmental Center. Harry Lee's time is full of gaps, but right now both he and his brother look short of motive, too."

"The only one with a motive couldn't've done it, huh? Maybe Jessup's airtight alibi has a leak, partner. What about the feds an' the *Ahvin Rivak?* Anything?"

"Cass's notes have a lot of suspicions and a couple of threads. What we've checked out so far doesn't seem to be going anywhere. All we have is motive. The *Ahvin Rivak* would rather not have peace and light brought to human-Tenctonese relations. I gather they figure it slows down the eventual exodus back into slavery. They have over eighteen hundred local members, so take your pick."

"The connection to the FBI?"

"I don't know. Paul isn't speaking to me. Not about this."

"A mess, George. Gotta feeling we're gonna be too late." He was silent for a long moment, then Matt frowned as images floated before his eyes. "I'm scared, George. Did I ever tell you, angry people make me scared? They do. I fight 'em, but they make me scared. Gonna see some angry people as a Tenctonese. Lots of angry people."

"You'll do fine, Matt. We'll have you covered."

"Mmm." It seemed very dark. Matt realized his eyes were closed. He didn't have the strength to open them. He felt George's fingers take his hand and hold it. He went limp and swam himself to sleep.

ELLISON ROBB
Slag Like Me

Those Cards And Letters

You know how you feel when a problem you think has been taken care of long ago turns out still to be a problem? It's like the resurgence of TB in this country a few years ago. TB was like the plague, something from the past, no longer a problem. Then, oops! Here it is again. The same thing happened with polio. The same thing is happening with my mail right now.

Those of you who read my previous columns might recall that the issue that caused this series to come into being was anti-Newcomer sentiment; human racism; slagging. It is an important subject, and if I were a reader, I could think of upwards of a million questions I could ask and suggestions I could make.

Physically, how was the transformation from human to Tenctonese made? Describe the surgical process. What was the thing that marked you as a human on your first abortive attempt at impersonating a Tenct? What was the process of change like? How does it feel knowing what that look is in some human's eyes? And, what about private business? Housing? The gangs? What about the rest of the United States? Are there any Newcomers in Canada? Why? If not, why not? When are the political parties going to push for Tenct candidates (what if the best "man" for the job isn't a "man" but a Tenct?)?

There are countless interesting issues readers might have raised, but questions and suggestions regarding the investigation of human-Tenct relationships represent less than two percent of the mail received thus far. The rest of the mail, frankly, makes me cringe.

"Because of your obvious African-American bias against the police department, the rest of this so-called investigation must be suspect. There are very real problems with the Tenctonese and how they are treated, but using this forum to grind the traditional anti-police ax carried by the black community does a disservice not only to the police and to the Tenctonese but to African-Americans."

"It's all too clear your Latino rage against the police department . . ."

"You white Jew liberals, in your attempt to put down Arabs and promote gun control . . ."

". . . white ultra-libertarians who never had to do an honest day's work . . ."

". . . sexual deviates attempting to force your perverted values onto innocent children . . ."

". . . wacko conservatives who want to do away with welfare and a woman's right to . . ."

"It was very clever to have a Slag write a column pretending to be a human pretending to be a Rubberhead, but simply the way you use words gives you away."

"As an Asian-American myself, I see in your

good-natured attempt at enlightenment nothing but the encouragement of discord. Although police reforms are certainly in order, having Vietnamese ancestry does not give you a special cross to carry . . ."

". . . and you damned Indians can't even figure out what to call yourselves. American Indians? Amarinds? Native Americans? American aborigines? Hell, we can't figure it out, so let's go after the cops!"

And those, dear reader, were a few of the more educated responses. I will spare you the venom of the rest, including a rather rabid representation of Latvian-Americans who were offended by my unfortunate example of a narrow agenda. They all assure me that Latvia has not a single native black gay midget biker within its borders (I assume they are all married).

Here are the very discouraging statistical results on my "race" thus far:

Ellison Robb is a:

Hebe	14.1
Whitey	16.8
Blacky	26.3
Tenctonese	06.1
Taconese	19.7
Gookese	08.0
Redskin	01.3
Other	04.2
Unspecified	03.5

"Other" includes Arab, Italian, Irish, Iranian, and a substantial portion convinced that I am from New Jersey(?). Out of a total of 26,588 responses there were

8,612 threats to life, limb, and property toward me, my family, the publisher, and staff of the Times, particularly against Martin Fell, who invited me to do the column (have a great vacation in Uzbekistan, Marty).

Interestingly enough, 922 correspondents confessed to believing that I am a retired, fired, or otherwise exed police officer; 612 accused me of being homophobic; 1,104 accused me of being gay (including lesbian); 2,238 claimed I was female; and 2,322 accused me of being male (one correspondent, who claimed to know me, confessed to knowing as well that I am a hermaphrodite). I'll spare you the breakdown on my political affiliations, except to assure you that communism, socialism, fascism, capitalism, and cannibalism appear to be alive and well at the Times.

This is what it must be like to run for political office. You want to talk about America's self-image, business prosperity, putting people to work, crime, drugs, education, environment, health, and human rights, but all anyone seems to be able to focus on is: "When he went on that college panty raid back in '72, did he, or did he not, put on the panties?" (We only want to know where he's coming from).

People, you don't get it!

Neither this issue (human-Tenctonese relations) nor this column can be seen through the filter of a black agenda, a white agenda, a pro-cop/anti-cop agenda, gay/straight, GOP/Demo, or any other kind of agenda.

"But how can we tell where the man is coming from?" (Which assumes that I am male).

A thing, a person, an event is what it is, and only what it is, itself. I report to you what I find through the perspective of one individual: a being on this planet called, for the purposes of this column, Ellison Robb.

"Yeah, but who in the hell is Ellison Robb? That's just a name (Yes! Yes! It is just a name!) How can we know how to look at his or her (or its) views if we don't know his (her or its) sex, political, national, or ethnic background?"

The answer is to look at the view, not at the viewer. Too simple for you, Goober?

Very well. I suppose a confession is necessary. Ellison Robb belongs to a minuscule racial minority known as Intelligent Life. He has both a masculine side and a feminine side, and he has the organs suitable to exercising the appropriate side's inclinations at any particular moment. In other words, dear reader, the ax in my hand is neither black, white, male, female, gay, straight, pro-cop, or anti-choice. The only ax in my hand is this column and an overwhelming desire to have people do the right thing.

What's the right thing?

There is a probably misguided piece of me that honestly believes that if you readers see the wrong thing and its effects clearly enough, the right thing will become unmistakably clear. Moreover, after such a view, the desire to do the right thing will become overwhelming. Perhaps it is just a fantasy of mine. It is for this reason alone, however, that I write.

Two more items of business:

First, among the countless bags of confused letters sent to the Times, came a request from a person who did sign his name, but whose name I will not print for reasons soon to become obvious. His letter didn't have anything much to do with the subject matter of this column, but neither did most of the others. He wrote:

"In your first column you said you studied the Tenctonese and know a lot about them. I know they were slaves and were controlled by strong addictive drugs before they crashed here, and I also know a lot of them don't do drugs anymore. How do they stay away from the stuff? I want to. More than anything, I want to stay away from it. I can't and it's killing me. Worse than that, it's killing everyone I love. How do the Tenctonese stay clean?"

I don't know how every Tenct stays away from drugs. I suspect most of them aren't addicts. In any event, a very wise anonymous person once said, "When you've had enough, find a telephone book, look up the number for Narcotics Anonymous, call the number, drag your ass to a meeting, and ask for help." They probably won't be able to tell you how Tencts stay clean, but they can help you to figure out how to get and stay clean yourself.

Finally, there was a big brown envelope from a person who works in the personnel department of a rather large and powerful institution. Inside the envelope were hiring stats, revealing memos, cover-up orders from on high, and a rope trail leading all of the way to Washington, D.C. that could stretch some very prominent necks. After meeting with my correspondent, we've estimated that it will take a week or so to set up my infiltration of the outfit. It should be very interesting. Meanwhile, there are intriguing doings down in the barrio. Stay tuned.

CHAPTER 13

As HE AND Paul Iniko stood and waited, George Francisco looked around the incredibly white living room in the Jessup home. The walls, furniture, rugs, trim, lamps, shelves, even the covers of the books on the shelves were white. The color was not a muted orchid, eggshell, nor off-white. It was white white, operating room white, snowflakes soaked in Clorox for three weeks white. George glanced at Paul and the former Overseer was looking down at the rug.

"What do you think?"

Paul raised his eyebrows. "I've never before felt quite so impure. Do you think we ought to come back after we get our heads buffed?"

"I don't understand why we're here at all. We have Ramos's report. Jessup has an airtight alibi. He was at that convention of English teachers, then he and some of his friends were in custody for setting the hotel on fire. The Boston PD confirmed it. According to them,

Jessup was locked up and in no shape to do anything but scream and vomit for most of the time." George held out a hand. "His wife and children, the housekeeper, and the gardener have the rest of the time covered."

"There are some things upon which I need to satisfy myself," said Paul.

"Things?"

"A hunch."

They were interrupted by the owner of the house, school superintendent Duke Jessup, entering the room. He was in his middle fifties, balding, wearing gray balloon slacks and a ripped red and yellow rugby shirt. He hadn't shaved for a few days and he looked as uncomfortable in the center of all that whiteness as Iniko and Francisco. He glanced nervously at the two Tencts and put his hands into his trouser pockets. "My wife said you wanted to talk to me."

"Yes," answered Paul. "Thank you for seeing us."

"You're here about the Cass thing, I imagine."

"The Cass thing?" George repeated.

"Yes," Jessup answered with no change in expression. "He's missing, I hate his guts, two plus two equals five, and here are the police back for the second act. The cops have been here already, you know."

"We have Lieutenant Ramos's report and your statement, Dr. Jessup," said Paul. "I'm Agent Iniko of the FBI. This is Sergeant Francisco with LAPD homicide. We're both working on the Cass investigation. There were just a few things we wanted to clear up. According to what you told Lieutenant Ramos—"

"Could we go to another room?" asked Jessup. He removed a hand from its pocket and gestured toward the door. "We might be more comfortable."

"Certainly," answered Paul.

Jessup turned and led the way through an equally white hall lined on one side with windows that looked out over the gardens. Potted plants had been strategically placed on the balcony outside to block the view of Micky Cass's house. As Duke Jessup walked, he remarked, "Lois is rather compulsive about cleanliness."

"It is some rather striking decorating," said George.

"You think that's white? Wait until you get a load of the bathrooms. I don't mean to sound crude," said Jessup as he glanced back, "but I sometimes wonder where in this house one can take a guilt-free dump." He smiled without humor. "Actually, I did mean to sound crude." At the end of the hallway was a closed door. Jessup opened it and held out his hand. "We can talk in here."

The room was a combination den and office paneled in honey-colored woods and furnished with worn leather upholstered chairs and rough hardwood tables. The windows from the hallway continued along the curve of the room's western wall overlooking the gardens. There was the stale smell of whiskey in the air.

George stood at the window wall and looked down. There were no strategically placed plants. Cass's eyesore virtually served as the centerpiece of Jessup's garden. At the far end of the garden, however, near the wall separating the Jessup property from Micky Cass's rose garden, the gardener and a helper were pulling three evergreen trees from the back of a metal-scrap-filled pickup. The trees were already over a dozen feet tall and the burlap-wrapped root balls were extremely heavy. The holes next to the wall had already been dug. It would take four or five years, guessed George, but eventually the trees would spare the Jessups the sight of Micky Cass's nightmare.

George turned and saw that hanging on the opposite wall were numerous plaques, trophies, and awards. He stepped over to them and noted that Duke Jessup had received several teaching, literary, and appreciation plaques. The trophies and awards were all for competition target shooting, for both rifle and pistol. George noted a glass-enclosed display cabinet at the end of the room designed to hold perhaps a dozen assorted rifles and pistols. The cabinet was empty.

"You may sit there." Jessup held his hand out toward two modular chairs. As George and Paul seated themselves, Jessup sat down in a third chair facing them and the window wall, with an unobstructed view of Cass's house. As they talked, he stared at the eyeball painted on the roof below.

"Very well, Sergeant Francisco, Agent Iniko, what can I do for you?"

George looked at Paul Iniko, and the former Overseer stared at Jessup with an unblinking gaze. At last Iniko said, "Tell me what life is like for you, Duke."

Duke Jessup's eyebrows shot up as his eyes grew ever wider. "Life?"

George frowned at Iniko as Jessup's eyebrows dropped into a threatened scowl. "What in the devil are you—" Jessup shook his head. "I don't see what business it is of yours what life is like for me. I've given your Lieutenant Ramos all the facts to which the police are entitled. How the elements of my world plan are meshing is no one's affair but my own."

George studied the superintendent. Jessup's face was red, his hands shaking. He repeatedly moistened his lips with his tongue, yet sweat beaded on his forehead. He looked terribly unhealthy, even for a human.

"Dr. Jessup," said Paul, "I assure you that my interest is not one of idle curiosity. Despite your alibi, you are still a suspect. Now, if you did participate in the abduction of Micky Cass, you have several very good reasons for refusing to answer my question. If you are innocent, you have nothing to lose by answering my question save my company and the company of Sergeant Francisco here. As soon as my question has been answered to my satisfaction, you see, we will leave."

"I didn't kidnap anyone."

"In which case, you may as well answer my question."

Jessup glanced at George, took a deep breath, and let escape a sigh of exasperation. "Sure," he said to Iniko as he looked down at Cass's house. "Why not? You want to know what my life is like?"

"Yes."

His eyes narrowed as his lower lip trembled. In a voice that was barely audible, he said, "My life is excrement."

"Because of Micky Cass?" offered George.

Jessup moved his gaze from Cass's house to George's face. "Cass?"

"Yes. You said your life was excrement. Is that so because of Micky Cass?"

Duke Jessup looked back at Cass's house, and George watched in astonishment as tears streaked down Jessup's cheeks. After a moment the man wiped the tears away with the backs of his hands and answered as though the tears had never existed. "Cass has contributed a small part to the project." He nodded toward the window. "The one place of peace and beauty in my life, the one remaining piece of sanity, my garden, Micky Cass fouled with what he did with his damned house." He looked at Paul. "But that was only one last turd on a very tall shit pile."

"What do you mean by that?"

"What do I mean, the FBI man wants to know." He snorted out a bitter laugh and shook his head. "Well, thanks to the notoriety following my return from Boston, I've been asked to resign as superintendent of Saint George's. Is that enough?"

"What about your family?" pressed Iniko.

Jessup looked at the FBI agent and seemed to slump inwardly. It was as though Iniko already knew all the answers, making it impossible for Jessup to either shade or evade them. "I'm losing my family, Agent Iniko. Is that what you wanted me to say? My wife and I haven't slept together for over two years. Last month she filed for divorce and for the custody of my two children, both of whom hate my guts. All the money I have in the world is tied up in this house, and I'm going to get killed in the settlement. My every waking moment is spent staring at the underside of hell. Now, is *that* enough?"

"Not quite," answered Paul without emotion. "Do you hold Cass responsible for your family troubles?"

Jessup glanced down at the hardwood floor, then let his gaze slowly rise until he was again looking through the window wall at Micky Cass's house. "No. I can't say that. Cass moved in less than a year ago. Lois has been threatening to leave me since before I even knew that anyone called Micky Cass existed."

"So what is responsible?" asked Paul.

"Responsible? Responsible for what?"

"For your troubles, Duke."

The use of Jessup's given name seemed to make his

neck twitch involuntarily. "How in blazes would I know what's responsible? Air pollution? The hole in the ozone layer? Defective karma?"

"Do you think you might have a problem with alcohol?"

A look of such incredible loathing leaped upon Jessup's face, it startled George sufficiently to cause him to reach involuntarily for his weapon. His hand moved no more than an inch, but George knew where his hand was headed when he brought it to a halt. He knew that Jessup had frightened him.

"No," answered Jessup. "I do not have a problem with alcohol. The thing in Boston was an unfortunate, but quite isolated, incident. I do not have a problem with alcohol."

"You're certain of that?"

"I think I'm honest enough with myself to know whether or not I'm a drunk."

Paul nodded as he rested his elbows on his chair's armrests and clasped his hands together. "At an earlier English teachers' convention, in '89 according to your records, you were charged with driving while intoxicated by the police in Minneapolis. Do you remember that, Duke?"

"I don't understand," said Jessup, his voice constricted by anger. "Am I being charged with some kind of drunk-driving thing?" He looked somewhere between rage and terror, as though the rage might not be justified, and that if the truth of that escaped into the light, he would die.

"No," answered Paul as he stood. "I simply needed to satisfy myself on a point, and you have done that admirably. Thank you for your cooperation."

"I have a question," said George as he got to his

feet. "I noticed the shooting trophies." He nodded toward the display case. "Where are the guns?"

"Gone. I don't own guns anymore."

"You sold them?"

"Some I sold. Some I gave away. They're all registered and they've all had ballistic tests in accordance with the new law, so it doesn't matter whether I sold them, gave them away, or tossed them in the Franklin Canyon Reservoir. They're gone. Why don't you two do the same."

Later, in the car driving down Beverly toward Wilshire, George took a moment to glance at the FBI man. Iniko had his arms folded across his chest and he was staring straight ahead from beneath a severe frown. "Why didn't we press him about the guns?" asked George.

"Guns? Oh." Iniko shrugged and looked through the passenger window at the passing scenery. "No one's been shot, George. We don't need a gun until then."

"Paul, Jessup obviously worships guns. Did you see all of those shooting trophies? He loves guns and appears to be an expert in using them. In addition he gives every evidence of being an alcoholic in full flower, with all of the denial, anger, violence, and impaired judgment that implies. Therefore, doesn't the absence of guns in his house strike you as just the least bit convenient?"

"Not really. For Duke Jessup guns are out right now. For the time being he has another god, a god that makes having guns in the house an immensely terrifying matter."

"I don't understand. What's so terrifying about having guns in the house?"

"What you said yourself about him being a late-stage addict." Iniko faced George and asked, "If you were obsessed with constant thoughts of suicide, murder, or both, would you keep a gun in the house?"

"How do *you* know that Jessup is obsessed with thoughts of suicide or murder?"

"If I could explain that, I'd have to be a great deal more intelligent than I am."

George frowned. "Do you mean this is another thing you can't tell me?"

"Just let it go, George. It's not important."

"Not important?" George waved a hand at Iniko and divided his attention between the traffic and the being in the passenger seat. "You're telling me that Duke Jessup being constantly obsessed with thoughts of murder is unimportant?"

"That's right."

"I would think Jessup being plagued with thoughts of murder would make him our number one suspect."

Iniko shook his head and returned to looking out of the window on his side. "Curious as it may seem, George, it pretty much eliminates him. Duke Jessup is not our man."

CHAPTER 14

MATT'S FACE FELT like a stretched drumhead, tight and incredibly dry. It was brittle, too, as though his skin would shatter if he smiled, turned his head, or wrinkled his forehead. It was the Realskin he was feeling, rather than his own. His own skin, covered and desensitized by the artificial skin, had moved the sensation of touch to the surface layer. To Matt's sense of touch, if not his mind, the sculpted Realskin was now his real skin.

Over the days since his operation, he had looked into his room's bathroom mirror several times, but his head and face, to protect the Realskin from infection, were completely bandaged making him look like the invisible man trying to be visible. The one difference he could see was the eyes.

The emotionally sensitive gel contacts were functioning, if not well. His eyes were pale green, reflecting

133

a degree of pain, except that he did not feel any pain. Nevertheless, the gel had remained green for so long that Matt had almost forgotten how the world looked without a green tinge. There were other things to do, however, while the Realskin healed, the cellular bonding continued, and the swelling went down. Those other things were the province of the *rama vo* and Ivo Lass.

"Rape and incest victims, concentration camp survivors, and former slaves all have something in common," she stated.

Matt shifted uncomfortably in the easy chair in his room and looked through his bandages at the *Hila* from the South Gate *Rama Vo*. She was Tenctonese and one of the few who looked ancient. She was well over the median Tenct life expectancy of 140 years and her name was Ivo Lass. She sat in the opposite easy chair looking quite relaxed. Every other Tenctonese Matt knew spoke English with some variation of an American accent. Ivo Lass talked like Margaret Thatcher.

She was the one who had helped Micky Cass to "emerge" as a Tenct. Although she was a suspect, Matt could not stay completely detached from what the woman was saying. She seemed to know everything about life, living, and about Matt Cross. He suspected that she knew, as well, that Matt Cross wasn't Matt Cross. He didn't think she knew he was a police officer, but she could add two and two. She knew where he hurt, how he handled it, and why he handled it the way he did. He hadn't told her any of this; she just seemed to know.

"What do they have in common, Matt?" she asked.

Matt mentally shrugged. Physical shrugs pulled painfully on the new skin of his neck. For the same reason he had learned not to purse his lips, grimace, frown, or engage in body language with his eyebrows. "Anger?" he guessed.

"Yes, Matt. Anger." She pointed a thin, graceful finger at him. "But the anger is not allowed to be felt, you see? The anger happens in a context where it is considered wrong, immoral, dangerous, even suicidal. Because of it, the anger is warped and hidden. It becomes twisted, corrupted. It's turned into shame."

"Shame?"

"Yes. You know about shame, don't you?"

"Shame?"

She raised an eyebrow. "There seems to be a terrible echo in here."

"I heard you. I just can't think of anything to be ashamed of." He shrugged beneath the force of her constant gaze and winced as the healing Realskin on his neck pulled painfully. "Okay, there were a few things I did back when——" Matt stopped himself from revealing his past as a patrolman. "Well, I did a few things in the past I'm not real proud of. When I was a kid and later. Is that what you mean?"

She leaned back in her chair, narrowed her eyes, and allowed her gaze to bore into him. "The shame to which I have reference has nothing to do with something you did. It has to do with what you are."

"Ashamed of what I am?"

"There's that echo again."

Matt writhed uncomfortably on his chair as he avoided eye contact with the woman. He noticed that his hands were clasped together and that the Realskin across his knuckles was very, very white. He folded his arms across his chest. "I'm not sure what you mean."

"How you do feel, Matt?"

"Feel?"

"More echoes?"

"Feel?" Matt spat again. "I'll tell you how I feel! I feel pissed off!"

"Pissed off isn't a feeling, Matt. It's a vulgarism used to avoid admitting to a feeling."

"Well, then, how about frosted? Salty? Madder'n hell? How about shitting razor blades?"

The old woman didn't bat an eye, but then Matt was in a mood sufficient to make him wonder if Newcomers could bat their eyes. "Shitting razor blades is close, Matt, but try again," she instructed.

"Okay," said Matt, his voice rough. "Angry. How about angry?"

Ivo Lass smiled with only the left corner of her mouth. "That was better, Matt, but your anger is a mask, too. It hides what you feel. Don't look for any sarcasms to throw at me, boy. Right now. Tell me how you feel."

Humans sweat and Tencts don't. Matt wondered in passing how the surgeons had handled that problem because he knew he was sweating beneath the *Hila*'s grilling. The old woman was missing out on a great career as a police interrogator.

The word was there, right on the tip of his tongue. He felt his tongue reach for his upper front teeth. "Threatened," he answered flatly. "Threatened. Frightened. Scared."

"Ah," she said, her eyebrows raised as though they were two hairless flags of victory. "And what are you frightened of, Matthew?"

He frowned in confusion as tears welled in his eyes and the green tinge of the world grew a shade darker. His breathing came hard. "I'm afraid . . ."

He tried to shut out the *Hila*'s image. Ivo Lass was

136

not his mother or his father; she was not a figure of authority. She was just another being. It would be much easier to say it if she wasn't there, however, because that was what he was afraid of—other beings. Afraid of their judgments. Afraid of their rejections. He felt tears dribble down his cheeks. "I'm afraid to let you know what I really feel." He allowed his gaze to fall on the old woman. "I'm afraid to let you know who I am."

Ivo Lass averted her eyes and looked through the room's window at the hazy sky. "Matt, before we continue, I need to know something. Is Micky Cass in some sort of danger?"

It had come flying out of left field and it took Matt a moment to piece together the implications. "What makes you think that?"

An amused expression touched her lips as her eyes crinkled at the corners. " 'Slag Like Me' has failed to appear for weeks. You are a police officer pretending to be a reporter, apparently tracing Robb's footsteps in disguising himself as a Tenctonese. I take it I'm even a suspect?"

"What makes you think I'm a cop?"

Her eyebrows went up again. "The same way I know that Robb's columns have failed to appear. I read newspapers. I watch television. You and your partner have appeared in both several times, Detective Sikes."

Matt held his hands to the bandages covering his face. "But you can't see me."

"I can hear your voice." Her expression grew serious. "What about Cass?"

"Unofficially, he's missing."

"And unofficially you're investigating?"

"Yes."

She nodded slowly, her gaze again on the window.

"Matt, I want to do everything I can to help you. During the time Micky Cass and I were together for his training, I came to admire him a great deal."

Matt drummed his fingers on the armrests of his chair as he weighed Ivo Lass's value as a suspect versus her value as an ally. It didn't really matter, he concluded. If she wasn't connected with Cass's disappearance, her help would be indispensable. If she was responsible, nothing would prove it more quickly than having her betray him. It would be sort of like looking for a gas leak with a lit match.

"I can use all of the help I can get. About the training?"

"Yes?"

"Cass wrote that it took eleven weeks. If it takes me that long, Micky Cass's trail will be long dead and gone before I get to it. Is there any way to speed it up?"

"There's no need."

"No need?"

"That's correct."

"What about the eleven weeks? He must have had something that needed fixing. What did Micky Cass have that I don't?"

"Self-esteem."

Through sheer force of will, Matt restrained himself from echoing her statement. Since that statement was all that filled his mind at that moment, however, he was left somewhat speechless. At last he said, "I don't understand."

She nodded her approval at his response. "Very good, Matt. Now, what don't you understand?"

"Who's making echoes now?" Ivo Lass laughed, but Matt persisted. "You said that Micky Cass had self-esteem and I don't."

"You don't and neither do most Tenctonese or other

138

kinds of slaves. It's his positive feelings about himself that revealed him as a human in his first attempt at passing as a Newcomer."

"You're saying I don't have positive feelings about myself? And what about my partner? He's a Tenctonese and sometimes he can be insufferable with how confident and self-assured he is."

"I've never met your partner, but perhaps he does the same thing you do—he pretends."

"Pretends?" Matt held up his hands. "Sorry." He lowered his hands as anger attempted to cover up his feeling of being threatened. "I don't see how you can know any of this."

"It's very simple, really. In your case, I can feel it. In the case of your partner, he's Tenctonese. A slave—any kind of slave—has to conform to survive. Whatever the prevailing mood, attitude, desire, the slave must instantly adapt if he is to survive. He must become an emotional—even political—chameleon. Particularly if one is born into it, there is little or no struggle involved. Everyone around you thinks and acts that way, and you do as you were shown."

"Who are you talking about now? Me or my partner?"

"Both, actually."

"We were both slaves? Is that what you're saying?"

Ivo Lass nodded. "I don't think I have to explain your partner's past, do I? You're satisfied that he was once a slave?"

"Yeah. Sure. What I don't get is you saying that I was once a slave. You sure you don't have your human history a little confused?"

The *Hila* leaned forward in her chair, rested her elbows on her knees, and looked deep into Matt's eyes. "What was your childhood like, Matt?"

139

"My child—sorry." Ignoring the pain of the new skin on his neck, he shook his head. "I guess like everybody else's. School, peanut butter, baseball, girls."

"Did you like school?"

"No. I hated it." He shook his head slowly. "I didn't get very good grades. Not much in the way of friends."

"What about baseball? Did you like baseball?"

Matt frowned. "Yeah. I liked it. Some. I played it because my father was a fan and I wanted to impress him." He gave a tiny shrug as he pulled his mind back from the past. "He only ever showed up to a couple of games." He held up a hand, "And before you ask, the peanut butter seemed to be the only thing I ever got to eat at home. There was never any food in the house, and I bought my own bread and peanut butter and stashed it."

"The girls?"

"One or two dates. They were disasters. I was the kind of kid fathers don't want their daughters to date."

"It's interesting, Matt, the parallels between slavery and certain dysfunctional family systems. Liot Mrysvi, the Tenctonese family therapist, published an incredibly interesting study on it titled *The Invisible Tattoo.*"

"I've seen it in the stores. I never read it."

"What was it in your family, Matt? Gambling, incest, eating disorders, physical abuse, drug addiction—"

"What?" Matt almost came to his feet, then dropped back into his chair. It was frightening how the *Hila* could see into his heart, his past. When George had gone though *riana,* the Tenctonese male

140

menopause, he had gotten a little smarter. It showed as an almost two percent gain in his intelligence quotient. Tenct women had a similar experience, Cathy had informed him, and Ivo Lass was over a century and a half old. When she was born, slavery in the United States was still a going concern. She must've been through *riana* a dozen times. But, thought Matt, how smart can you get before your head explodes?

"What was your childhood home like, Matt?"

He looked down at his hands, remembering the Adult Children of Alcoholics meeting he had attended. He never could understand how those people could talk about this stuff like it wasn't something swimming in shame. The image of his father drunk, his mother wiped on prescription drugs, the countless times he bit his tongue, closed his eyes, covered his ears. The back of his father's hand, the long silences, the longer arguments. Moments after the one time he had opened his mouth and wished his father dead, he watched in horror as some thug shot him down. Matt moistened his lips, glanced at the *Hila*, and said quietly. "Alcohol. Drugs. Some physical abuse." He looked down at her hands. "A lot of physical abuse."

"And you survived," said Ivo Lass. "How you survived, however, had certain effects. One of those effects was to crush your self-esteem. It is quite similar to what happens to any slave."

"I was *not* a *slave!*"

Ivo Lass looked into Matt's eyes, her expression something of steel wrapped with compassion. "Were you forced to do things against what you knew was right?"

Matt thought for a moment, then shrugged. There

had been only a couple of hundred thousand times. Being the man of the family at the age of five because the man of the family was passed out and the woman of the family was locked in her bedroom talking to people who had died twenty years ago. Lying to friends at school because of the endless shame. So many things. "Yes. There were some things. Lots of things. That's how it was in my family."

"Were you punished no matter what you did?"

Matt's mouth suddenly went dry. The stupid scene with the bike when he was eight flooded into his mind. He had left his bike in front of the house. His mother, citing everything from what the neighbors might think to a world filled with potential thieves, beat him with a wire chair leg for leaving the bike in front of the house. He looked at his knuckles, remembering the blood there from the wire cutting his fingers as he tried to protect himself. Once she was exhausted and went to pop a few more Valium, young Matt put the bike away in the garage. His mother beat him again for that. It seemed she had wanted his father to see what an irresponsible slug his son was, and the bike in front of the house was valuable evidence that Matt had fouled. He had been beaten again when he asked his mother if he should put the bike back in front of the house. . . .

"Okay. So what?"

"Matt," continued the *Hila*, "were you denied because those in authority were serving an even greater authority?"

Frowning, Matt held out his hands, grateful to be angry instead of rocketing down that well of self-pity. "What in the hell does that mean?"

"Think."

"Think?"

Ivo Lass nodded and pointed between Matt's eyes. "With your brain."

Matt raised his eyebrows and folded his arms. "Getting just a touch testy, aren't we?"

"Answer the question."

The question: Had he ever been denied because those in authority were serving an even greater authority? He stared into a dark corner of the room. He had certainly been denied. There had been no childhood. No real friends; he couldn't afford them—the shame, the lies, the endless embarrassments. All of the things he had never had because there was never enough money. Matt's bike had been purchased with money he had earned cutting grass, raking lawns, shoveling endless mountains of garbage.

When his father had stumbled in late the night of the great bike episode, he had not been beaten again. Instead he had watched as his father took out his rage on the bicycle, reducing it to scrap in a matter of minutes. The mother and father that were never available for him except for guilt trips and beatings, and then not even for that. And what higher authorities were his mom and dad serving? Mom worshipped at the feet of Prince Valium. Dad's god was the great deity, Al Cahol, and his consort, Mary Jane. He felt his eyes grow moist as he nodded.

"Matt, were you free to change your nightmare? Were you free to leave?"

He slowly shook his head. "No."

"Then, you were a slave." As she raised her brows and smiled, Ivo Lass seemed to stop herself with an effort. "I am not your enemy, Matt. It is not even my province to treat you against your will."

"What the hell were you doing, then? Ambush counseling?"

"I was answering your question about the training. You don't have the same obstacle to overcome as Micky Cass. You don't have the same self-esteem."

Matt took a deep breath and let it out in a rush of frustration. "You're telling me that Newcomers can tell a human with too much self-esteem."

She burst out with a laugh and shook her head. "No, Matt. Tell me something."

"If I can."

"When I first came into the room, when you first saw me, how did you feel?"

Matt knew that if he repeated the word *feel* as a question, he'd just be stalling for time. Not only would he be stalling for time, it would be an obvious stall. How had he felt? He thought back and nodded slightly. "I guess I felt a little like what I feel a lot like right now."

"Which is what?"

"Threatened." His eyebrows crouched into a frown. "Maybe a little envy. Maybe a lot of envy."

"Matt, that's how that prostitute felt when she caught sight of Micky Cass in his disguise. Tencts have come to associate the feelings with humans, but they are the same feelings felt by every emotional cripple next to someone who is healthy."

"Come again?"

"I don't need to prove anything to you, Matt. I don't need you or your good opinion of me. I don't need to justify my existence to you or to anyone else. There is absolutely nothing within me that makes me either need or want your approval. That makes me very scary to someone who feels that he constantly needs to prove his worth to others."

"I don't feel that way."

"Then why tell me?"

"Tell you?" asked Matt, completely forgetting his little speech habit. "You asked." Matt paused as he thought on the past few moments. "Didn't you?"

"No, I didn't." Ivo Lass stood up and walked to the window. Her eyes studied the cityscape outside as she said, "There is an easy test of your need to justify yourself to others, Matt. I will tell you what it is and ask you to make no response. After all, I am not in a contest with you. I will tell you what it is, and you may do what you will with your conclusions. Do you understand?"

"Okay." For some reason Matt felt more threatened than he had experienced before.

"Very well. Matt, do you have a boyfriend or a girlfriend?"

"Girl," he said, realizing as he did so that his response involved disassociating himself from a particular life-style because Ivo Lass might judge it somehow. Already he was up to his ears attempting to prove something to the old alien. "Yes," he said. "I have a friend."

"Intimate friend?"

"Yes."

"Now, this is the question the answer to which I want you to only think about, not express. Do you understand?"

"Yes."

"When you're relaxing—watching baseball on television, say—and your intimate friend walks into the room from doing dishes or balancing her checkbook, or from whatever unknown activity, how do you feel?"

The feeling? It had only happened five hundred times. Matt's eyebrows went up in recognition of the *Hila*'s point. When Cathy came in when he was goofing off, that's how he felt—like he was goofing off. He felt guilty.

There was that stupid joke he'd heard after mass as a kid. In the Vatican, the pontiff's secretary comes running in and screams, "Your Holiness, He's out there! He's out there and He's going to be in here in a few minutes!" The pope asks, "Who are you talking about, Father? Who's out there?" The secretary pulls at his hair and wails, "It's Jesus, Your Holiness! The son of God! He's out there and He'll be in here in just a minute! What'll we do? What'll we do?" The pope frowns, picks up some papers, and says, "Look busy."

That was how it was when someone, anyone, interrupted him while he was taking a break or relaxing. He felt guilty; as if he should "look busy."

Then he did feel as though he constantly had to prove himself to everyone, to justify his existence. He turned in his chair and faced the *Hila.* "I have one question, Ivo Lass. If slaves have no self-esteem, and that's how Tencts identify Tencts, how come it's just the opposite with us?"

"How you look at things, Matt, including yourself, is something that can be changed. Many—most—Tenctonese are still slaves in their minds. I've done the necessary work and am no longer a slave in mine. What you are to your own mind is something you can change, although you don't want to change it right away. After all, it's an important part of your disguise. When you are ready to change it, though, there are all kinds of help available. Micky Cass is a good example. He, too, came from an addictive home—drugs, gambling, food addiction, and so on. He had become so healthy, however, it took eleven weeks of training to make him sick enough in his view of himself to impersonate a Tenct."

Matt stood up, his hands at his sides, a strange feeling of panic and longing in his heart. "Will I be seeing you again?"

She turned from the window, her eyebrows up again. "I'm a suspect, aren't I? We'll be seeing each other again."

CHAPTER 15

IT WAS NOT long after Sikes's session with the *Hila* that the FBI's unofficial investigation became officially official. The pulley of time strained against the belt of reality, the great shaft creaked on its rusty bearings, and the necessary prerequisites popped up in their respective pigeonholes. The unofficial bureau assistance became an official FBI investigation and, in a rare display of cooperation with local authorities, the bureau continued to operate through the Robb investigation command center in the LAPD, making it the core of the federal task force. In other words, nothing changed except Captain Grazer became second in command under Special Agent Stillson Landry.

Landry was a human with an overly polished manner who only insisted upon two things: (1) he and Captain Grazer were co-commanders of the joint task force, and (2) Stillson Landry was in charge. It was an accounting thing to enable some FBI number cruncher in Washington to defend his organization before some congressional committee bent on saving thirty-five cents worth of paper clips while stuffing billions into personal pork barrels.

There was one other change that occurred by making the investigation official. It then became part of the public record. George expected any moment to see Amanda Reckonwith, the self-proclaimed queen of the Slagtown news beat, come bursting through the door and start sticking her damned microphone in everyone's faces. That also meant increased pressure from the chief's office. The task force was a truck with a powerful engine, a heavy foot on the pedal, and no gas.

In the task force's command center, as Landry put on a primo performance of "Stuff Everybody Already Knows," George Francisco watched Captain Grazer twiddle his thumbs while the police officers and agents assigned to the task force doodled on notepads, whispered among themselves, stared blankly out of the windows or, in at least two cases, dozed. One officer, Burke from crisis control, was playing a hand-held video game.

Why not? thought George. Some writer with more poison in his pen than sense in his head trashes the police department, throws gasoline on the coals of anti-Tenct racism, and jumps into the middle of a crowd of killers just to make a big publicity splash, then vanishes and expects the aforesaid police officers to pull his cookies out of the fire? As far as George was concerned, the only interest he had in the investigation was twofold. First, Matt was going undercover in a bizarre masquerade and might be killed for his efforts. Second, what was it that Paul Iniko had found that was so secret he wouldn't—couldn't—share it with his fellow investigator?

George pulled out his own notepad and leafed to the previous day's notes. He and Iniko had been up in Coldwater Canyon at Duke Jessup's house overlooking Micky Cass's big eye. Jessup hadn't appeared particularly distraught at the possibility of Cass's kidnapping, but he appeared to be solidly covered with alibi plate. From the time Cass had last made an appearance until the two days before Martin Fell came into Grazer's office to raise the alarm, Jessup had been at a national English teachers' convention in Boston, accompanied by his wife, Lois, and the chairperson of Saint George's Academy department of English, Randolph Trassler.

The next thirty-six hours were covered by the Boston PD who had arrested Jessup, along with several other academic merrymakers, for making a public disturbance and damaging hotel property. The remaining time had been filled in and testified to by Mrs. Jessup, the two Jessup children, the Jessup's housekeeper, Gloria Salcines, and the head gardener from Coldwater Nurseries, Jimmy Lee.

He turned to another page. There was an incredibly ripe odor coming from former police officer Michael Hong's alibi. George went back two pages for his notes on the second Mike Hong interview. After everything had been plotted out, the corroborated times filled in, and every benefit of the doubt given, there were still forty hours of former officer Michael Hong's time unaccounted for. A very critical forty hours, too. They began shortly before Cass missed his first copy drop and went for a day and half after that. Michael Hong's answer?

"A fired cop doesn't have to account for his time, shoo-fly. Maybe I did kill the bastard and just don't remember." He had shaken his head and said with a cruel smile, "Naw. I wouldn't have forgotten killing him. Not him, I wouldn't."

George flipped his notebook closed and placed it in his coat's inside breast pocket. When they had returned to the car, Iniko had only commented, "Well, forty hours isn't so hard to lose." Terribly understanding for one who had been reared his entire life to be a watcher, an Overseer investigator.

After seeing Hong, while they had been at Jessup's, Paul Iniko had made a telephone call the content of which he refused to share with George. He then told George to take the car, he called a cab, and left. No explanations; no excuses.

Iniko couldn't do that. It was insulting, stupid, senseless. What in the hell was so goddamned secret the FBI man couldn't share it with a lowly detective sergeant who was on the same investigation? Perhaps now, with the FBI officially running the task force, Paul Iniko's games would end. Perhaps they'd simply grow worse.

George looked around the room again, caught Grazer's eye, and made a gesture toward the door with his head. The captain nodded sympathetically and George stood and turned around. Dobbs was at the door, leaning against it, his arms folded across his chest. He nodded at George and cocked his head toward the hallway. Once they had left the assembly and Dobbs had closed the door behind them, Dobbs called out, "Hey, George."

Francisco walked the length of the hallway and pushed through the doors into the squad bay. Once he was at his desk, he dropped into his chair, picked up his telephone, and began punching in a number. Dobbs pushed down on the button, breaking the connection. "What are you doing, Dobbs?"

"George, we have to talk."

"I can't think of a single thing to say to you, and I can't thing of anything I want to hear from you."

Dobbs took his finger off the button and sat on the edge of George's desk. "You know, Francisco, you are one hard dude to apologize to."

"Apologize?" said George suspiciously. "What do you have to apologize for?"

"You know. The Slag Slasher thing. You're right. It is the same. I'm sorry."

George shrugged, frowned, held out his hands, and said, "I'm sorry, too, for what I said."

"Okay, forget it. It just makes us even."

George shook his head. "Not really. I knew what I was doing. You didn't know any better."

Dobbs's face grew considerably darker. He closed his eyes for a second, and then took a deep breath as he mentally entered a ten count. As he let the breath escape, he opened his eyes and asked, "What about Matt? How's he doing?"

"The bandages were supposed to come off this morning. I tried to call him before the meeting in there, but they were right in the middle of it and couldn't be interrupted." He pointed at the telephone. "I was about to try again."

"In a minute. There's something I wanted you to see first." Dobbs walked to his desk, picked up a thick file, and returned, placing the file in front of George.

"What's this?"

Dobbs looked around the squad bay, virtually deserted save for himself, George, a records clerk, and the eternal custodian, Albert. Both the records clerk and Albert were on the other side of the large room oblivious of anything except the work before them. Dobbs bent over and said in a hushed voice, "You know that column Robb wrote where he talked about some big and powerful institution he was about to investigate and expose?"

"Yes. What about it?"

Dobbs tapped the file's jacket. "This is what he was after."

"What is it?"

"Would you believe the FB of cotton pickin' I?"

George's eyebrows jumped up in surprise, then slumped into a frown. "Iniko."

"Yeah, ol' massa Iniko. He was part of an FBI cover-up before with the MDQ business. It looks like he's still holding down the same old slot."

"He has been acting quite suspicious." George looked up at Dobbs. "Where'd you get this file?"

"Don't ask. Let's just say someone in the command center is real concerned about Matt and that no one really seems to be on the Robb case, despite all this cover-our-asses shit with the task force and the bureau."

George's frown grew deeper. "You mean the investigation is all a sham."

Dobbs stood, placed his hands on his hips and glowered at George's desk top as he bit at the inner skin of his lower lip. "The FBI end of it sure seems to be. Maybe our end of it, too." He looked up at Francisco. "You ever play poker, George?"

"Yes. A few times."

"You ever been in a game where everybody in it disliked the new player?"

George shook his head. "No. The games in which I participated seemed rather friendly unless I won several hands in a row. Then the irritation level went up rather abruptly. But that happened to whoever won several in a row. It wasn't directed at any individual."

"Friendly games." Dobbs folded his arms across his chest and leveled his gaze at George. "Back when I was in the navy, stationed in the middle of nowhere with nothing to do, a bunch of us used to play a lot of poker. Some days you'd win, some days you'd lose. We all knew each other and it was a way to kill time and throw money away. One time when the usual crew was settling down to play a game, this new guy comes along and asks if he can sit in. I didn't like him. I could tell by the looks on my buddies' faces that they didn't like him, either. It was just a feeling. There were only six of us, however, and seven is better for poker. Besides, none of us had what it took to tell the guy to get lost and cause a lot of bad feelings."

"Anything to avoid a confrontation," said George.

"Yeah."

"I can relate to that. Back on the ship that was the story of my life. Go on."

"It's not complicated. The guy sat in and within an hour he was cleaned and pressed. He wasn't a bad player, either. It's just that everybody disliked him. There was always someone who hung in and called every bluff. If he opened at all, no one called."

"In other words, you didn't allow him to play. You only avoided calling it that."

Dobbs nodded. "You've got it. That's what I figure the task force is doing to Micky Cass with this investigation. It's nothing official. I don't even think it's conscious. He threw a turd on the bureau, made the cops look bad. Cops cover cops, Micky Cass is the enemy, and that's how that tune is played. I don't think there's anyone that was in that room who's serious about this investigation except you, Grazer, and me."

"You?"

"Yeah, me. And you know why that is?"

"Not because of Micky Cass," said George. "It's because Matt's going to be out there with his neck on the chopping block."

"That's part of it." Dobbs smiled and scratched his chin. "With me, I think I want to find Cass, also."

"You?"

"Yesterday I hit a couple of used-book stores until I found that old paperback of Griffin's, *Black Like Me.* I never read it before. It was a gutsy thing Griffin did, George. It was before I was born, but I could taste the fear, the shame, the unfairness of it all. Maybe for the first time I got a hint at what my parents had to endure every day for most of their lives." Dobbs nodded. "What Micky Cass is doing is gutsy, too. Important. More important even than cops taking care of cops. It's doing the right thing." He reached down and tapped the jacket of the file. "Watch your ass, George. There are some big names in there."

Francisco drummed his fingers on the file for a moment, then looked around the squad room. "Where's Kirk?"

"Over at DMV trying to hunt down Archie Panek's four-by-four."

"How did you two make out with Goober and friends?"

Dobbs shook his head. "Kirk thinks he's hot on the trail, but I don't think these guys are insane enough sober to do anything, and they sure as hell don't seem to be able to handle anything drunk."

Francisco nodded, leaned forward, and opened the

folder. "Thank you for this." He looked up at Dobbs. "But you never said why you and your poker buddies disliked the new fellow who wanted to sit in on the game."

A streak of guilt flashed across the detective's face, followed by a sad smile. "He was white." He smiled sadly at the use of the term. "White. Anyway, that's where our heads were at back then. Now that I think about it, he was kind of gutsy, too."

CHAPTER 16

MATT STOOD NAKED, his eyes shut tightly.

Ivo Lass had said, "When you first behold yourself as a Newcomer, know all your feelings and know as well why you feel as you do."

"Tall order," he muttered as he opened his eyes. He looked into the full-length mirror attached to the closet door in his hospital room at Mt. Andarko's. He looked, but he didn't look. He studied the reflection in the glass of a mark high on the wall behind him; he examined a flaw in the mirror where a flake of silvering had fallen away; and he scrutinized a scratch in the glass near the bottom of the mirror as though determining the extent of the scratch, its origins, and the motivations of He Who What Done the Scratchin' somehow contained the key to the secrets of the universe.

"I am jerking around," Matt muttered.

Each surreptitious peek at himself with his periph-

157

eral vision startled him. It was as though a stranger were in the room and Matt Sikes was curiously absent. "Sort of an in-body out-of-body experience," he joked, attempting to laugh himself out of how he felt.

He moved his gaze until it was centered on the eyes in his reflection. The special mood sensitive contacts had turned green. Still the pain. Emotional pain. Old stuff never expressed. As the *Hila* had taught him, he closed his eyes and focused on the swirls and flashes produced by the pressure of the fluid in his eyes on his optic nerves. After a moment there was a brightness, and he dove into it, allowing it to fill him, surround him, calm him.

He opened his eyes again and the green was gone— for the moment. The causes of the pain were still with him. Old tapes. Emotional baggage. All of life's garbage that he had never taken out.

There was a strange smell in his nostrils. It was something of rot—an old fishy stench that left him as soon as it arrived. The green was back in his eyes. It was like a fuel gauge for pain, and right then Matt was registering a full tank.

Again close the eyes.

Again the light, letting it flow around him, remaining suspended in it, listening for wordless peace. He felt his skin tingle and then grow warm. The muscles in the back of his neck and shoulders relaxed, and he opened his eyes again. Once more the green was gone.

The eyebrows, too, were gone. He touched them with the fingers of his right hand. They had been shaved, treated with a hair growth retardant, and covered with a thin film of Realskin. He could feel it and it was his skin now. His nose, his cheeks, his head . . . *his head*.

He stared at the spotted baldness facing him and

allowed feelings of shock to fill him. He had imagined it a hundred times. Seeing it, however, placed him on a new plane of reality. This was no disguise. This was *him*.

Moving his fingers across the top of his spots, Matt felt for the tiny video recorder that had been implanted beneath his new skin. He examined very carefully the area where it was supposed to have been implanted but could not detect it. He lowered his arm and looked down the length of his reflected body. Looking at the front of his left thigh, he smacked it with his open hand and watched where his fingers had struck. No redness appeared, only a pale anemic pink. He looked into the image's eyes again. He was not a human disguised as a Newcomer. He was a Newcomer with some rather eccentric memories of being a human.

There was a knock at the door, and he felt some small portion of his head warp as he reached for his robe. Everything he could intellectualize told him that he needed no robe. Everything that was the body of Matt Sikes was covered with Realskin. Everything he felt, however, said he was raw naked, and the nakedness was of a more extreme degree than he had ever felt before. As he tied the sash to his bathrobe, he called to the door, "Yeah?"

"Matt?"

The door opened a crack and Cathy Frankel poked in her head and looked. When her gaze located Matt standing before the mirror, she went speechless. Matt turned slowly and looked at her. "Well?"

She entered the room, closed the door behind her, and leaned her back against it. She studied his face, his head, the portion of his neck and chest visible through the open top of the robe, and his hands.

"Well?" he repeated. "What is it? Am I a freak? An obvious *nugah*? Spit it out."

"No, darling," she said quickly as she pushed away from the door and walked to his side. When she stopped she did not touch him. Instead, she examined his face very closely. "Celine's mercy, Matt, but you are absolutely beautiful."

"Beautiful?" he repeated, catching his echo as he did so.

"What is it, Matt?"

"Nothing. I'm trying to shake the question marks out of my talk. It isn't easy." He pointed at his own face. "Wouldn't handsome be a better word?"

She frowned, touched a finger to her cheek, and cocked her head as she studied his face. "No. Not handsome. You are beautiful. I love your skin. How do you get it that way?"

Matt snorted out a bitter laugh. "How? I buy it by the goddamn square yard. How in the hell would I know? I just got the stuff." He pointed again at himself. "Well, what about it? I'm serious."

She nodded slowly. "From what I can see, Matt, it looks excellent. Even your hands."

Matt looked up at her. "They didn't just cover my hands."

Her eyebrows went up. "Everything?"

For a moment he felt the skin beneath the skin blushing. "Yeah. Everything."

"May I see?" she said, maneuvering to stand in front of him, very close. Her long, delicate fingers parted his robe and reached around his waist until her hands came to rest upon the small of his back. "How does this feel, Matt?"

"It feels."

She looked into his eyes and asked, "Did you say *everything?*"

"Yeah."

"How do you know it works?"

Matt raised his eyebrows and smiled wickedly. "Oh, they brought in a Tenct sex therapist and she put me through the usual rehabilitation exercises: spaceman on top, alien on a bone, Cool Whip and waders—"

She pushed away from him. "I don't think that's very funny."

He pulled her back and held her closely. "It works. If you need proof, keep feeling me up and you'll be getting a rude nudge real soon."

"Now?" she asked, a smile of her own tugging at the corners of her mouth.

"I think we'd better go home, first. You know how loud we Tenctonese get when we're getting it on."

"Seriously, Matt. Can you go home now?"

"My time's my own until tonight. That's when Matthew Cross, alien boy journalist, goes undercover in Chayville and hangs with the bangers."

A worried look crossed her face. "Matt, what about the training?"

"I'm trained. Just as long as I don't have to give a speech, I'm *debah.*"

"How can you be so certain? It took Ellison Robb eleven weeks."

"Do you get any weird vibes off me?"

"No." She frowned and looked thoughtful for a moment. "That's strange. I never did." Looking into his eyes, she repeated, "I never did. Why?"

Matt shrugged and glanced down. "As far as my mentor, Ivo Lass, is concerned, there are all kinds of slaves in the universe. I was just lucky enough to be one of them."

The room's telephone rang and Matt disengaged one of his hands from Cathy's waist, reached out, and picked up the handset. As he placed it against his earfold he was again startled at how natural it seemed. "Yes?"

"Matt?" answered George.

"Yeah? What's up?"

"We just got the word. It's Micky Cass. They think they've found his remains."

Matt felt something within him turn dark and brittle. "Cass," Matt repeated, his new skin tingling.

"It was in a dry lake bed east of Barstow. According to the officers who found the body, there's hardly anything left. He was mostly dissolved in a bath of some kind of acid. Judging from the condition of the head in relation to the deterioration of the rest of the body, Cass's head was left out of the bath at first." George's voice broke. "He was alive when he was placed in that bath, Matt. He was alive and awake."

If Looks Could Kill

In Black Like Me, Griffin wrote about "the hate stare," a look he would receive from "whites" as he walked southern streets in the late fifties masquerading as a "Negro." The stare was more than a look of disapproval. Rather, it was an exhibition of such extreme abhorrence it was virtually an attempt to kill with one's eyes.

Looks such as that are not the thin yields of idle choice, preference, or the mere habits absorbed through a regional upbringing. The roots run much deeper. The person who aims "the hate stare" at someone is looking at an entity that threatens not only existence, but one's reason for being. Thief of job, home, neighborhood, and nation; defiler of humanity and all that is good; God-killer. The impact of "the hate stare" is quite shattering. The first one that was fired at me was in Santa Monica walking along Ocean Park Boulevard.

There are few Tencts in Santa Monica, and I suppose there is some weight to the argument that "we" can't be everywhere. There are still less than a million Newcomers on earth, and since two out of three are mired between L.A. and East L.A., it spreads the rest fairly thin. Nevertheless, there are only a few in Santa Monica, which is why I chose to stroll its streets. I wanted to look at the faces, make eye contact with my fellow beings, and see if I could attract "the hate stare."

I began my odyssey on The Promenade, turned up Pico, and made my way down Lincoln, turning onto Ocean Park pleasantly surprised that I had not run into a single shattering look. Mostly what I found was indifference: indifference to me, to everyone else, to the street, to the city, to reality at large. I had the feeling that I could have sprouted tentacles and grown fangs and began snatching little boys and girls off the street and devoured them and no one would have noticed, with the possible exception of the little boys and girls. Perhaps self-absorption is the mark of our age.

There were a few frowns aimed at me, and although some were disapproving frowns, the majority were the "strange to see one of them in this neighborhood" looks. There were also a few of the upraised eyebrow variation of the "what's that?" look. The disapproving looks were generally the same sentiment coupled with a "something might be wrong" streak. These were the same faces, looks, and frowns that every human gets on city streets. I was looking forward to writing a column about tolerance in Santa Monica.

Then I saw it coming from a woman waiting at a bus stop.

The hate stare.

She was in her late forties, dressed in slacks, blouse,

and sweater. She carried a tote bag containing her shopping scalps of the day. Her face was set with narrowed eyes, black with raw, rabid loathing.

I was literally knocked back a step. Perhaps those who believe in perceptible auras emanating from living beings are right on the money, because I could feel a physical pressure that smacked my face and reached right into my soul, compelling me to feel worthless and evil about myself. To be honest, it frightened me to such a degree I was ready to tell Marty Fell to stick it. I wanted to pack in the project and go home. I had never before wanted to hide my face in shame, and the feeling bubbled over until it outraged me.

I walked over to the woman, faced her, and asked, "Was there something you wanted to say to me?"

"No. There's nothing I want to say to you." The look in her eyes, if anything, was more intense.

"Did I do something to you? Cause you some kind of injury?"

She shifted her weight from one foot to the other. "I didn't do anything to you. You got no right to question me."

"I never did anything to you," I insisted. "Why do you hate me?"

For the next ten seconds I watched her face erupt in such extreme hatred, tears came to her eyes. All of a sudden I no longer feared her or felt ashamed. Her hatred was a cancer that ate at her heart, mind, and soul. I felt sorry for her and it must have showed in my face. That ripped it. She could not bear to have a Tenctonese pity her.

There was a Tenct man waiting at the bus stop and he gave me such a disapproving look, it visually smacked my knuckles. "Don't cause trouble," said the look. "What's the matter with you? Blend, go along, look down. Do not protest, confront, insist. No slave ever survived through confrontation. Are you crazy?"

Perhaps I was crazy. The injustice of that look seemed to drive me toward a dangerous edge. Nevertheless, the bus arrived, both the woman and the man got on the bus, the doors closed, and they roared off in a cloud of environmentally approved fumes. There was a coffee shop across the street, and I decided to get a cup of tea and either scribble some notes or call Marty Fell and tell him to roll up the Sunday Times and pound it up his ass.

As I was waiting for the light to change, a boy of about seven or eight stepped off the curb and into the path of an oncoming Oldsmobile. Instinctively, I grabbed the back of the kid's electric green tank top and jerked him back to the curb. The whole thing took about a quarter of a second.

Before looking to see what had snatched him out of the street, the boy saw the near miss with the car. Hence, when he looked at me, his face was frightened and words of gratitude were on his lips. "Thanks. Thanks a lot, mister. I didn't see any—"

Despite the fact that I had already released my hold on the boy, a man, presumably the boy's father, clasped the lad to himself as though to shield him from my touch. I looked into the man's face and beheld something that struck me quite speechless. It was "the hate stare" with the man's lips writhing in a grotesque attempt at saying "thank you" that never quite made it to an audible level.

I nodded and turned away, grateful that my surgical disguise prevented the flush in my face from being visible. I was ready for that cup of tea. The light changed and I lifted my foot to step off the curb when I felt a heavy hand on my shoulder. I turned and it was the boy's father. His face was literally warring through a succession of conflicting emotions and there was a five-dollar bill in his hand. "Here," he said, shaking the bill in the air. "Take it."

"It's okay," I said, turned away, and tried once more to catch the light.

He pulled me back and shook the money in my face. "Here! Take it! I want you to take this." He nodded. "For my boy."

"It's okay," I repeated. "I was glad to do it."

He did not release my shoulder. "Take the money."

It was standing before me, a thing I had read about but had never before seen: a sociological Sasquatch. He could not be beholden to a Tenct and still find life livable. He would've found his son's death by Oldsmobile easier to handle. I pulled my shoulder free and said "Forget it" as I stepped into the traffic, now that the light was against me. Again the hand dropped on my shoulder. "Look, I want to pay you for my son."

I stepped back on the curb, and I can only imagine the expression on my face as I said, "You think five dollars is enough?" Then his pain and mine did this little dance.

"What . . . what do you mean, enough?"

I looked at the boy. "What do you weigh, kid? How much?" The kid didn't want to play so I turned back to his father. "Say, sixty-five, seventy-five pounds?"

"So what?"

"That's only seven, eight cents a pound. Hell, man, I have to pay at least a buck ninety a pound for ground chuck. Your kid ought to be worth at least that much, and that doesn't even include sentimental attachment. Round it off, say, and you give me a hundred dollars."

"What? I'm not giving you any hundred dollars."

"Then, let's forget about it, okay?" The light changed again and I turned to cross the street. Again the hand dropped on my shoulder. "Look. You take the five dollars! I'm not going home owing a favor to a damned slag!"

"I'm not taking your money, Goober. So what're you going to do? Throw your kid back out in the street?"

For a split second I almost thought he was going to do it, proving this particular point seemed that important to him. Instead, he crumpled up the five dollars and threw it on the sidewalk. Perhaps fifteen or twenty persons walked by before a druggie snatched it up. It just goes to show how bad inflation has gotten. Just before I entered the coffee shop on the other side of the street, I glanced back in time to see the man smacking his son's backside for being rescued by a rubberhead.

There's no point in naming any names here. Who could inflict more pain on that man than he inflicts on himself? What would be the point? It takes a teachable person to learn from pain more than the fact that it hurts.

CHAPTER 17

IT MADE MATT think of the Miadi gang execution three years before. Old man Miadi's two ambitious sons attempted to dissolve their father in acid. The Miadi boys, however, hadn't gotten their gold stars in chemistry, and there was a lot left of Daddy. The two sons hadn't been any better at finding lawyers than they'd been at chemistry and were currently housed along lethal row at the new facility at Tujunga. To get them there, however, Matt had needed to see the father's remains. The images of the corpse had never left the shadows of his memory.

The air in the autopsy theater felt corrupt enough to stain anything it touched. Matt's lungs felt raw. The lump on the slab had been barely recognizable as a primate, much less a human. The lower extremities were completely missing, while from the empty frame of the remaining ribs hung the tail of the few remaining vertebrae, rounded and pitted by the action of the

169

acid. On the shoulders, neck, and skull the epidermis and a considerable portion of the underlying muscle tissue had been eaten away, leaving the skull looking like an incompetent anatomy student's cadaver at semester's end. Although the teeth could be seen amid the white foam that had bubbled through the gaps in the cheek muscles, the tissue of the lips and nose was mostly intact. The acrid, rusty smell of blood and acid hung in Matt's nostrils long after they had left the horror behind, making the air in the staff lounge seem close and filthy.

They all stood, no one really feeling comfortable with sitting down or touching anything. George Francisco kept staring at Matt, fascinated still at the transformation in his partner's appearance, though he had found no opportunity to comment upon it.

The assistant pathologist, Arthur Rivers, looked ill, his face edged with Newcomer gray. Chief Pathologist Kim Nishida pushed her glasses up and perched them on top of her head, revealing almond eyes capped with a frown. "The body was fed feet first into a bathtub filled with concentrated hydrochloric acid. Enough of the scalp was eaten away to expose the miniature video recorder, which is missing. The remaining Realskin tissue around the mouth and nose indicates the use of some sort of mask, perhaps a respirator, that protected somewhat that portion of the lower face—"

"Why?" asked George.

"Why the mask?"

"Yes."

Dr. Nishida thought for a moment and looked at Matt. "The fumes from that amount and concentration of acid would kill a human after a moment or two if he breathed them in. If the objective was to cause the deceased the maximum amount of pain, as the evidence would suggest, there would have to be some way for him to breathe. A respirator of some kind would be a possible explanation."

"Sweet Celine," muttered George.

"Wouldn't there be something left of the respirator? Some parts?" asked Matt.

"It looks as though the mask was removed before the head and upper body were dropped into the bath. We're fortunate that the porcelain coating on the tub was shattered in one place allowing the acid to eat through the metal and drain out. If the mask had been thrown in, the medical examiner would've found something. Whoever did this took the mask."

"The site was cleaned up, as well," said George. "No prints, no tracks."

Matt closed his eyes and swallowed. The stench in the autopsy bay had been a twisting rope of repugnance: the lung-searing stink of acid, the heavy smell of blood; and . . . there was something else. "Kim, what in the hell was that sickly sweet lemon peppermint rot stink in there? I thought it was going to make me puke."

"Maalox. It was in the corpse's mouth. The officers on the scene poured it in to protect what was left of the teeth. One of the cops had an acid stomach. The other one had some high school chemistry. Lucky she did, too."

"And that thing in there is what's left of Micky Cass?"

Nishida nodded. "We've had his dental records on

file since he was reported missing. Everything that's left matches. I'm satisfied it's Micky Cass."

"Except that Micky Cass was a pseudonym," interrupted George.

"Let me put it this way, then, George. I'm satisfied that the teeth in that thing in there are the same as those appearing in the X rays provided by Micky Cass's dentist. The blood type is the same and the lips and nose are covered with the remains of a Realskin surface, which is consistent with the operation he had to disguise himself as a Tenctonese." She glanced at Matt.

A sad giggle escaped from Matt's lips. "I'm sorry," he said as he held out a hand. "It's just now we'll never find out if Cass was male or female."

"It depends on your definition," said Nishida. "Cass's blood shows that either he's female or perhaps undergoing hormone therapy in preparation for a sex change operation. Perhaps he was a hermaphrodite. There are many degrees of in between. However, if I had to bet the barn on it, from the bone structure I'd say he came into the world male. Maybe. Probably. Possibly. I've seen plenty of exceptions cross my table. Male. Maybe."

"Hell, anybody can flip a coin," said Matt. He shook his head and tried to get his mind to focus. "There's something flapping loose here. This stuff, concentrated hydrochloric acid. I remember it from chem class. HC1. Mrs. Yates, our chem teacher, used to treat that little bottle like it was nitro. To fill up a bathtub would take a hell of a lot. It would also take some pretty specialized equipment to get it there in the center of that dry lake and then put it into the tub. In other words, somebody went to one hell of a lot of trouble to kill Micky Cass in this particular way. Why?"

He looked at George and his partner was looking at the assistant pathologist. Dr. Rivers allowed his gaze to fall upon Matt. "If you took a Tenctonese and dipped him into salt—"

"Salt water," completed Matt. "I saw it happen once. It acts just like a very corrosive acid. You're saying someone wanted to give Micky Cass the full Newcomer experience?"

"I can see the *Ahvin Rivak* or some other purist fanatic group doing something like this," said Dr. Rivers. "You were right about something else, sergeant."

"What?"

"It took whoever did this a considerable amount of trouble to do it in the middle of that dry lake."

"What's your point?"

The pathologist looked toward George. "Whoever did this knew how to handle HC1. What I don't know is why they'd perform this act in a place where it was bound to be discovered and done in such a fashion that they made certain there would be enough left behind to make an identification."

"Are you saying that it was intentional?"

"I'm saying it's very likely," answered Rivers. "The medical examiner's report as well as the investigating officer's report suggest that the portion of the tub where the acid ate through, the porcelain was shattered by a small-caliber bullet. Pieces of the slug and bits of porcelain were found on the ground near the point where the acid drained from the tub. The shot was enough to knock the porcelain coating off both sides of the impact point without puncturing the metal. Once the acid ate through the metal, the tub drained. If it's not deliberate, it's a fortuitous circumstance indeed."

To Matt it was very clear why the perps had done what they had done and in this particular manner. It wouldn't be much of an object lesson if no one ever knew about it. It was a message to anyone who might dare to follow in Micky Cass's footsteps.

CHAPTER 18

OUTSIDE IN THE parking lot Matt leaned against his car, his arms folded, his head down. George stood facing him. "I'm sorry, Matt."

"Sorry? What about?"

"Micky Cass. I know how much he meant to you. I'm sorry we didn't find him in time."

"In time," Matt repeated, his voice low and menacing. "I wonder if he even had any kind of chance. I can already hear the cops and the Tencts cheering."

"Not all the police officers are cheering, Matt. Dobbs is working hard to help, and so is the captain. So am I. Murder is still murder, Matt. Not all of the Newcomers are cheering."

"Sorry." Matt looked off into the distance and fought to keep the tears from his eyes. With an effort he returned his gaze to George. "A good person—a very brave person—is in there, dead, eaten away, unrecognizable, tortured to death. The really sad thing is that the very ones he fought for and died for will probably be relieved at his death. No more probes into police racism and brutality, no more Tencts embarrassed by Ellison Robb rubbing Goober's nose in the racist mess, no more corporations or government agencies scrambling to cover up the stink in their personnel departments. Rubberhead Robb is dead; everybody is off the hook. And when nobody really wants to find the killer, nobody is going to find the killer. Isn't that how it goes, George?"

"I want to find the killer, Matt."

Sikes glanced around suggestively. "That's more than we can say for the feds. Where's Iniko?"

"Paul doesn't confide in me. He's off investigating something he can't talk about."

"Can't talk about? What in the hell is that supposed to mean?"

"Unknown."

"What's Grazer doing about it?"

"There's not much he can do, Matt. He's got no real authority over the federal personnel in the task force."

"What if we turn up a big red arrow pointing right at the FBI? What about then?"

George frowned. "Dobbs said the same thing. He gave me some stuff to look at, and there are some big names in the bureau that Cass could've gotten pretty dirty if he'd published only half the stuff he's got on them."

"Chase it down, George. Somebody's hands are bloody as hell, and it could be the bureau."

"Do you really think that's possible?"

"Right now I wouldn't be surprised to find out the FBI director and L.A.'s chief of police personally paired up to lower Cass feet first into that acid."

George looked sympathetically at Matt and raised his eyebrows. "At least you won't have to go through with that absurdly dangerous undercover assignment. Too bad, really. You look much more distinguished this way. You can help me chase down the FBI leads Dobbs turned up." He studied Matt's face. It was as unmoving as a granite cliff. "You're not going undercover."

"My man, I have to track down a certain banger down in the Chay. It might be the bureau, and then again it might be the Nightshade or someone else he ran into down there, like Goober and the slaghunters."

"You're trying to see Danny Mikubeh?"

"That's what I said."

"That's absurd. Matt, once the news of this gets out, the Chay is going to erupt in flames. There's no need to take the risk."

"George, you know that Edward Lear quote that was left at Micky Cass's home?"

"What about it?"

"You know how we figured it might've come from Jessup, the next-door neighbor?"

"Yes. His professional background is in English literature."

Matt's eyes narrowed. "You'll never guess who else has a background in English lit."

George frowned, then raised his eyebrows. "Not Danny Mikubeh."

"Yes, Danny Mikubeh. It was right there in Cass's notes. Mikubeh's under another name at Pepperdine in his third year of journalism. How about that?"

"That *is* interesting."

"I'll say it's interesting, partner. I can't wait to get

together with him and have a heart to heart to heart to heart about owls, pussycats, and things that go kill in the night."

"Still, there's no need to go right now, Matt. We can wait for things to at least calm down a little."

"We don't have any time. There's something suffocating out there, partner, and if we don't get to it fast, what little of it that's left is going to flat out die. Back when I was young and stupid I used to call it 'justice.'" Matt turned and opened the door of his car. He climbed into the driver's seat and pulled the door shut behind him. "There is no time, George. No time at all." He started up the car.

"Matt, I have a very bad feeling about how the city is going to react to the news of Cass's death. Have you checked in with Landry or Captain Grazer today?"

"Nope. I haven't checked in and I haven't been home. I don't intend going home. I am officially undercover right now, and you haven't seen me."

"What about your backup?"

"Screw the backup. The way the task force is dragging its feet on this thing, we'll see the Cubs take the series before we catch Cass's killer."

"Matt, it was dangerous enough before. Going without backup is suicide."

"You're right about one thing, George. This city is going to come unglued once news of this hits the street. Shit, fire, storm, death, and destruction. In the middle of that all the rules get holes in them. Their rules and our rules. When the rules rip I have to be there."

"Why? For what purpose?"

"To see it. To pick up what falls out."

Matt pulled away and drove the car out of the lot.

As his car pulled into traffic, a young adult human male on the crosswalk raised his fist, shook it and bellowed, "Fuckin' slag!"

George watched the car become swallowed by the traffic. "Take care of yourself, partner," George whispered. "Stay low."

CHAPTER 19

THE NEWS OF Ellison Robb's execution hit the streets and flamed its way around the globe at the same time as the news that the author of "Slag Like Me" was political satirist, columnist, and best-selling author Micky Cass. The news also came with video of prominent L.A. politicians and police officials placing their profound indifference to Cass's death on the record in addition to startling full color images of Cass's acid-ravaged corpse. The combination pulled the plug on an ocean of devastating frustration and rage. Protest demonstrations in the large cities of the United States were mirrored by spectacles in London, Dublin, Paris, Berlin, Moscow, Tokyo, and even Beijing. In Detroit, New York, Philadelphia, Atlanta, Miami, and L.A., however, the demonstrations immediately turned violent.

Most network and cable commentators were rather confused by the whole thing. None of the cities paralyzed by demonstrations or going up in flames, barring Los Angeles, had significant Tenct populations. Most of them, in fact, had no Tenctonese at all. The Rolodex experts hypothesized about violence on television, the alienation of self, the dichotomy of poverty and plenty, making it easier to hire the unemployed *v.* protecting union jobs and pay scales, the dregs of the "me" generation, and the second amendment to the Constitution. No one seemed to be able to grasp the obvious: a great wrong had been committed; an archaic spark of justice had been quenched. It awakened a much neglected sense of what's right felt by a great number of persons both human and Tenctonese.

The Tenctonese usually didn't participate in demonstrations. Former Overseers and slaves alike knew how to keep their places and keep their feelings to themselves. Before they had come to Earth, sense and safety for a Newcomer had always been along the path of compliance. For most of them, nothing had changed with the coming of freedom. There were, of course, exceptions. There were the young Tenct gang bangers down in the Chay. There were the other kinds of criminals, as well; robbers, muggers, second-story artists, serial killers, and a complete spectrum of addicts and dealers. Together they were the evidence that the usual Tenctonese compliance was a survival mechanism, not a genetically mandated program.

With the death of Micky Cass, the generally expected Newcomer acceptance evaporated in smoke, flames, and gunfire. In offices and supermarkets, on assembly lines and street corners, the usual smug comments, rubberhead jokes, insults, and brush-offs were no longer ignored. Instead they drew retaliation times ten. At the command center, a rebellion of a more subdued nature was taking place. Most of the personnel had been pulled for duty at riot control central, leaving the desks, phones, computers, and piles of documents unattended. A lone Tenctonese investigator sat in a cone of light, frowning at a few scraps of newspaper on the desk in front of him.

"Iniko, where in blazes have you been?"

Paul Iniko looked up from his desk and saw the enormous scowl of Captain Grazer looking back at him. "Is there a problem, captain?"

"A problem?" Grazer stabbed at the air with his finger. "A problem? The G-man wants to know if there's a problem! Micky Cass is dead; the headlines are a foot tall; Landry and your field office have the chief crawling up my ass; the damned city is coming unglued; we're looking at a goddamned war down in the Chay; Sikes is off on a one-jerk crusade; I team you up with Francisco and the last time Francisco laid eyes on you goddamned Santa Ana had the goddamned lease on the goddamned Alamo! Would you call that a problem?"

Iniko looked down at his hands, his expression troubled. "I apologize, captain."

"Apologize?" Grazer sat on the edge of Iniko's desk and raised his thick dark eyebrows. "Apologize? I'm sorry, captain, and everything's all right again? Listen to me, buddy. Stillson Landry is smokin'! Your boss, Nate Crook, is putting out a contract on you. Man, you haven't even checked in with your own field office! What in the hell is going on?"

"Perhaps, captain, it's a two-jerk crusade."

"This isn't funny, and you're not a privileged character. You don't have any special ass to swing around here, pal. Your own boss is even more pissed off at you than I am. You want to tell me what's going

182

on before they throw a net over you and drag you off to El Segundo for the stupids cure?"

The former Overseer leaned back in his chair, his gaze still fixed to the top of his desk. "Captain, I think I know something about Micky Cass. If what I think is true, it's something he didn't intend anyone to know. It might, however, give me a clue to who did this."

The captain waited a moment and then said, "Well? What is it?"

"I'm sorry, captain. I can't tell anyone without breaking a confidence."

Grazer held out his hands. "So, break a confidence! Feel crappy, see a counselor, eat some weasel jerky, and see me in the morning! This isn't the world's biggest problem, Agent Iniko. Spill! Start talking!"

"This is not the kind of confidence I can break, captain. I suspect what would be lost far outweighs what would be gained. This is why I couldn't tell George about it."

"About it? About what? You haven't said anything yet!"

Iniko looked up at Grazer, his face impassive. "I'm not going to, either."

"Are you sure you want to work it this way, Paul?" A look of concern came over Grazer's face. "Buddy, unless you can get back on the team, the bureau is going to yank your tail feathers. Landry burned off my ear not more than an hour ago. If you don't pick up that phone and square things with him, it'll be badge and gun time and you with a handful of want ads looking for a slot on Pico bucketing fried chicken."

"Everyone has to do what they have to do."

Grazer studied the former Overseer for a long time. He lowered his voice and said, "You know Cass's notes on the FBI?"

"I haven't seen them."

"They point a pretty big finger at a bureau cover-up of an official no-Tenctonese hiring policy."

"What are you driving at, captain?"

"Well? What about it?"

"It's possible. As you know, the bureau has covered up things before."

"That's right. I also remember you were part of that cover-up."

"For a while."

Grazer scratched the back of his neck. "Would getting rid of you be part of a new cover-up?"

Iniko looked up at the captain and allowed his gaze to settle upon Grazer's eyes. "Confidentially, captain, I doubt it. If I had to make a guess as to why Stillson Landry and Nate Crook are upset with me, I would venture to say it's because I haven't been following orders very well—at all."

"His or mine?"

"No one's."

The captain sighed and rubbed his chin. "Look, Paul, can't you even give me a hint about what you've been doing? Give me a little something I can use to square things with Landry and the chief."

"Instead, captain, let me ask you something."

Grazer sighed and folded his arms across his chest. "Yeah. Okay."

Iniko leaned forward and rested his elbows on the edge of the desk. "Everyone has something that is most important to him. What's most important to you?"

"Most important to me?" The captain thought for a moment and repeated, "Most important." He nodded once and looked down at Iniko. "My daughter. That's what's most important to me. Why?"

"Captain, if the only way you could do your job by the book was to place your daughter's life in jeopardy, would you do it?"

"What kind of a question is that? How would it endanger my daughter's life?"

"For the sake of argument, captain. If the only way you could do your job by the book was to place your daughter's life in danger, would you do it?"

Grazer stood up, grimaced, and placed his hands upon his hips. "Why do I feel just a little sandbagged? You already got from me what's most important, so you already know the answer to your question."

"Yes, I do."

"So what's most important to you, Paul?"

"Serenity, captain."

Grazer snorted out a laugh and raised his eyebrows. "I don't suppose you'd care to get a little more specific."

"If I could do that, Captain Grazer, we wouldn't be having this conversation."

The police captain averted his glance. "Look, Landry told me to get you to call in or to collect your ID and gun. If you aren't here, I can't collect anything. Understand?"

Iniko leaned back in his chair, took his ID case from his pocket, opened it, and glanced at the card that had once symbolized a high degree of acceptance in a world that wanted no aliens and wanted alien Overseers even less. He placed his ID on the desk, took the gun from his belt, and placed it on top of the leather case. "Thank you, captain. It looks as though I have to do what I have to do without these."

Grazer picked up Iniko's gun and ID and looked at them as he said, "Officially, Iniko, you no longer have any authority regarding this investigation. Officially, you're to stay away from it." He looked at Iniko and held out his hand. "Off the record, good luck and stay in touch."

The former Overseer stood, shook the captain's hand, and said, "I'll call in if I learn anything I can tell you." Iniko released the captain's hand, closed the file on his desk, and walked from the command center, Captain Grazer still looking down at the former agent's gun.

"Cap?" came a voice from the doorway. Grazer turned and looked to see Dobbs and Kirk leaning through the doorway into the room. Sergeant Dobbs was wiggling two fingers in a walking motion, his eyebrows raised.

Grazer nodded and said, "George is in position out front. Give him the signal and tell him to be careful."

"Right."

"And, Dobbs, Kirk."

"Yeah?" they both answered.

"You two be careful. I'm not really sure who our friends are in this. Watch your back."

"Will do, cap."

As the pair left, Grazer returned his gaze to Iniko's ID and gun. "You watch your back, too, you stiff-necked bastard."

The Color Pink

"Pink" in Tenctonese is tjai (pronounced and spelled "chay" in the Tenct barrio). Pink is the Tenctonese color of death. This isn't the pastel pink of a rose or tomato soup made with milk. Tenct death is hot pink; ski-slope pink; the neon stuff that makes Day-Glo look subdued. You can find the color on most of the Tenct gang jackets anywhere within Chayville, the area east of the Golden State Freeway to Lorena bounded roughly north and south by Brooklyn and Whittier. In this one and one-third square mile area there are fifteen main gangs, eight of them Tenct.

This is the armpit of what Goober calls Slagtown. It probably wouldn't be very smart to take a drive down there to check out the fashion statements, however. If you're Tenctonese, you may be mistaken for a cop, a member of a rival Tenct gang, or someone from out of the neighborhood with significant potential as a victim. If you are not Tenctonese, it would be radical chumphood to show your face in the Chay. Too many

Tencts in the area have been maimed and shot dead in drive-by slaghunts by Afro, Hispanic, Anglo, and Asian gang members, and by Goober and his buddies on their regular Saturday night exercise of their right to be alcoholic handgun owners. Between the Tencts and the drive-by shooters, they racked up more than three hundred reported murders in the Chay last year. That's better than half the city total.

Danny Mikubeh, hivek of the Nightshade, had been told about my column, "Slag Like Me." He read the pieces and then extended an invitation to me to come down to the Chay and run awhile with the Shade if I wanted a real look at how the fehn treats Tencts. Fehn means "hair," and that's what humans are called in the Chay. Hair, fur, fuzz, lint, they're all names for humans. To designate ethnic groups among humans, those in the Chay use the usual abuses.

Personally, I believe Danny wanted me to return to Shade turf in order to punish me in some manner. My maiming or death as a human in Chayville would make a traditional Nightshade statement, of course, but Danny Mikubeh is less complicated than that. When officers Hong and Kent dumped me at his feet on Eagle Street the week before, my disguise had fooled him. The leader of the Chay's biggest gang does not easily forgive such breaches of etiquette.

Still, I accepted, walked in all alone, and stood up to Danny like a person who had a right to be there. There was a piece of Danny that admired my demeanor, and before that wore off, the disguise took over. After an hour together, Danny was talking about debah and "us," referring to Tencts, and "them" and the fehn, referring to humans.

He talked about his youth on the slave ship, the terror of the crash, the hopes and dreams of his family

188

as they looked out upon the vistas of earth and the staggering prospect of freedom. And then there was the welcome.

"Yes, we're so teddibly opposed to slavery, and we're so teddibly pleased you're free, and now go like a good rubberhead and be free someplace else." And then, "Mira, we know what it's like, man, to be oppressed, you know? And, bueno, you free now. So go do your libertad anyplace but here, comprende?" And "Ah so. Hajimemashite dozo yoroshiku. Happy you no longer slave. Not so happy you here. Sayonara."

Danny, when he "talks fehn" and does "the welcome," is hilarious. His face becomes plastic and his body liquid as he takes on outrageous accents and becomes the grotesque ethnic stereotypes in which the backs of multicolored hands have caused him to believe. It was easy to imagine him doing stand-up comedy in some really insensitive club. Danny Mikubeh is a natural performer, but I don't think you'll ever get a chance to catch his act. He'll never live that long.

There's only one thing upon which the fehn gangs on the borders of the Chay turf agree: Danny Mikubeh must die. Danny and his friends formed Nightshade three years ago on Breed Street, and then proceeded to fight, run, bludgeon, and kill the fehn gangs out of the area, bringing Chayville into existence. He initiated the treaties between most of the Tenctonese gangs, and keeps the relative peace within the Chay with a heavy fist. Any gang on the borders of the Chay who ventures to cross the line will find Danny Mikubeh on its case.

We walked the streets of the Chay, Danny's bodyguards on point, trailing behind, and gathered around him and his inner circle of lieutenants. I saw the way the people on the street looked at Danny and his gang.

In a few cases it was stone-faced fear, but for the majority it was respect ranging from the grudging acceptance of a necessary evil to unabashed worship. I even saw how they looked at me. Ellison Robb took a moment and basked in the fantasy of one permitted to walk with the hivek, or leader, of the Shade. I got a little taste of what it was like to own the street. It felt good, empowering.

My surgical disguise, I should add, besides making me appear Tenctonese, also made me look as though I was in my mid-twenties. The image, to Danny Mikubeh, was more powerful in the short run than the reality that I was fehn. To Danny I became a new friend, one of the Chay, a great addition to the leader's entourage and world plan, up until he introduced me to his sister. Her eyes went wide, hearts went all pitty-pat, there was a suggestive hum, and a self-satisfied look on Danny's face that would have rivaled any matchmaker's. That self-satisfied look suddenly vanished to be instantly replaced by the grotesque expression of one who suddenly realizes one has placed one's foot in a bucket full of rattlesnakes.

He screamed his sister back indoors, ordered two of his lieutenants to drag me along, and stormed up the street to a storefront that served as Shade headquarters where I found him sitting behind a table, his eyes wild with anger and confusion. Upon Danny's signal, the two aides vanished into the woodwork. The comfortably furnished room was hung with gang jackets torn from the backs of defeated Shade adversaries. There had been no attempt at hiding the brown patches of dried blood that stained most of the jackets. They were Shade scalps.

"You really aren't Tenct," he stated in Tenctonese.

"No, I'm not," I replied in kind.

"Man, that disguise is good," he said in English. "Your accent is right off the ship. You move Tenct. You feel debah. It really messes me."

"Thank you."

He shook his head. "You look and feel debah, but you're all hair. Just another lint ball."

"Not just another lint ball, Danny. I'm a unique lint ball."

"How much did all that plastic cost?"

"The paper paid for the surgery and training. It cost about half a million."

I expected an outraged protest concerning the price of the plastic surgery, but Danny simply sat there, thinking. While he was thinking, it occurred to me that half a mill to the hivek of the Shade was chump change. They run protection inside the Chay, which amounts to millions by itself. Add to that the tributes from the other Tenct gangs, and the cut Nightshade gets from every burglary, mugging, bet, drug deal, and trick in the Chay, and it soon becomes obvious that Nightshade is one of the state's major corporations.

"You suppose they could make me up like a human?" he asked.

"I don't know. Probably."

"Why would I want to, man?"

"Maybe to see what it's like, to look through someone else's eyes, to walk in their shoes."

Danny's quick gaze fixed on me. "Is that what you're doing, man? Are you taking a stroll in slag sneakers?"

"Something like that."

He snorted out a laugh and leaned back in his chair. "Yeah. Maybe you are. You got your spots on for only a couple of hours and the cops hammer the shit out of you." Again he laughed. "But maybe you aren't. You're trying, but see, the Blues sometime thump the fehn sickies they catch hanging around outside the schools, not just the Tencts. You didn't get lumpy because you're Tenct, my man; you got it because you had your dick out."

"I did not!"

Danny held out his hands. "Smooth down, man. Just a figure of speech." He let his hands drop into his lap. "It's like this: a couple of bad looks on Ocean Park don't make you Tenctonese. Getting the shit kicked out of you by a couple of cops don't make you debah. Not in this town. You haven't walked my street; not yet."

"I'm here now," I answered. "What do you suggest?"

He raised his eyebrows at me. Danny Mikubeh never made a suggestion in his life. He gives orders. Danny grinned. The grin faded slowly as he pondered something. Danny looked out of a window facing the street as his eyes narrowed. "I got something." His grin became quite wicked. "Yeah. I got a suggestion."

"I'm listening."

"I think I'll take you on a stroll tonight down on The Place." He nodded. "Yeah, we'll go and pull those rubberhead rubbers over your bunions and see how they fit. If you live through it, you ought to get something to write about. Maybe you can do a book on the complete Tenct experience, Slagging on Five Dollars a Day."

He took me home to his mother's house for dinner. There was nothing strange about the food; no weasel jerky or roach croutons on the salad. He didn't reveal my secret to his family, and his sister Varina kept coming on until I let it drop that I was married. Mrs. Mikubeh was a very good hostess and cook, although very quiet. She seemed to make a practice out of not questioning her son about anything out of fear of the answers.

Her husband as well as Danny's Binnaum had been shot and killed the year before by a Korean gang during an East Eighth Street slaghunt. Immediately afterward, some of the unidentified Chay rode onto White Dragon turf, captured the shooters, and executed them by suspending them, one at a time, between the back bumpers of two pickup trucks: the left leg and right wrist over the chest tied to one bumper and the right leg and left wrist behind the back tied to the other bumper. When the cars are driven in opposite directions the suspension arrangement and length of the ropes causes the upper body to wrench about, breaking the back, just before limbs begin being ripped off. They call this "doing the twist."

It's amazing how much of this horror one can listen to and not vomit. It's even more amazing how many of these horrors never make the news, they're so commonplace. But it's just bangers killing bangers. Not really newsworthy. There are times when I wonder why the riots in this city are so far apart.

While dinner progressed, Danny's bodyguards stood watch on the house and at both ends of the street. Beyond the street was a network of eyes and ears that covered the Chay. Twice while we ate I heard shots. Both times one of the Shade came in, whispered to Danny, then went back out. Both times Danny faced the table and said, "It's taken care of."

Watching Danny hold court at his mother's dinner table while, at the same time, controlling the eyes, ears, scams, and forces of the Shade, made me think of Mario Puzo's *The Godfather*, and how every time a group is crushed by being set apart, cheated, humiliated, and subjected to brutality, a certain kind of defender is wrung from the ethnic pulp. Vito Corleone was a fictional representation of the original "Moustache Petes" that rose among exploited Italian immigrants. They are not heroes, for they add to the exploitation and abuse. They are, however, grass roots community leaders.

Talk about your worst nightmare. Among all of the gangs, fehn and Tenct, there are close to two thousand Danny Mikubehs in the L.A. area. Despite the public spin put on for the media, there is no desire among the police or the city or county administrations to end the warfare between the gangs. This is for a very good reason: if the gangs should ever make peace and join together, they would become an army of some ten divisions manned by hate-filled, tough, experienced fighters who think they have nothing to lose. There is no danger of the gangs getting together, however, so long as the "us" and "them" mentality governs what we call ourselves and, hence, who we will be to ourselves.

Danny took me for a stroll on Third Place. Danny and I walked together up front while Iron Roc, Sticker, Slice, and Tank were strung out behind, forgoing Danny's usual careful security. No one was wearing the pink. Instead they dressed down, civilian clothes. Just six unattached Tenct youths on the town looking for a little lethal excitement. We were fishing. What I didn't know at the time was that we were the bait.

The Place, as it's called by all of the gangs, is the southern border of the Indiana and Lorena streets triangle on the western limit of East L.A. "The Angle" lies between Nightshade turf on the west, the White Dragon and the X south of Lanfranco, and the Choya east of Indiana. Above the apex of the Angle, north of the Evergreen Cemetery on Bernal, is the southern outpost of the Jets. (I am not kidding, and yes, they took their name from the musical. Although they are exceptional killers, they can't dance very well. Anglos, you know.)

There is a sixth gang allegedly contesting the area: the Blue Crew—the LAPD. It is only alleged, however. There was no evidence of their existence on The Place that night. Third Place is where all of the surrounding gangs come to socialize with each other, push the edges of tolerance, and settle a few old scores without resorting to formally declared warfare.

"Here you can roam in some rubberhead Reeboks, Robb man." Danny nodded his head toward the street where the colors, strangely enough, weren't at each other's throats. A group of five Choya, flashing their bright green, was holding up a wall outside a liquor store actually laughing with and talking to three Jets, who wore black with orange blazes on their backs. Each of the Jets wore one black sock and one orange sock ("When you're a Jet you're a Jet all the way . . .").

A closer look, however, showed Choya and Jet lookouts between buildings and on rooftops keeping a close watch on the social scene in front of the liquor store. An even closer look revealed sentinels for the X, the Dragon, and the Shade. There were platoons of reaction raiders waiting in the wings for the signal to launch.

A wrong word, a rude gesture, a suspicious move. None of these were on The Place. Everyone was very polite, except to the few *T*enctonese who were on the street. All of the fehn gangs had become an "us" by making the *T*encts the "them."

"Now, check this," said Danny. "Before the crash, the newcomers were the Koreans, Viets, and Bozzies. *T*he day they let the *T*encts out of the quarantine camps, though, the White Dragon, the Deltas, and the Splits organized to keep us down and out. Suddenly they were the natives and we were the invasion." His train of thought was interrupted by something he saw. Suddenly he raised his hand and pointed. "Scan the man, Stan. I thought we'd have to hang half the night, but here they are."

At *T*urd & *T*urd (where *T*hird Place and *T*hird Street intersect), a big red Dodge 4 x 4, its roof rowed with headlights, came roaring onto *T*he Place. *T*here were three fehn in the cab and four more in the bed. *T*he one in the passenger seat and the four in the bed of the truck all had weapons. *T*hey weren't carrying colors and were ethnically diverse. Red and yellow, black and white, they are assholes in his sight. My God, Goober, it was you and your alcoholic buddies after a hard day at the plant out on a slaghunt.

*T*here must be a new name for this emotion that exploded inside me; this incredible compound of rage and terror. I could see them all: Choya, White Dragon, Jets, and X; Hispan, Asian, Anglo, and Afro, and they were all watching. No one was running and hiding, save the *T*encts: the homeless, the meek, the dispossessed, the addicted, and the Nightshade. *T*argets all. No one was the least little bit concerned about being shot, except for the *T*encts. Whitey and the Latinos were hanging together, the blacks and the Koreans, all of them watching rubberhead catch it. *T*hey weren't the ones I was the most angry at, however. I was ripped at the Shade. Danny Mikubeh had made me a goddamned duck in his personal shooting gallery for some kind of bizarre object lesson. This was his mosey in another man's moccasins bit.

I turned to run west toward Nightshade turf, but Danny stopped me with a muscular arm. "C'mon, man. It's time to climb on the monster and ride. You want to see through Tenct eyes? This is it, man. In Technifuckingcolor."

Danny and his soldiers simply stood there, waiting, as the truck full of yahooing jerk-offs fired shots at anyone without hair, streetlights, store windows, and the halt and lame. (Joke: hey, man, what's that pink stuff stuck in your tire treads? Bubble gum? No. Slow slags.)

I saw a Tenctonese woman hit in the leg and a Tenctonese child struck in the chest. It wasn't just Goober and his buddies that were cheering, but all of the fehn on the street. "Get him, get him, get him!" yelled an X as the truck bore down on a Tenctonese male on crutches. He was missing a leg. Two shots hit him. One in his remaining leg and one in his back. His crutches went flying as he sprawled face down on the filthy concrete. A cheer went up from the fehn.

"Wait for it," Danny urged his companions. "Wait for it," he repeated. We were the only Tencts left on the street. Everyone else had either fled or was down and bleeding. The red Dodge wheeled about and one of the fehn leaned on the top of the cab and fired two shots over the cab. The first shot went through the window of the storefront behind us. Tank took the second one through his left shoulder. He looked like a mosquito had nipped him. Tank didn't let his gaze stray from the truck for a second.

"Now," Danny said calmly.

I saw him reach into his jacket and pull out a rather large automatic pistol. I turned my head and saw Tank pull a revolver from his belt while Slice, Iron Roc, and Sticker reached for their weapons. They all opened up on the truck at the same time. The windshield exploded, the man sitting in the middle caught a face full of shattered glass, the shooter leaning on the top of the cab was knocked back into the bed, and the truck jammed hard right and proved for all time that you really can drive on flat tires. One of the four in the back raised a rifle to make a parting shot, and caught at least two rounds in the gut. He tumbled out of the bed, landed headfirst on the pavement, and crumpled into a still lump. In a second the truck was gone, the street empty.

Feelings.

Victory, nausea, outrage, terror, guilt, exhilaration, hate. I had become a Tenct racist, instantly an anti-fehn, complicated somewhat by still being a fehn myself. The moment called for something, but I didn't know what. Goober and his friends went off to hospitals, rehabs, and other repair and burial facilities, as did the wounded on the street, all except for the lump that fell from the back of the Dodge and the little Tenctonese boy who caught one of Goober's shots through his chest. They both stayed until the coroner showed up. Danny and his friends went back to the Chay, and Ellison Robb went home to a place that once seemed part of a moderately understandable universe.

At home I couldn't sleep. I couldn't relax. The monster that had always been under my bed was now out in the open, and what to do about it? The aimless claptrap about jobs programs, money for schools, community groups, education, police training, and all of the Jesus-jamming everybody-love-one-another bullshit flying from countless pulpits made me choke, want to cry, hide my face in shame.

I don't have answers to anything. Gang violence, racism, the hole in the ozone layer, nothing. I'm beginning to suspect that no one has any answers. Hell. My job is to walk in those rubberhead rubbers and tell you about it. That's all. My job is to find the questions. Someone else will have to find the answers.

Incidentally, the official police report on the Third Place shootout listed the dead Tenctonese boy and Goober's dead buddy both as victims of a gang drive-by shooting. There were "some" reports of other shootings in the neighborhood that night, and no suspects. It got six seconds on one nightly news broadcast and nothing on the rest. My own newspaper gave it two and a half column inches on page seven, which also included eleven other shootings that resulted in three other deaths in the barrio that night.

Bangers killing bangers, sez Blue. Tough. And that's where the cops plan to leave it. Maybe that's where everybody thinks it's going to be left, but scan this, Goober:

I have what is called a photographic memory. I can draw every face I saw that night in detail from memory. I remember the make, model, year, and license number of the truck. I even remember who shot which victim. I have at my disposal the resources of one of the great newspapers of the world. Some of those wounds you and your alcoholic friends received that night had to be treated, and doctors and hospitals keep records. Your dead buddy has a name, a place he worked, a home, family, friends, people who know where he was that night, and with whom. It may take a little time, Goob, but I'll track you down.

Once you're nailed I can't say it will accomplish anything. The Tencts will still be down, the Chay will still be in there killing and dying, and the next crowd of Goobers will be frying out their brain cells and going down to Turd & Turd to smoke the slags. It will make me feel better, though.

CHAPTER 20

THE AUTHOR OF "Slag Like Me" was dead. As an automatic reaction the city used the writer's murder to once again try to kill itself. As Matt Sikes walked the city, trying to arrange a meeting with Danny Mikubeh, stores were looted and burned, people were killed, and those old enough to have been through it all before wept. A meeting was arranged, and as Matt waited, there was a light drizzle as the fog rolled in on the Chay, making the streets slick, but not clean, leaving the smell of wet ashes on the night air. The moisture was not enough to keep itinerant looters, eager TV reporters, and opportunistic clergy persons indoors, although it did lower the temperature of the violence somewhat. Perhaps the damp allowed a few to reflect on why they were doing what they were doing. After all, pondered many Tencts, Micky Cass was *fehn*. Avenging his death was a human matter.

Many humans, however, had a different view. Micky Cass, with his offensive column, was out carrying a banner for the slags when he died. Let the rubberheads take care of it. Curiously enough, none of the special interests had an interest. No one was really certain of Cass's sex or orientation, so women's and men's groups, hetero and alternate, were silent. No one was confident of Cass's race, so none of the ethnically militant groups had a comment. Cass's political interests had been gathered under no label, hence none of the political parties or organizations issued a statement. No one was even certain of Cass's citizenship, so none of the nationalistic organizations chose to go on record.

The mayor made a vague declaration deploring all violence everywhere in the world, and the President of the United States expanded this to include the universe, both known and undiscovered. Neither mentioned the columnist by name. The Author's Guild did hold a news conference to deplore Cass's murder, but it was a hot news day and no one showed.

One editorial in a Palmdale weekly observed that there was in the world not even one pro-human group, much less any pro-intelligent life groups. The ever-present problem, of course, was the standard for determining intelligent life. No one wanted a definition that excluded them. However, any working definition that didn't exclude the bulk of humanity was generally meaningless.

On a popular TV talk show, a teenager (female, black, Libertarian, Jamaican-American) stood to say that Micky Cass was a human being trying to do the right thing. For that reason alone his murder was an outrage. A large percentage of the audience hooted her back into her seat. After all, she had a very narrow slant on things. She was a she, she was young, she was black, she was neither Democrat nor Republican, and she had a funny accent. The test for intelligent life continued to go begging.

Still, at the closing of the third day of the mayhem, since no one's ox appeared to have been gored, save Micky Cass's, tensions appeared to ease somewhat, which was mostly because TV news blinked for a moment to look at a few other things. Hence, as the new Mobil refinery in Wilmington went up in flames, lighting the skies a hundred and seventy miles out to sea, city hall, citing peace in our time, decided against asking the governor to call out the National Guard. Even as the body count reached a new U.S. riot record, the networks were momentarily drawn to a farm in Ohio where a cow gave birth to a three-headed calf named Hueydeweylouie.

In sports New Englanders were again calling the home team the Red Sucks, and down in Homestead, Florida, a family whose home had been flattened years before by Hurricane Andrew finally received its insurance check from those friendly folks. The barrio and its flames fell through the cracks into page six.

In Slagtown, however, those with earnest business on the street were still at it. Nightshade and its Tenctonese allies were locked in battle with a ring of *fehn* gangs. The LAPD was patrolling the streets with maximum force, and as long as the killing was kept down to double digits and within the Chay, no one was very alarmed. The civil war had calmed even further to occasional sniping over newly established gang borders.

The power grid in the Chay and surrounding areas had gone down. That night Matt stood nervously in the dark on Olympic west of Rio Vista, the dull glow of flames against the sky toward the north. Two black-and-whites, sirens yelping, passed him racing east. He felt his buns tighten as the officers scanned him. He couldn't make out the faces, but he knew what the occupants of the speeding cruisers were thinking. Just outside the Chay, a rubberhead standing alone in the dark, he had to be up to no good. The Blues were running somewhere fast and scared. Otherwise they would've stopped and hipped his hop.

He knew why. In this part of town a badge was a target. Some TV commentators, several politicians, a few rap artists, and thousands of bangers thought those targets deserved to be perforated. Near the Chay a smart cop needed to treat any kind of colors as the enemy. And near the Chay, spotted baldness was the color to watch the most.

As the police cruisers were swallowed by the dark, a nondescript gray station wagon pulled up in front of Sikes. In the distance, its lights off, a second car pulled to a stop behind the station wagon but twenty meters farther back. Matt's fingers wrapped around the grip of the Beretta in his jacket pocket. The electric window on the passenger side of the station wagon wound down and a voice came from the darkened interior. "So, you're the big-time reporter jock in a rubberhead suit? Hey, man? Halloween is just around the bend. You gonna get a prize?"

"Are you Danny Mikubeh?"

"Hey, man! Look at the spots on you. Ain't you worried about taking a dip in some joker's HCl Jacuzzi? That's the acid test, you know."

"You're not going to believe this, banger, but I don't think you're funny."

A face appeared in the window. It was a very young face with fresh scars on the left cheek and above the left eye. There was not a hint of humor in his expression. *"N'ak hivek Mikubeh. Zirak nas tiruda Krakor."* With effort, Matt pieced together what Danny had said. "I'm leader Mikubeh. Get in and ride the beast."

"This car isn't that bad," answered Matt.

"You know about the *Krakor,* then?"

"I know what the word means. What'd you mean by it?"

Danny Mikubeh turned his head and nodded at the street. "I was talking about the night, reporter Matt Cross. I was talking about the night." He gestured with his head. "Get in."

"I didn't think you were going to show." Sikes climbed into the passenger seat and closed the door. Danny picked up the mike from the dash, keyed it, and said, "Let's go." He pulled away from the curb and followed the same direction taken by the black-and-whites. Matt turned in his seat and looked through the rear window. The second car was following at a distance of twenty meters, its lights still off.

"I know I said I'd take you up to Eagle Street," said Danny as he hung up the microphone, "but that's off for right now. I got to get back to the flames. If you want to come along, you're welcome."

"What do you mean 'flames'?"

"Where it's going up, man. Haven't you checked it out? There's a war going on in the Chay."

Matt caught himself about to say "Don't sweat it." He shook his head and said, "I don't care about Eagle Street. I got other things to do."

"Are you going to answer my question?"

"Your question? Which one?" A building engulfed in flames could be seen in the distance. It was too far away to tell if the fire department had arrived.

"You really a reporter come all the way down here to bring the light and truth to the great hairy public all the way out there?"

Matt turned his head and studied the young Tenct behind the wheel. There were all kinds of gambles. In a strange way, Micky Cass had trusted, even admired, the *hivek* of the Shade. The reporter cover no longer fit. Matt shrugged and looked at the street as Danny turned the car up Soto. "As far as I'm concerned, Danny, the Tenct and *fehn* bangers can blow the hell out of each other. It's less work for me. I'm down here for only one reason. I'm after the bastards who killed Micky Cass."

"You a Clark Kent? A reporter?"

Matt allowed a pause to fill the moment. "I'm a police officer." The leader of the Nightshade stood on the brakes and broadslid the station wagon into a complete stop.

"Cop? Man, I thought there was a bad smell in here. Is that your name, cop? Matt Cross?"

Matt allowed the breath he had been holding to sigh from his lungs. "My name's Sikes. Matt Sikes. I'm a homicide detective."

"Sikes." Danny's eyebrows went up. "Matthew Sikes? The *fehn* cop that teamed up with that *Ubi Dugi,* Sam Francisco?"

"*George* Francisco. He changed his name to George, and unless you want to mix it up right here with me, banger, I'd stop calling my partner names like *Ubi Dugi.*"

The gang leader looked at Matt for a moment, then aimed his attention toward the street as he turned the wheel and pressed the accelerator, once again heading the car north toward the Chay. "Man, you are either one badass cop or the biggest asshole I've ever seen.

What in the hell do you expect out of putting on spots and walking the Chay by yourself? You figure the bangers're all gonna be impressed and bend over 'cause you swingin' that big macho stick?"

"Why do you talk like that, Danny?"

"Talk like what?"

"Like a bad cross between Cheech Marin and Huntz Hall?"

"Who're they?"

"It's not important. What I don't understand is the way you talk. Micky Cass's notes say you have three years of college. Pepperdine, right? Journalism?"

Matt was gratified to see Danny Mikubeh's jaw drop. "There's no way he could know that."

"Because you went out of the Chay? Because you used a different name? *Mikubeh* means black, and you want to know how hard it was for Cass to track down a Tenct named Dan Black? Two phone calls, and that was because he misdialed the first time."

"So, cop, I've been to college. So what?"

"Have you ever heard of Edward Lear?"

"Lear?" Danny Mikubeh frowned and pursed his lips. "Yeah. Poetry. He wrote some children's stuff."

"You don't sound like you like it much."

"No kidding. 'The Owl and the Pussycat'? 'The Courtship of the Yonghy-Bonghy—' whatever the hell it was? I'm down on the block, cop, watching guns, drugs, racism, poverty, cops, and indifference turn little kids—Tenct and *fehn* both—into corpses, cripples, bums, killers, and junkies. You think I give a rat-fuck about an owl and a pussycat in some beautiful pea-green boat? What I care about is coming down on the Jets, the X, and the Dragon hard enough that they never ever think about crossing Lorena Street again. What's Edward Lear got to do with Micky Cass?"

"Somebody left a quote of Lear's on Cass's door-step shortly after he disappeared. The sense of it was good riddance."

"And so, I'm a suspect because I can read?"

"Maybe. Cass also gave your Goober hunt on Third Place a pretty big write-up. Maybe you didn't want your adventures reported in 'Slag Like Me.'"

"Ellison Robb makes me a hero and I toss him in the acid? That doesn't make much sense."

"Did it make sense to go down to The Place and hang yourself out as bait for the slaghunters?"

"He made me a hero, man."

"Hero?"

"Yeah. Don't you ever read the letters to the editor, Sikes? Man, when you read what the readers wrote in about the "Pink" column about me and the shootout, I could probably run for mayor right now and win."

"Right now, so could goddamn Saddam."

"Sikes, you know I was even offered a movie deal?"

"What are they going to call it? *New Jerk City?*"

"I don't know, man, but it was for enough bread even to impress me. It wouldn't make any sense to dissolve my relationship with Robb, so to speak."

"You're a real comic, Danny. I bet you have a great dead baby juggling routine."

"Cop, if you want to show a *fehn* what being Tenct in L.A. is all about, it makes sense to walk The Place. There's nothing like sitting in the center ring of a target to clear away the fog and sharpen one's senses."

"I wonder what that line would sound like in front of a judge and jury."

Danny Mikubeh laughed and shook his head as the car crossed East Eighth and approached the first of the series of underpasses leading beneath the Pomona and Santa Ana freeways. "Cop, did it ever flash on you that I got about the tightest alibi in L.A.? Look out the back window." Matt turned his head and saw the dark car following them, its lights still out.

"Your boys?"

"That's right. I don't go anywhere without Iron Roc, Sticker, and Slice. They can account for my whereabouts just about twenty-four hours every day. In addition to them, there's the almost constant surveillance of half a dozen snitches, undercover cops, and blue fuzz technoweenies. Where in the hell did I come up with the time to kill this Micky Cass and trot his body out to Barstow unobserved? And the acid thing. I wouldn't even know where to begin getting that stuff."

"Danny, gang bosses haven't changed since the days of Attila the Hun. You give orders. What you don't know or don't have, you take or buy."

Danny Mikubeh nodded. "Yeah, cop. So all you need now are a couple of witnesses who saw and heard me hand out the contract to Guido and Dr. Strangelove. It'd probably help to come up with a motive, too. Why'd I do it?"

"Do bangers need a reason for killing?"

"I do."

Danny glanced at Matt then returned his gaze to the street, twisting the wheel to avoid the burned-out hulk of a police van. "You know why I'm here, cop? You know why we're riding around together right now? There's a war on, the cops and every hair ball pack of jackals in the Chay is for crushing the Tenct gangs, and here I am giving the grand tour to someone who told me he was a reporter following up on the Cass killing. He turns out to be a cop, though, and a rather stupid one at that."

"Stupid."

"Yeah, stupid. You think I like being in the middle of a damned war twenty-four hours a day? Ellison Robb—this Micky Cass—was working to end that. You must've read his column on the slaghunt."

"Yeah?"

"Don't you get it? He set himself up, cop! I got your number, Goober? I can draw your face from memory? I'm comin' to get you and your alcoholic buddies, Goob? What kind of a damned road map do you need, cop?"

"We've been through all of Micky Cass's files. There's nothing in there about that night on The Place except for a couple of drafts of his column. No names, no numbers, no drawings."

"No kidding, cop. Look, that *fehn* in the rubberhead suit was so damned scared he wouldn't've recognized his own mother behind the wheel of that truck. He didn't get any license number and he didn't memorize any faces. Those are tough things to do when the lead's flying and you're trying to find a hole to pull in after you."

"What about his photographic memory?"

Danny grinned. "He was lucky if he could remember his current pseudonym from one minute to the next. Sikes, Micky Cass did the same thing with his column that we all did that night on The Place. He set himself up as a target. I'll bet you your killer is one or more *fehn* called Goober."

"You got anything better than a guess that the perp was one of those slaghunters?"

"Let me ask you something. There was a body that fell out of that truck. The body had a name. He lived someplace. Maybe he had a family, a job. We know he hung out with some stellar citizens. What've the few and blue done about tracking down his playmates?"

"That's not my end of the investigation."

Danny laughed as he shook his head in disgust. "Shit, cop, it's not *anybody's* end of the investigation. A body drops in Slagtown, and, well, that's the way it goes. It was just a couple of working stiffs cutting out the props. Boys will be boys. They were just shooting up a few rubberheads. You don't want to ruin a man's life over a thing like that."

"You finished, Danny?"

"Not near as finished as your so-called investigation, cop."

"Look, banger, every lead will be followed just as soon as the damned city stops burning down."

"Right. What do you got that says I did it, cop?"

Sikes raised his eyebrows and smiled. "A guess." He pointed toward the street ahead. "Where're you headed?"

"Fourth near Saratoga. A meeting with Rina Vatu."

"Hivek of Wolfsbane? Don't they have *fehn* members as well as Tencts? I thought Wolfsbane and Nightshade were big-time enemies?"

"When you got a choice between making peace with Wolfsbane or getting eaten alive by the *fehn*, you get tight with the Wolf."

"Fourth and Saratoga? That's deep inside your territory, isn't it?"

"It was last night. Right now it's on the edge of White Dragon turf. If the Dragon keeps going, it'll run over us in a couple of days."

There was a crackle of static and Danny picked up the mike. "What?"

The crackle came back. "Police officers coming up from behind."

Danny glared at Matt. "Yours?"

"No. Nobody knows where I am except for you."

He frowned for a moment as he thought about George. His partner knew he was going, but he didn't know where he was going to meet Danny. "No. Nobody knows."

"Get out your ID, hair ball. If they don't know you're a cop, cop, then you're in big trouble."

"Nobody's in trouble, Danny. Just tell Iron Roc and his boys to do what the officers tell them."

"Hey, man, you never heard of Rodney's Rule? Don't get out of the car. Even if it's on fire, don't get out of the car."

Sikes looked through the rear window and saw the blue flashes of the black-and-whites against the night. Danny keyed his mike and called to his lieutenant. "Roc, can you see how many watchers are on you?"

"At least two cars," came the answer. "Five thumpers in the one right behind us. I don't know about the other. Want us to split off?"

"As soon as we hit Seventh, hang right and head for—"

"No!" Matt interrupted. "If they run for it, they will be in for it! Tell 'em—"

"Man, if the cops get hold of me right now, the best I can expect is to spend the next couple of days lost in the system hopping stations! I can't take the time! I got a war to run!" He keyed the mike again. "At Seventh, go right to Marietta then start working your way up to Inez. Lose the cops at the school then meet me at the Breed Street Station."

Iron Roc's mike clicked. "Run free, *hivek*. Your signal, Danny."

They roared out from beneath the Santa Ana Freeway into a thick, oily cloud of smoke from several burning cars. Past the cars, Danny opened up and both cars were doing ninety by the time they reached the intersection of Soto and Seventh. "I hope you got your seat belt on, cop." Danny keyed his mike and said, "Now!"

Both Danny and Iron Roc climbed on their brakes forcing the officers driving the black-and-whites to swerve around them to avoid a collision. The police cruisers spun out as they lurched up Soto while Iron Roc headed east on Seventh and Danny swung left and went west toward Breed. As Danny's foot fell on the accelerator, Sikes was pushed back in his seat and the black-and-whites left far behind.

"Are you an idiot!" screamed Sikes. "You take off like that, and there's a whole different set of rules they go by! This is a riot situation! They can open up on you now with automatic weapons if they feel like it!"

Danny shook his head as he swerved the car around a school bus that had been rolled onto its side. "I can't believe you never did a beat down here, Sikes. You were hanging too loose back there on Olympic to have done your probies in Hollywood. Maybe it was before the Tencts crashed in the desert, but you've been down here before. You know the score."

"It's not like that anymore!" Sikes insisted. "We have new rules, better training. Hell, almost half the cops are women and Tencts now!"

"What are you, Sikes? Some kind of sexist? You never had the shit clubbed out of you by a policewoman? Get with the decade, *debah!*"

Up ahead were a row of flashing blue lights. "Ahead, Danny! Slow down!"

"Shit!" muttered the leader of the Shade. Danny braked, spun the wheel, and reversed direction. He jammed his foot on the accelerator, and the tires smoked and squealed as the car sped back toward Soto. More blue lights came at them from out of the

smoke ahead: a police assault vehicle and two cruisers.

Sikes pulled his gun from his pocket and aimed it at
Danny Mikubeh's head. "Stop this car! *Now!*"

"Man, you—"

"Now!" Sikes repeated, touching the muzzle against
Danny's head. "Slow down and stop! Put this heap in
park and turn off the ignition. Open the door, get out
of the car slowly, raise your hands, clasp your fingers
behind your head, and stand still. When an officer
tells you to do something, don't give him any shit. Just
do it. Just do it and no one'll get hurt."

The car slowed to a stop and Danny killed the
engine and put the car in park. He raised his eyebrows
and smiled at Sikes. "And now the lesson begins."

As Danny opened the door and stepped out of the
car, Sikes began putting his gun back into his pocket.
Before that could happen, however, the door on his
side was yanked open, a baton came down on his
wrist, and a rough hand grabbed his collar and yanked
him from the car.

"Down! Down! Down, rubberhead! Eat asphalt!"

As his knees hit the street, Matt looked up at the
woman and bellowed, "F'crissakes, you assholes!
We're—"

He felt a baton strike his back, and he realized that
he was rising from the pavement. As long as he was
rising, he wasn't in strict compliance with the police
instruction, hence a legitimate target for a baton rally.
Matt fell to the asphalt and tried to remain still as
batons struck his back and legs and then stopped.

"I got the piece," said a voice.

"Ridin' armed with Danny Mikubeh, rubberhead?
Tch, tch, tch," said a second voice.

"I'm on the job, asshole," said Matt, reaching

toward his hip pocket for his ID. Again a baton came down on his wrist, a foot stepped on his head, grinding his face into the surface of the street. A hard blow stuck his left kidney and the tears came to his eyes as, for just an instant, he looked beneath the car to see four cops on the other side bringing their batons down repeatedly on the writhing shape of Danny Mikuheh.

There was a grotesque ballet that Matt seemed to witness from a place elsewhere. As the Tenct suspect struggled to his feet and tried to defend himself, five officers, one Tenct male, one human male, and three human females, swung their batons with regulation strokes, attempting to beat the suspect into submission.

One of the officers fell, and all of them turned and drew their weapons as a hail of gunfire came from the shadows. Matt saw his Beretta fall to the pavement as the officer who had been holding it grabbed his face and fell against the car. Matt reached out, took the weapon, and replaced it in his pocket just as a baton was brought down on the back of his head. The universe exploded and went very soft and dark.

CHAPTER 21

THE SMELL OF burnt rubber lingered in the air even in West Hollywood where only a few cars had been overturned and set ablaze. Sporadic gunfire signaled a few nervous shop owners and residents blowing neighbors and pedestrians out of their socks or mistakenly wounding or executing partners, employees, spouses, offspring, or house pets. One reformed NRA member, after being fired upon three times by nervous neighbors, went down to Melrose and torched a sporting goods store that was making a killing doing a cash-and-carry trade and to hell with the waiting period. Still, there were a few havens within the firestorm, even if their starting times had been delayed. Late that night there were words being read:

". . . There are no strings attached to NA. We are not affiliated with any other organizations, we have no leaders, no initiation fees or dues, no pledges to sign, no promises to make to anyone. We are not connected with any political, religious, or law enforcement groups, and are under no surveillance at any time. Anyone may join us regardless of age, race, sexual identity, species, creed, religion or lack of religion. . . ."

As he listened to the opening reading, Paul Iniko stood leaning with his back against the white-painted brick wall at the rear of the church basement, his eyes looking at the human and Tenct men, women, and children at the meeting. On an assortment of chairs and on the floor they were sitting, four and five deep in a huge circle. Many of the faces he knew. Some of them, however, were at the Narcotics Anonymous meeting for the first time, afraid they wouldn't be accepted, afraid they *would* be accepted.

Paul's thoughts were still on the fire outside and the things he had read in the "Slag Like Me" column. The hints—the magic words—had been in Micky Cass's writings. At least he thought they had been there. How much was design? How much was coincidence? How much was just plain wishful thinking? Had he thrown his career away over a guess, a misunderstanding?

Operating a slaver hadn't been a complicated matter. Neither Overseers nor slaves had been trained in subtlety or double meanings. Puns came hard to the Tenctonese. Yet there had been time enough among humans to see the things that had been hidden before by lack of experience and understanding. There were now Tenctonese who laughed or groaned at puns, who could see hidden meanings.

Paul was certain he was right. He raised his eyebrows as the next recovering addict in the room read "How It Works," including the twelfth of the Twelve

Steps, the step containing the clause that might have been used to lure Micky Cass to his death: ". . . we tried to carry this message to addicts. . . ."

Paul was certain, but too often his past certitude had been the signal that he was dead wrong about something. Luis had pointed that out to him more than once.

Paul scanned the circle of faces once more, looking for that familiar countenance. Luis Arévalo, retired California Highway Patrol cop and recovering addict, was not in the room, and repeated examinations of the occupants would not conjure him. Another opportunity to develop some patience. What a difficult thing for some to learn: patience. That familiar pang of guilt skittered across Paul's guts. He hadn't been completely honest with Luis in the past. That honesty might be the price to get the information he needed from his friend.

Paul's hand fell upon the empty holster on his belt. There had been something so very special to have been accepted in the FBI. Even when he had been paraded around as the bureau's token Newcomer. Even when the bureau had attempted to use him in its illegal cover-up of the MDQ affair. Even so, the bureau had been his cause to make Earth his home, his thread to make a meaning for himself. To every particle of that which he seemed to know, he needed to be in the FBI. And now what? Now that he was out, what would he do? Look for that slot wearing a peppermint-striped paper hat bucketing squirrel nuggets at Bucky McBeaver's?

Two faces came in from the church's kitchen carrying cups of coffee. Paul checked them out but neither of them was Luis Arévalo. He looked again at the circle. The small meeting room was crowded with over sixty recovering addicts from the surrounding West Hollywood community. Iniko knew this particular meeting well. Its usual weekly discussion gatherings were considerably smaller, perhaps two dozen on a normal night. This was a special night, however. Elaine, Annie O., and Bad John were celebrating anniversaries. Sometimes Luis skipped the Tuesday meeting, but he never missed a sponsee's anniversary night, and Luis was Bad John's sponsor. He had to be here.

Paul checked his watch, wondering if the riots were continuing to cool down. It was a little after ten. Paul let his arm hang at his side as he shifted his weight from one leg to the other and leaned back against the wall.

According to the messages George Francisco had left for him, Matt Sikes had gone down to Chayville to follow up on a multitude of leads. The write-up in Cass's "The Color Pink" column had named a few names. There were the heavy hints in the column pointing toward "Goober" and his buddies, as well. The Chay was up in flames, but Sikes had gone anyway. No backup at all. *Nada.* Sikes had much of the same brand of courage as Micky Cass, even if he was not quite as flamboyant. Paul's first impression was that it was foolish courage. Childish. Tenct survival had always been along with the flow. There was the order of things, and survival demanded one's obedience to the order, even when it was clearly in error. He frowned as he amended his thought.

It was not so much obedience to the order; it was the *apparent* obedience to the order. So many times the slaves had bent every effort to appear in conformance with authority while exercising little violations: stealing a little extra food, stealing a little extra time, failing to see someone else who was breaking a rule. Even the watchers would go around a rule and cover it up with an obscure reference or a cryptic entry on a computer report when the rules made progress on an investigation impossible. Sometimes there were even more serious violations. Slaves had occasionally killed Overseers. Watchers had sometimes ignored it because the victims themselves were murderers by a different standard of justice—the justice of the hearts.

Taking risks and going against authority were heady matters. It had been frightening enough for Paul to cause him to trust Luis Arévalo enough to tell the human that he, Paul Iniko, was addicted to zhabbies, also called zabs by humans, the synthetic street version of the substance used by the Overseers as part of the slave control system on the ship.

It seemed like yesterday. On the ship, long before the crash, a few of the Overseers decided to bend one of the rules. Their eyes blinded to the sole purpose of the drug, they experimented with it on themselves because it felt good. They would be careful. They weren't like the slaves. They were too smart to become addicted. Long before they became exposed to the concept of partying, the Overseers partied. The drug did what it was designed to do, and more slaves were created.

The combination of the crash, the destruction of the *zhabrokah,* and a new career in the FBI had temporarily kept Paul clean. But then zabs hit the street. Paul had run into the imitation *zhabrokah* at a friend's house at a time when he was feeling in need of a lift. He touched the blue liquid to his tongue and trembled as his slave chains were hammered back into place. It had been a brief, hideous plummet through shame, despair, and suicidal depression. The night-mare ended only when a former bust of his, a human named Federico G., brought him to his first NA meeting the year before. It was strange how the powers of the universe worked. Paul had gone to question Federico regarding his possible involvement in a crack lab, and he had stayed behind to learn. The former dealer had saved his life.

The reading of the Traditions finished with the reminder that anonymity was the foundation of the program; that without it, the millions recovering now through Twelve-Step programs would die. Paul knew beyond a doubt that he never would have entered the program without his membership in NA being kept from his superiors.

A huge human, swarthy and black-bearded, stood and began talking. It was Bad John. He related the chronology of his addiction from when he was sipping wine as a Methodist minister in Brookline down to when he was dealing crack off the back of a motorcycle in Boston's Combat Zone to earn enough to feed the dragon. Between using, dealing, and stealing, Bad John was trapped in the squirrel cage chasing after his high and trying to outrun his monsters: the law, his creditors, and withdrawal.

Bad John talked about going to L.A. on a geographi-cal cure, getting arrested for assault, and attending his first Narcotics Anonymous meeting in jail. He talked of how getting straight had been a rebirth for him, a chance at a new life. Iniko felt himself nodding as he glanced to his right.

Holding up a piece of the wall next to Paul was a slender young human male of about twenty. His hands were in his jacket pockets and his legs were crossed at the Reeboks in a studied pose of indifference. Although his face remained as still as cast iron, the fear in the young man's dark brown eyes betrayed him. Bad John finished his story and left the podium as the recovering addicts applauded. Iniko held out his hand to the young man. "Hi. I'm Paul."

In response the young man glowered for an instant, then looked flustered as he tried to pull his hand free from his pocket.

"Yeah, man. Hi. I'm Spence."

"First meeting?"

Spence gave a nervous grin as they shook hands. "I must have a neon sign on my head. I just got out of rehab yesterday. My aftercare counselor told me to come here."

Iniko gave the young man's hand another shake. "Welcome to the club. This is a good group and we need you."

The young human grinned widely. "Thanks. Thanks a lot. Paul was it?"

"Yes."

Spence's voice became a whisper as the next speaker took the podium. "I thought drugs was supposed to be a black problem. Aren't there an awful lot of white dudes in here? Asians? Tencts? Women? Look at all the kids. Thirteen, fifteen years old. That one kid looks like he can't be more'n ten."

"He's eight," answered Paul. "It's a very democratic disease." As Paul turned his head he noticed a familiar face making its way from the door at the rear of the room toward the kitchen where the group kept its coffee urn. Luis had shown after all.

Paul squeezed Spence's shoulder and whispered, "I have to see somebody. Keep coming back."

Spence grinned and Paul waved good-bye as he

began threading his way through the addicts toward the kitchen. As he did so he received waves, pats on his back, a handshake here and there. He knew most of the faces there, which was a piece of the guilt he carried. He knew them, but almost no one knew him, except through a rather convoluted indirection. That was one of the things he needed to change.

When he reached the kitchen, he entered the white-painted room and closed the door, reducing the sounds of the meeting to a dull mumble. In front of the coffee urn was Luis Arévalo, a toffee-colored paunchy man in his late fifties wearing tan slacks and a red windbreaker. His upper lip was crowded with a massive salt-and-pepper mustache.

"Luis?"

The man at the coffee urn looked up. "Damn, is that you, Paul?" His face broke into a huge grin as he put down his coffee cup. "Paul, man, where in the hell have you been for the past month?" He met Iniko in the center of the room and gave him a bear hug. "You go out to do some more research?"

"No. Nothing like that. It was just business that took me out of town." There it was again: the automatic half truth.

Luis held Iniko out at arm's length. "Why didn't you call me? I was worried about you. Hell, I even missed you."

Iniko shrugged and looked down, not quite able to look Luis in the eyes. "That's what I wanted to talk to you about. You mind if we talk here for a couple of minutes?"

"No. Let's go over by the sinks away from the door." On his way past the coffee urn, Luis picked up his cup. "You set?"

223

"Nothing for me."

When they were at the end of the kitchen the farthest from the door, Luis leaned against the edge of a sink and sipped at his coffee. "Okay. I've got nothing but time and ears. Let me have it."

Paul shoved his hands into his pockets and leaned his back against the counter adjoining the sink. "I'm at something of a loss, Luis. It's not that I don't know where to begin; I don't even know if I should begin."

"It's up to you, man, but it's like they say, you're only as sick as your secrets."

Iniko lost control of a giggle. "If you only knew how sick that makes me." When the giggle had finished running its course, he looked up and asked, "I need to know something about anonymity, Luis."

"Shoot."

"Whatever I say right here, whatever I tell you, is confidential?"

"Yeah. That's right. What you hear here, who you see here, stays here. Or as a group in Philly says, 'You speaka my name, I breaka you face.'"

"What if there was something that I'd done where I had broken the law? If I told you about it, is that confidential?"

Luis took another sip of his coffee, swallowed, and nodded. "You've heard people share at meetings, man. A lot of that stuff could get them into big trouble if it was carried outside. Our business is recovery. Squaring yourself with the law is your business. That's why the cops in the program leave their tin outside the meeting."

"I have to be certain."

Luis held out his hands. "All I can do is give you my word that whatever you tell me goes no further." He placed his coffee cup on the counter and folded his arms. "Paul, without anonymity the Twelve-Step programs like AA, OA, and Narcotics Anonymous would collapse overnight. To recover we have to get our issues out so they can be dealt with. To do that we have to be able to count on not finding our stories in the headlines or on a police blotter the next morning. If you've broken the law, that's between you, your conscience, and the law. Between you and me we have to have trust. Now, what is it?"

Iniko thought for a long moment and then began. "Only part of it's about me." He pulled up his sleeve and then smiled as he remembered he no longer had the tattoo.

"Had it removed, huh?"

Paul's eyebrows went up. "You knew?"

"I guessed. Hell, man, out of all the Tenct brothers and sisters in there, you're the only one who never shared anything about before the crash."

"And it doesn't change anything?"

"I'm still here."

Paul nodded and raised his eyebrows. "There's just one other thing I didn't tell anyone. Up until a little while ago, I was an agent with the FBI."

"Well, the way you always showed wearing a suit and tie, you were either a fed or a lawyer, and you're way too nice to be a lawyer." Luis grinned. "Don't go hide your face in shame over it, Paul. We got all kinds of cops in the program; everything from guards at the mall to Interpol. They leave their badges outside the door, though." Luis Arévalo paused for a moment, then frowned. "Back up a sec. You said up until a little while ago."

"Yes. I'm out."

"What happened?"

"I was asked to turn in my ID and weapon earlier this evening."

Luis sipped at his coffee and nodded. "Okay. I'm listening."

"You know the 'Slag Like Me' column?"

"We're burning down the damned city over it, aren't we?"

"I was part of the task force assigned to the investigation of Micky Cass's disappearance. I ran into a bind; something where if I followed procedure I might have to break the anonymity of someone in the program. That's part of it."

"And?"

"From what Micky Cass wrote in his column and in some other pieces under different names, I thought I saw the program. The magic words."

"Easy does it? First things first? One goddamned day at a time?"

Paul nodded. "I thought Cass might be in the program. That would provide a possible explanation for how he was abducted. Luis, he got a phone call right before he left his home. Micky Cass kept meticulous phone records, yet he kept no record of that last call before he left the house."

"A Twelfth-Step call, maybe?" said Luis.

"That's what I think. Another recovering addict calls for help. Because of anonymity he wouldn't keep any record of a Twelfth-Step call, and he'd go if he could, wouldn't he?"

Luis shrugged. "If the caller was in the program, and if it was a Twelfth-Step call." He raised his eyebrows. "That's it?"

"I know it sounds flimsy. I've been looking into it,

trying to find out for certain, but I couldn't tell my superiors without breaking Cass's anonymity."

"He's dead, Paul. Even the program Nazis don't worry about anonymity once someone's dead."

"There was still my own anonymity to consider, too. Once the bureau found out that I was a recovering addict, that would be the end of my career. The bureau isn't terribly enlightened about the disease."

"I'll give you that much," said Luis.

Paul folded his arms across his chest and continued. "There were two other considerations, as well. First, if the task force had decided to investigate my suspicions, there would've been agents and police officers hanging from the rafters at every meeting."

"From what I hear, most of 'em could use a meeting."

Paul folded his arms across his chest. "Don't you think it would've put a bit of a cramp in our claim that we're under no surveillance at any time?"

"I was just kidding. What was the second consideration?"

"You know how Cass kept his sex, race, religion, and so on secret?"

Luis nodded. "So his stuff wouldn't be looked at as some group's slant on racism." He nodded again. "Yeah, I see it. The recovering junkie's view of human-Tenct relations."

"Exactly. If he was in the program and it became public knowledge, everything he's tried to do would become compromised."

"So, what can I do, Paul?"

"You know a lot of those in the program in this area. Was there a Micky C.?"

"I thought the feds pulled your ticket."

"That's right. I'm just a private citizen trying to piece together an answer or two."

"Yeah, right." Luis nodded, frowned, shook his head, and nodded again. "Man, you sure know how to put a strain on the Traditions. Okay, you're not a cop, you're in the program, and Micky Cass is dead. There was a Micky C. I've known him from meetings for years. In the last few months I ran into him a few times at meetings over in Westwood and Beverly Hills. Now, what do you expect to do with that information? Hang around meetings in the area and grill the addicts for anyone who might've had some contact with Mick?"

"I'm asking you."

Luis went to take another sip of his coffee but found his cup empty. He turned and headed back to the coffee urn. "Damn, son." He poured himself another cup and came back to the sink and leaned against it, his face troubled. "Paul, I got a boy in that meeting out there tonight, his first time since he got out of rehab. My youngest son."

"Is his name Spence?"

Luis nodded. "Yeah. That's what he calls himself. Did you meet him?"

"Yes. He looks scared."

"He's scared, all right. He finally heard the angel feathers and decided to duck in out of the shitstorm for a bit and see what getting clean can do for his world plan. He bought his first shit in the school yard when he was eight and in a year was dealing in the same place to feed his dragon. He's had another twelve years on the streets since then, and you don't keep up those three-hundred-dollar-a-day payments bagging groceries. Know what I mean?"

"Yes."

"Paul, I think we might safely assume that he has some old issues with the law to get squared away—possibly any and everything from mugging and B&E to murder. Now, me, I'd like to see this boy keep coming back, wouldn't you?"

"Of course."

Luis nodded. "It's more than him being my son. It's the same with any of them out there, including the cops in the program. I'd rather have them trying to stay clean than killing to stay high. Besides, if they want out of the nightmare, they deserve the chance to recover and to square themselves with the people they've hurt." He glanced up at Paul. "You want to guess at how long my boy will stick around if you start asking cop questions? Or even if he hears about you asking questions of other addicts here or anywhere else within a hundred miles by using the program or its meetings? Hell, buddy, you'd clear out the halls everywhere they hear about it. That's one hell of a lot of death, destruction, and mayhem to cause just to chase down one lead that may turn out to be nothing. Anonymity's bigger than you or me or Micky Cass, murder, or even that riot out there."

"It's not like attorney-client confidentiality or other privileged information. It has no legal status."

Luis nodded. "True. Without it, though, millions of us are dead."

Paul Iniko rubbed his eyes and let his hand fall to his side. "So, if it was a bogus Twelfth-Step call that suckered him out, Luis, how do I turn up the perp? There's still a killer out there. It was one of our brothers he tortured to death. It's triggered the bloodiest riot in L.A.'s history, and I want him. He's got a lot to answer for."

The retired highway patrolman lifted the hand not

occupied with the coffee cup and scratched the back of his neck. "Okay, man, let me think. Jesus, you get into more shit." He frowned and talked as the thoughts came together. "Mick had some time in the program, understand?"

"I'm not certain."

"Time. I mean, he was here when I came in eleven years ago. The guy knew what was going on; the ropes; the drill. What I'm trying to say is that he knew better than to go on a Twelfth-Step call by himself. He would've gotten hold of another NA to go with him. Did he make a call himself after the one he got?"

"According to his wife, there was just the one call, then he left. He didn't try to get in touch with anyone else. . . ." Paul's eyebrows went up. "But what if someone called him to ask him to assist on a Twelfth-Step call? Would he have gone?"

Luis scowled as he nodded. "Like a hooked salmon." He placed his coffee cup on the edge of the sink and thrust his hands into his trouser pockets. "Son of a bitch!" He shook his head and looked at Paul. "Don't even think about cruising the meetings to try and track down the perp."

"How else am I supposed to track him down?"

"I don't know. But, like I said, keeping the people in this program anonymous and free from surveillance is more important than who killed Micky Cass. If I have to dog your heels twenty-four hours a day and rat you out in front of every meeting you show up at, I'll do it."

"What do you suggest? I'm looking for someone in the program, right?"

The big man frowned, looked at a blank spot in space, and slowly began shaking his head. "No." He shook his head again. "No. I don't think so." He pulled a hand from a pocket and pointed at Paul. "Look, in a fellowship made up out of addicts of all kinds, you're going to run into an asshole or two. I'm not saying it's impossible. It's just not very likely. If you hang around the program long enough, you get better. Whoever pulled this stunt, using the program to kill someone, is one sick and sorry bastard. I don't figure Mick would go out Twelve-Stepping with someone he hadn't even met before unless there was something very unusual about the call." He looked up at Paul. "Where's his car?"

"At home in his garage. He didn't take it."

"Did his wife see him get into a cab or a car?"

"No. She didn't see anything. We checked all the cab records, and no one picked up a fare anywhere near his house that night." Paul folded his arms across his chest. "So, what do I do?"

Luis held out his hands to his sides, palms toward the ceiling. "So, I don't know, man. I'm guessing you're looking for someone who isn't in the program but knows enough about it to know about Twelfth-Step calls. He also had to be able to get Mick's unlisted number. Maybe the perp's an early dropout; just hung around long enough to pick up a few telephone numbers and a bit of the routine. Maybe it's a friend or relative of some blabbermouth in the program, or the perp might've gone to a few open meetings with a friend or relative to keep him company. Take your list of suspects and start shaking the tree for a druggie."

"You think the perp is an addict?"

"Not necessarily, Paul. But, whoever it is, he's had some kind of contact with the program or with someone who's in the program. Nobody shows up in NA by accident or out of a desire to be sociable.

Usually it's someone in a dead heat with the nightmare. Find the chemical, buddy, and I'm betting
you'll be on the trail leading to the killer. You run
across any addicts yet?"

"Three of them. The father of one of the children
Cass mentioned in his 'Policeman's Lot' piece, Cass's
next-door neighbor, and the cop from the first column."

"The one called Davenport?"

"Yes. Davenport's alibi was a doctor and his lieutenant supplied the doctor's name. He's a psychiatrist
who specializes in treating alcoholics by substituting
an addiction to prescription drugs."

Luis shook his head. "Diagnosis—acute Valium
deficiency. I take it this Davenport isn't exactly familiar with the program."

"You're right. His alibi isn't exactly seamless, but
dissolving someone in acid for getting a department
reprimand would be a bit of an overreaction even for
Davenport."

"What about the other two?"

"Both of them are into alcohol, at least. Maybe
other drugs, as well."

"Alibis?"

"They both have excellent alibis and neither one
has even a clue about recovery or the program—any
program." Paul held out his hands. "So?"

"So, keep looking. Your junkie is out there, Paul,
not in here. If he was in here, the city wouldn't be in
flames."

When he and Luis left the kitchen and returned to
the meeting, Elaine G. was sharing her story. Good
girl, sexually abused as a child, addicted to food,
moved on to diet pills, and the entire range of

over-the-counter and medically prescribed relaxants, tranquilizers, antidepressants, and sleeping pills. Her addiction had cost her a family, a home, several jobs, considerable physical and mental damage, and left her screaming out her guts locked up in a psycho ward where they introduced her to a whole new series of drugs with which she promptly fell in love. Then a sister of hers who was in NA dragged her to her first meeting putting her at the bottom of her long climb back to sanity. Throughout it all she had not done a single illegal drug. To thunderous applause, she picked up her two-year key tag that night.

Annie O., a Tenctonese addicted to zabs, shared how her immigration joke name, Ann O'Nymity, had eventually led her through her nightmare to the doors of NA. The name designed to shame and degrade her had saved her life. Annie picked up her one-year tag that night. As she did so, Paul felt the one-year tag in his own pocket. It represented a million battles and just as many victories. Later, the young man named Spence picked up his white beginner's welcome tag.

As they stood and formed the traditional closing circle, their arms around each other's waists and shoulders, one of the addicts read out the reminder of anonymity, followed by a moment of silence for the still-suffering addicts outside the halls of NA. While Bad John read "Just for Today," Paul looked across the circle to see George Francisco serving as an extremely uncomfortable part of an otherwise serene group hug. As the addicts said the Serenity Prayer, George mouthed the words to Paul, "We have to talk."

CHAPTER 22

YOU OKAY, MAN? *Baffa, pim vot niyim?* Hey, *debah,* we gotta get moving!"

An all-encompassing numbness, a mental syrup that stood between awareness and the raw edges of unbelievable pain. Not all of reality was menacing, however. There was light.

Sunlight? Morning?

Maybe it was some of that out-of-body near-death stuff they talk about on Oprah.

He squinted his eyes open just a crack and looked. The light. It was a building on fire. Several buildings on fire. Green flames.

Green. Green?

Green is pain.

And pain is pain whether or not it is felt. He remembered being taught that. He couldn't remember who taught it to him. There was a line from a song, "It's not easy being green . . ."

"No goddamn shit," he whispered, the effort sending pains through his eyes.

Motion.

Something was moving. He looked and saw wreaths of oily black smoke against the flames. The sky was blotted out, filled with a hairless head.

A man.

Tenct.

Greenish face looking down at him.

Tenct, chunky, scarred, bleeding that pinkish green blood. Flames going up; smoke coming down. The face began spinning.

"Nya ve! Nya ve!"

"I'm awake," he heard himself say in response, although he wasn't quite certain what it was that he had been commanded to do. The effort of talking brought on pain. Different pain. Pain that could be felt. His jaw hurt; his neck; the right side of his head; his back and legs, arms and wrists—everything.

His head felt as though it had been crushed. Sharp pains from his sides and back. His organs felt as though they were on fire. The comforting dark, the anesthetic syrup of unconsciousness, remained just beyond his reach. He heard himself moan as he once more opened his eyes and watched again the spinning face.

"What is it?" he whispered.

"Man, we got to move! The Dragons and the Jets caved in and the Blue'll be here in a couple of minutes! The Shade can't hold 'em. Without Danny and the Roc we're nothin'! Man, we got to move!"

There were footsteps and another voice. "Breaker, who's that?"

"Danny picked him up late last night. He was in the

car when the Blue stopped it. The cops did a thump on him, Hooks."

The one called Hooks squatted down and looked into his face. Hooks's face and spotted scalp were blackened with soot. In his hands he held a Micro Uzi 9mm. "Looks like a bit of hardball on him."

"Hardball, hell. Looks like the whole damned World Series took place on his face."

"Who is he?" asked Hooks as he stood upright. "I don't know him."

He felt hands moving over his body. "Hey, he's got a piece. Look at that. Nice one, too." Breaker went back to the search.

"Let me see." There was a moment, then Hooks said, "A Beretta. What about some ID?"

"Nothing. If he had a wallet, it's gone."

"What's that chain?"

He felt something tap his chest. "Hey, Hooks. Look at this, man. It's a press pass. He's got a press pass."

"What station?"

"Not TV. This guy's with the papers. He's from the *Times,* you know, like that Ellison Robb."

"He got a name?"

"Cross. His name's Matt Cross. I remember Danny saying something about this guy."

This guy.

Matt Cross, he thought. *This guy. My name's Matt Cross.* There was something right about it—something terribly wrong about it, too.

Right; wrong.

There was too much pain in his head to allow thought.

Matt Cross.

Who?

Issues for another time.

"Another *nugah?*" asked Hooks.

"I don't know, man. He sure looks *debah* to me. If he's *fehn,* plastic man did one hell of a job on him."

"Get him up. We got to get off the street."

"No," mumbled the one called Matt Cross. He felt them try and lift his arms. "No. Don't. Please. I hurt. Hurt too much. Can't move."

Hooks squatted down. He was clad in a ripped Shade jacket, the neon pink muted by the ashes of the Chay. "Matt? Hey, Matt Cross? Earth to Matt. Earth to Matt."

"What?"

"Man, I don't know if you're *debah* or *fehn,* but right now you're beat up, bald, spotted, and sittin' in the middle of a pile of dead Blues."

"Cops? Dead cops?" A strange terror streaked through his chest. Beyond the face of Hooks, in the street were a number of bodies. There were Newcomers. Bangers and bums from the looks of them. And humans in blue riot gear. Two, three of them women. By the wreck of a smashed and burned gray station wagon were two more Tencts. One wearing blue, the other was Danny Mikubeh. "Dead?"

"Man, when the Blue gets here, they're gonna waste the slags and put the pieces together *mañana.* You got me, *debah?*"

The second Tenct held up the Beretta in front of his face. "Maybe some of those cops got dead with this? Hey, man?"

"No. *No.*"

"If the Blue gets here before you're gone, Matty boyo, the next thing you're going to *mira* is snoozo *grande.* You got to move! Now! *Wakaru? Xianzai!*"

The mix of street English, Tenct, Spanish, Japanese, and Chinese made Matt's head reel. He looked down at the blue plastic press ID suspended from his neck by a thin chain. The photo of a young Tenct male was on the front with the name Matt Cross appearing beneath.

Matt Cross.

Tenct.

There was something inside, working its way through the physical pain. A feeling. A sense that he had found the lead role in a horror flick; his worst nightmare coming true while all he could do was witness his own helplessness.

There was a line facing him: Freddy, Jason, Michael, the Alien, Charlie Manson, and the Thing. He looked at his own team, the L.A. Victims, and saw an endless chorus of scantily clad screaming girls, spilling eyes, intestines, and gallons of blood onto the Astroturf.

"Man," said a weirded-out voice, "What in the fuck is the matter with you?"

"I think I've seen too many movies."

Godzilla was calling the signals, "Tora, Tora, Tora!" Yamamoto snapped the ball to Genda, and Matt's team was Larry, Moe, and Curly playing patty cake, patty cake, all fall down.

There were flame-illuminated figures squirming in the shadows of his mind. The Blues bringing down their batons. Beneath the car, the look in Danny Mikubeh's eyes as the four officers brought their sticks down on Danny's struggling form. Danny's look was calm. It said something, the look did.

What did it say? I told you so?

I told you so.

"Danny. What about Danny?" he heard himself ask as the world kept spinning faster and faster.

"He's dead," stated Hooks, his voice breaking.

"The others? What about the others? Following us. Iron Roc? Sticker?"

"They tried to nab Iron Roc and his boys over on Inez. The word is they all died in the pile-up. Burned to death."

Maybe the look from Danny hadn't been an I-told-you-so. Maybe he had just been dead. *Then*, thought Matt, *that was the ultimate I-told-you-so.*

"Forget the honor roll, *debah*," interrupted Hooks. "There are way too many blue bodies out here and nowhere near enough slags to blame. *Nya ve!* We got to become scarce! Come on, Matt Cross. If it hurts too much, just pass the hell out."

He felt rough hands beneath his arms, lifting him up, away from the street, away from the blood, away from the flames and smoke. He looked at the reflection in the remains of a storefront window and saw a battered Tenctonese being lifted by two other battered Tencts. As he fought to stay awake, he struggled to remember his name. There was something wrong. Something terribly wrong somewhere. He just couldn't put his finger on what or where.

Matt Cross.

He fell through the floor of hell into the darkness beneath, repeating the name Matt Cross, panic in his heart because he couldn't remember who he was, where he was, nor even why.

CHAPTER 23

GEORGE DECIDED TO try one last time. "Let me put it all together, Paul. You think Micky Cass was a recovering drug addict?"

Paul Iniko, sitting in the car's passenger seat, looked over at George Francisco as George turned the car onto Wilshire. "That's your deduction."

"I can't come up with any other answer to explain your behavior. Why else would you be at that meeting?"

Paul shrugged and smiled. "It might be because I'm a recovering drug addict myself."

"Are you?"

"N'ak debah" he answered. "All Tencts are brothers and sisters of the chemistryhood."

"Even Overseers?"

Paul nodded. *"Zhabrokah* is no respecter of occupational status."

"Are you a member?"

"It's really none of your business."

"Then what about Micky Cass?"

"I think I've already answered that."

"You can't tell me you think Micky Cass was a recovering drug addict because of some damned NA club rule?"

"You're an intelligent fellow, George. How many times are you going to pick at this before you figure out I can't answer you?"

"I don't get it. If Cass was in NA, some people in NA must know. I didn't see anyone in there wearing a mask."

"You're right, George. If Cass was in NA, some people in NA must know."

"Well?"

Paul smiled and faced forward. "Well, what?"

"For Celine's sake, Paul! It's more frustrating talking to you than it is trying to get two coherent thoughts in a row out of Matt!" He held out a hand and shook it in time to his words. "If those people in NA know, you can tell me."

"Are you a member, George?"

"No!"

"Then I don't choose to talk about it. If that's all, you can drop me off here and I'll get a cab."

"Wait. Wait just a second. What do I have to do to become a member of NA? Develop a drug problem?"

"No, George. The only requirement for membership is a desire to stop using."

"Using? Using what?"

Paul sighed and said, "Whatever your substance or behavior is, George. Mood-altering substances, which includes old milk."

"Very well, I have such a desire. I'm in. Do I take a pledge or sign something?"

Paul faced George and studied his face. "No pledges, nothing to sign, and nothing to joke about, either."

"Can you do that, Paul? Can you refuse me membership?"

"No. But membership doesn't entitle you to everything I know." He placed his left arm up on the backrest. "Look, George, there's no rule protecting the anonymity of the dead, but there are still those who are alive. I've had it itemized for me rather clearly that badges running around the meetings grilling the addicts would cost more lives than any answers would be worth."

"What's your point?"

"George, if you agree in advance to do this with me and my way, we can compare notes. Otherwise, let me out."

Frowning, George began slowing down the car until it barely crawled. He glanced at Paul, returned his gaze to the smoking skyline and pressed down on the accelerator. "Very well. Your way."

"Turn around and head for Coldwater Canyon."

"Why?"

"We're looking for someone with a chemical problem, George, either a user or someone who knows a user. Someone who hates Micky Cass and knows enough about him and NA to use the program to kill him. Also, it's probably someone he knows."

"What about Duke Jessup?" asked George as he turned the car.

"No. He hasn't a clue about either recovery or a Twelve-Step program. We're looking for someone we don't know. Or, perhaps, we're looking for someone we don't know well enough."

"What about the FBI? The bureau can find out about anything they want, including NA."

Paul rubbed his chin and faced George. "I don't think so. I'm not an expert in government conspiracies, but I have learned enough about cover-ups to know that the preferred method of eliminating a person is a quiet disappearance and a fading memory. An acid-ravaged corpse displayed nightly on all networks in prime time triggering off a citywide holocaust strikes me as just a shade too stupid even for government work."

George hesitated a moment, then said, "Maybe someone else working with the bureau. It's not like the bureau hasn't been associated with disreputable parties before."

"The mob? The cartel? Forget it, George. Now you're talking *real* professionals. We're after amateurs."

"What about the *Ahvin Rivak?*"

"On their own, perhaps. I can't see anyone in the bureau foolish enough to cooperate with the *Ahvin Rivak* on something like this. It's not that they're too squeamish; they're just not that stupid. To hook the bureau to it, you have to explain the acid bath and the remains that were left on purpose. Who? Why? Toward what possible end? To see how many incriminating witnesses and pieces of damning evidence that can be left behind?"

There was a pause, then George's call signal came across the net. He reached forward, grabbed the mike, and answered the call. There was another interval, then Captain Grazer's voice came on. *"Francisco, you find Iniko yet?"*

"Yes, Captain. He's with me right now."

"Where's Dobbs?"

"He's following us," said Paul.

George paused for a beat and said into the mike, "He's following us."

"I'm following them, Cap," came Dobbs's voice over the net, *"and if I drive much faster to keep up, I'll have to give myself a ticket."*

George looked at his speed and raised his eyebrows. He had been doing almost eighty-five. He slowed down to fifty and spoke into the mike. "What is it, captain?"

"Understand something, all of you: we've got men on this already, so don't go ballistic on me. It's Matt Sikes. There were a couple of shootings in the Chay tonight. Shootings, hell. They were battles. On Seventh west of Soto nine officers were either killed or wounded along with five civilians dead. They found Danny Mikubeh's body. Sikes wasn't one of the casualties we found, but he'd been there. We found his ID on the street. Like I said, we got a team working on it, so don't freak. I just wanted to keep you posted. Francisco, where are you headed now?"

Francisco felt paralyzed as his hearts jumped at the news. His hands gripped the steering wheel as he fought the desire to turn about and drive into the ruins of the Chay. "Sometimes doing nothing is the hardest thing to do," said Paul.

"Say again, Francisco? George? Where are you headed?" asked Grazer.

"Toward Coldwater Canyon," answered George, glancing at Paul. "We were chasing down a lead."

"Okay. Keep chasing and don't let that civilian in your car get into any trouble."

George glanced at Paul. "I'll take care of him, cap. Keep us posted on the effort to find Matt."

"Will do. Do you still need Dobbs?"

"No," answered George. "We . . . I can handle the lead."

"Okay, cut Dobbs loose. I want him in on tracking down Sikes."

"Got it," Dobbs's voice crackled. *"Stay low, George."*

George signed off and hung up the mike. As he stared at the darkness of the night, he glanced at the rearview mirror and saw Dobbs's car do a U-turn and streak east.

There was a sight there and it made George sick. There was a rosy sky in the east, and it was too early for sunrise. "Paul, with all the death and destruction happening right now, I almost feel silly trying to hunt down one lone murderer. It's like trying to stop and arrest someone for speeding in the middle of the Indianapolis Five Hundred."

"Even Micky Cass knew the answer to that, George. He said, 'You do the right thing. Even if it doesn't change a damned thing. Even if the only point in doing the right thing is to have done the right thing, you do it—'"

"'—so you can say to the souls in Hell, "I did the right thing. What's your excuse?"' You read that note he scribbled on the outside of the gang banger file."

"Yes."

They rode in silence for a moment, then George asked, "Was Micky Cass a hero or an asshole?"

Paul sat silently for a beat, and then said, "Yes."

CHAPTER 24

"VIOT ATI, DEBAH."

Matt felt something shove between his fingers. A piece of paper. It felt as though his back and head had been crushed; the pain of his headache was beyond description. He could feel he was sitting. Nausea hovered closely, and he loathed the idea of puking in his own lap.

Opening his eyes slightly, Matt frowned at the mush of images: a row of faces, some bleeding, others frowning or in pain.

Humans.

Tencts.

Bright lights.

Figures passing quickly.

Others standing, sitting, waiting. Some on the floor, others in wheelchairs. With great care Matt turned his head and noted that he was seated in a chair, the edges of the wooden armrests cutting into his arms. He added together what he could and realized in was in a hospital emergency waiting room.

A Tenctonese female wearing jeans and an embroidered buff cotton poncho turned and walked toward him. In her hands she had a sheaf of papers all cherry red. There was a death pink strip of cloth tied about her head, and for some reason Matt couldn't identify, she reminded him of his mother. Perhaps it was the look of cold, bitter anger in her eyes.

Mother?

Mom?

He frowned as he continued staring at the woman. Matt couldn't remember his mother. His frown grew deeper. Neither could he remember himself. The pain from his head and body thundered into every particle of his awareness. He closed his eyes against it.

Trauma.

Bop on the head amnesia. He'd heard about that before.

How?

A doctor?

Nurse?

Watch a lot of television?

Matt. He knew his name was Matt.

No.

Someone had told him his name was Matt. Someone very tough-looking, very scared. Bleeding. Tenctonese.

Breaker?

Breaker and Hooks.

What had happened to them? They were the only persons in the world that Matt knew; that is if his name really was Matt.

He opened his eyes and saw that his chin was resting upon his chest. "Must've passed out," he muttered to himself. He looked down and saw the blue plastic press pass hanging from his neck. Vaguely he remembered the two young Tencts, gang bangers, members of Nightshade, picking him out of the carnage on Seventh Street. They must have taken him to a hospital.

What hospital?

In what city?

What had happened on Seventh Street? Why did everything smell as though it were on fire?

"Are you a reporter?"

It had been a voice. A close voice. He knew it had been directed at him because of the piece of blue plastic hung about his neck. He looked up and watched as the room spun about the Tenct woman in the poncho. She was looking down at him, at his press pass, actually.

"I'm pretty confused," he croaked at last. "My head."

"You're looking mighty lumpy, *debah*. Matt, is it? Matt Cross?"

Matt Cross. He knew that's what it said on the piece of blue plastic. His heart, however, didn't know the name.

Heart?

Hearts? Something was wrong. Something was wrong, but he couldn't find a clear track upon which to run the investigation. Whatever it was, it would have to wait.

"Your name is Matt Cross, right?" she repeated.

"Yes. Matt Cross."

"I don't get it. Did you change it?"

"Get what? Change what?"

"I don't get the joke. What's the joke in the name Matt Cross?"

"Joke?"

"You know, like Claude Balls and I.P. Daily."

Claude Balls. Some issues were simply too complex to unravel upon demand. What was the joke in Matt Cross? Was it true, someone had once asked, that if the Tencts had crashed into ancient Rome, they would've been named things like Chromus Domus or Dickus Maximus?

Jokes.

"There isn't any joke," he answered. "Can't think of a joke, anyway. That's just my name—Matt Cross."

"You'd think they'd name you Woody Cross, Chris Cross, or H. Cross Buns, at least. Maybe Matt Finish or Matt Ress."

"I'm just deprived. What's your name?"

"Li Sinritu."

"Lighten up, Li Sinritu." He frowned as he said, "That's a Tenctonese name."

"Very good. You're throbbing on all lobes, you are."

"What?"

"Nothing. The immigration officials named me Rosy Scenario. Did you read the flier?"

"Flier?" There was something wrong with asking questions; answering questions with questions. Matt felt terribly afraid, but he couldn't remember why.

"The flier in your hands." The woman pointed at the sheet of red paper. He squinted and read the headline:

SANJA AHVIN RIVAK!
SALAS, TANARAH, NAS MIRIDAH!

"I can't make it out."

Li Sinritu pointed at the words. "'Join those who would return. Peace, safety, and dignity.'"

Matt looked up at the woman, wincing at the pain in his neck. "Are you one of these nuts? One of these idiots who wants to go back into slavery?"

"I'm a member of the *Ahvin Rivak.*"

He waved at an empty chair facing him. "Sit down, Li. Please. Hurts too much looking up at you." As she sat down he held out the piece of paper, the fog in his head clearing not at all. "You're the bunch that wants to contact the *Stallahraj,* the creators of the Tencts, right?"

"We're urging the development of the technology."

"Even though it means going back to being slaves? Maybe making humans slaves, too. I don't understand that."

Li Sinritu studied Matt for a moment then stated flatly, "You're not Tenctonese."

"What?"

"You're a human made up like that other *Times* reporter; that Ellison Robb—Micky Cass, the one who was murdered."

Matt looked down at his hands as the room beyond continued spinning. *I don't know,* he thought to himself. *Hell, every time I think I have a scrap of information, it turns out to be wrong. Now I don't even know what species I belong to.*

There were sounds. Li Sinritu was talking.

". . . ship's computer records. I've seen them. Since my family line was made part of the ship's production unit, one hundred and nineteen males and females were born, wed, had children, lived productive lives, and died peacefully."

"It sounds really fulfilling."

"You want fulfillment, Matt Cross? In the few years we've been on Earth, half the adults in my immediate family have been refused work and the other half have been forced into demeaning and degrading occupations that make labor for the *Stallahraj* slave masters seem most satisfying."

"Lawyers, are they?" At the stony expression on the woman's face, Matt glanced down. "Sorry."

"I'll fill you in on a bit of reality, human. Compared to the ship, my family now lives in Hell, eleven are chained by the nightmare of illegal addictions, three have been victims of murder, and five of them have committed suicide. There are worse things than being slaves, *nugah*. If you want to know more, come to a meeting." She stood and walked off, handing out fliers to other Tenctarians in the waiting room.

"Come to a meeting," Matt repeated. An electric tingle skittered across the back of his head.

Come to a meeting. Keep coming back. That's what they told him all those months ago.

Matt. Keep coming back, Matt.

Matt Sikes.

Sergeant Matt Sikes, LAPD.

He closed his eyes as it all flooded back: Cass, the endless operations, Danny Mikubeh, the city on fire, the beatings and the massacre on Seventh Street.

All of the dead cops.

All of the dead bangers.

How it had felt to have a foot grind his face into the street.

The rage.

The look on Danny's face.

Matt coughed, a streak of pain fired through Matt's left side, and he heard himself cry out. He didn't know what was worse: the physical pain from his beating or the pain in his heart knowing he had gotten it from his fellow officers—that those officers were now either dead or wounded—that the city was burning down. Again.

"Shut up!"

He squinted his eyes open. No one appeared to be looking at him. "What?"

"I said shut up!" The voice came from behind. Matt turned around, crying out again from the pain. There was a human wearing a white lab coat. He was young with a great shock of black hair above large dark-rimmed glasses. He had a clipboard in his shaking hands and his face was bright red. "You fucking slags burn down and loot the goddamned city then come in here and whine about getting a little bump on the head. Look, I'll treat you crybabies because that's the law, but I'll be fucked if I'll listen to you rubberheaded bastards piss and moan all night just because you got what you asked for! So, shut the hell up! Just shut the hell up!"

The waiting room was tomb silent, both human and Tenct patients shocked into silence. The healer paused, turned on his heel, and stormed back through the emergency room doors. As a dreadful sadness overtook Matt, he used the chair's armrests and pushed himself to his feet. For a moment he felt the blood drain from his head. The moment passed, and he slowly limped from between the rows of waiting patients.

At the glass doors leading to the parking lot, Matt stared with unbelieving eyes at the skyline in the first light of morning. Columns of black smoke reached into the sky, reminding Matt of Saddam's spiteful farewell when his forces retreated from Kuwait leaving behind hundreds of burning oil wells. The columns of smoke rising from the city, however, weren't from oil wells. Instead they were from cars, buses, trucks, homes, businesses, schools, government buildings. How many of those dark pillars, he wondered, marked more dead. Before he had gotten into Danny Mikubeh's car, the riot-attributed death toll had still been under one hundred. Where was it now?

The Tenctonese girl had mentioned something about a meeting. Matt frowned as it brought something back. The memory brought another thing back and it caused him to blush. The blush was for stupidity, or was it a disease, he asked himself silently. Either way, how much of the flames and deaths out there were the responsibility of Matt Sikcs?

"Who are you?" He turned and looked at the speaker. It was the *Ahvin Rivak* worker, Li Sinritu. "Are you a reporter?"

"No."

"What's your name?"

"Matt. Matt Sikes." He looked back at the burning city, the memory of the faces of those in riot gear bringing down their batons on him—women, men, human, Tenct. Brothers and sisters.

The Blue.

"I'm a police officer. Homicide." Matt closed his eyes as he felt himself blush again. It wasn't just the mistake he had made, nor even its consequences. It was *why* he had made it.

He turned his head and looked at the Tenct female. "Li, I have a headache that can digest rhino snot, my side is on fire, I can hardly walk, and I think I know who killed Micky Cass."

"So?"

He squinted as he looked at her. "That's what I was working on." He gave a bitter laugh. "Yeah, that's

253

what I was working on when my brother officers dragged me out of the car, killed Danny Mikubeh, and beat the shit out of me."

"Danny Mikubeh, *hivek* of Nightshade?"

"That's the guy. You know him?"

"I read about him. In Cass's column, 'Slag Like Me.' The cops killed him?"

"Yes. The cops killed him." The images, the entire bloody ballet, flashed before Matt's eyes. "He was beaten to death. Yes. The cops killed him."

Li Sinritu pointed at Matt's face. "Cops did that to you, too?"

"That's right."

"Too bad you don't have it on videotape. You could be another Rodney King, go on the talk shows, sell a book, help start another damned riot."

Matt reached his hand up and gingerly touched his scalp with his fingers. The skin was smooth and unbroken. He looked at the button on his jacket and jewel on his ring. Both microcameras were still there and still undamaged. "I just might have it on videotape." He felt his inner face blanch as he said it.

"You're looking very weird, Officer Sikes."

"The whole massacre on Seventh Street," he said, "the police dragging me and Danny Mikubeh from the car, the beatings, Danny being beaten to death, the Nightshade wasting the cops. All of it. It's on tape."

He winced at the pains in his back and closed his eyes against the throbbing in his head. "Is there a telephone around here? I have to call in. Where in the hell is here, anyway? I don't recognize this place."

"All the lines are down, cop. I just tried calling home a minute ago. Phone lines, power lines, the works. The hospital's power comes from a generator.

Do they have generators and radios at the police stations?"

"Sure. Why?"

"Well, I imagine if you flashed your badge and got pushy enough you could force the hospital to let you use their radio communications system even though they'll probably have to let a few lives slip through their fingers while you chat with your buddies down at the blue sty."

Matt reached to his back pocket. "My badge. It's gone." He patted the outside of his left jacket pocket. "I still have my gun." Frowning, he looked up at Li. "The two bangers who pulled me in out of the street, they left me my gun."

Li rolled her eyes in disgust. "They're not all thieves and killers."

Sikes held up a hand. "Oh, these two were both: thieves and killers. First rate, too. Now that I think about it, though, they were both carrying better artillery than this. They probably didn't want to weigh themselves down with inferior firepower. God, one of them had a Micro Uzi. But I still don't have any ID."

"And in the middle of a riot, cop, with the bodies stacking up and every available resource stretched way beyond limits," said Li, "what would you do if a beat-up Tenct without ID staggers up to you, claims to be a cop, and demands to use the radio on police business?"

"I guess I'm not going to try the radio. Where is this? What hospital?"

"Lafayette Emergency Center."

"Yeah," he nodded, immediately regretting the gesture. "Lafayette. The new one on Wilshire. Near the park." He looked at the young woman's face, moistened his lips, and took a grip on a wall railing to keep from swooning. "Tell me, Li Sinritu, do you have a car?"

"Why? You going to commandeer it?"

"No. I couldn't even drive. I'm going to be damned lucky to make it to the parking area without passing out. I'd like you to give me a ride."

"Why should I help you, cop? You just got a small taste of what the police have been doing to my people ever since we arrived on this love-forsaken planet. I'm certainly not taking you to any damned police station."

Matt, still holding onto the railing, leaned against it and sighed. "Maybe. Maybe you're right. This place—L.A.—looks like hell right now. Looks like it, smells like it, feels like it—it is hell, wall-to-wall shit."

"You're not much of salesman."

"Yeah. I really ought to take a night course." He closed his eyes against the pain, waited for a wave of nausea to pass, then opened them again. The woman with the fliers was still there. "There are a billion things wrong with this city, Li, but I think maybe I can straighten out one of the tiny ones—take care of one detail if you'll help me. I think I know who killed Micky Cass. Something you said triggered it. I think I know who, but I don't know why. If I'm right, though, someone else is in danger. I don't want to go to a police station. I want to warn that person."

"What do I care about who killed Micky Cass? The *Ahvin Rivak* denounced 'Slag Like Me' when it first came out."

Matt thought for a moment as a wave of nausea came and left. "Look, Li, let's say everything goes just the way you want. The government throws the deficit-reduction program out the window and gets behind your effort to go back to slavery with unlimited funding and technical assistance. The entire techno-logical might of the world is dedicated to reinventing and assembling the communications equipment that will bring the *Stullahraj* hotfooting it to Earth. Let's say they don't enslave the human race, and let's say slavery is just the way you remember it when you were a punk little kid. You want to guess how many decades it's going to take just to make the components for the communications? And while you're waiting, right here on Earth is where you'll be. How do you want to spend the next thirty or fifty years? In the middle of a war with each side trying to out-stupid the others?"

"I take it back, Sikes. You're better at selling than I thought."

"Will you give me a ride? I'm asking. Maybe we can even stop a riot."

She looked around at the waiting room to see the cherry red fliers she'd handed out. They'd been left on seats, on the floor, balled up and tossed into trash cans. No one seemed particularly interested in the *Ahvin Rivak.* "I guess I've done all I can here." She faced Sikes and asked, "If I give you a ride and the cops try to stop us, I'm not going to stop. You understand me?"

"Yeah."

"I'll drive right through the bastards and risk pull-ing bloody badges and blue fuzz out of my grill before I pull over for any cops in this town. Are we clear about that?"

Matt looked into her eyes for a long time, then nodded. "We're clear about that. No stopping."

"Okay. Where do you want to go?"

He held up his arm. "Crutch me out to your car, kid, then you can drive me to Coldwater Canyon and sell me the *Ahvin Rivak* on the way."

Her eyebrows went up. "Do you think I have a chance?"

"Maybe. After today, a little vacation below decks pulling an oar looks pretty good."

CHAPTER 25

GONE.

It was all gone. Just an oily stench left in the air. What did it smell like? Kerosene? Lighter fluid? Gasoline? That's right. They were still trying to get the refinery fire under control between sniper shots.

What the hell.

Sitting in the dark of his den, Duke Jessup looked with dull eyes at the black and gray towers of smoke rising above the city toward the south and east, the break of day filtering through layers of dusty haze. He finished his whiskey, placed the empty tumbler on the corner of the end table, and listened uncaring as it tipped off the edge and fell to the carpet. It was silent in the room, save for the sounds of distant sirens, the squeak of someone with worn brakes parking in the turn-off outside. Duke shook his head in disgust.

The city burning down, armies of looters and killers roaming the streets, still the *turistas*. Hell, the riot was a better draw than the Universal Studios tour and Rat Town combined. With real bodies, too. Danger, adventure. Check out the amazing special effects. Tickets for the week, only twenty billion dollars, including free identification of your remains.

Duke wondered if he should check the locks on the doors and windows and put on the alarm. There really wasn't any point, he concluded. The alarm required a working telephone system and the phones had been an on-and-off thing for days. It didn't matter. There wasn't anything in the house he cared about, including himself. Lois would be getting everything in any event. Screw her, wherever she was. Screw her and the lawyer she rode in on.

That's right, he reminded himself. She's gone. Liberation day. He looked around and sniffed at the air. It was time to do something about that filthy gasoline smell.

He reached to his shirt pocket, took out a cheroot, and lit it up, allowing himself an especial wallow in carcinogenic luxury. As he puffed and pulled the sweet smoke deep into his lungs, he thought again about locking up. No point, really. He had locked up the day before and hadn't gone out at all. At least he couldn't recall going out. So everything should still be locked up, he reasoned.

Besides, none of the rioting or looting was taking place anywhere near the canyon. Didn't matter anyway. It was all gone.

Out there, the city. It was gone.

In the distance the sky was a reproach. The screams, the dead, the flames, the never-ending smoke. The city, all of those lives, the school, the marriage, the money, the home, the children, the life. All gone.

Somewhere along the line he had lost Duke Jessup, too.

Micky Cass gone, as well.

Too much to think about.

He picked up the remote and pressed a button. The dim red lights on his entertainment center stereo went on. After a pause the melancholy cadence of Siegfried's funeral music filled the darkness. He had played the Wagner piece many times, each time berating himself for the low production values of his wallow in self-pity, yet wanting to hear it one more time.

The music.

There was something in it that pulled at him. The piece began in sadness, but it moved to uplifting hope, even a possibility of victory. Out of death comes life, the end is the prelude to new beginnings, there really is a light at the end of the tunnel.

Then it perishes. The hope is fantasy, the victory illusion, the light the open door to the eternity of the underworld. Damnation. In the end it is the end. Death. That mournful cadence.

A squeal came from the sound system, making him sit up straight. The squeal ground to a growl and then silence. Duke Jessup eased himself back into his chair and muttered a quiet, "Shit!"

He knew what the noise meant. He'd heard it before. As he sat there the tape deck was eating his Wagner cassette alive. He should have cleaned the roller and capstan some time ago. It had been, however, too much bother.

"Ah, hell," he muttered. He took a deep breath, sighed, and shrugged. "It was an old tape anyway."

Fourteen, fifteen years old. Used to be important to

261

him. That was a long time ago, though. A lot of things used to be important, a long time ago.

He looked down at the roof of Cass's house. It was still dark. The Newcomer girl Cass had for a wife, Tian Apehna, had failed to turn on the strobe lights ever since Cass's death had been reported. She was alone in her house; Duke was alone in his. She probably missed Micky Cass. Jessup frowned as a truth worked its way through the haze. He missed Micky Cass, as well.

He barked out a laugh as he surprised himself with his realization: he missed Micky Cass.

No, he corrected himself. He missed hating Micky Cass. With Cass in the world, Duke Jessup was a cause, a warrior, a man with a mission. Without the irritating bastard, Duke Jessup was nothing but another bitter old drunk waiting for another lonely death.

"Ah me," he said to no one in particular. "Who would have thought it would come to this?"

Something below crossed his line of vision, hazy though it was. A gray sedan pulled up next to Cass's house and Duke watched as the two Tencts who had questioned him the previous week climbed out of the car and disappeared around the front. There was a third person at the back of the house doing something in Tian Apehna's rose garden.

Duke turned and reached to the table for his glass and found it missing. When he remembered it falling to the floor, he decided against looking for it and flopped back in his chair, wondering if he ought to turn on the air-conditioning. It wasn't very warm, but the stench from outside seemed to make the air seem very close.

He reached out, picked up the beautifully puckered

bottle of Haig & Haig, and took a long swallow. As the liquid drug burned its way down to his gut, he rested the bottle on his belly, placed his head back against the chair, and closed his eyes.

Murdered.

Micky Cass murdered.

The media and the police didn't know who, they didn't know why, but there was a hint about how. There had been a telephone call, not logged as usual, then he wandered out into the night without his car and was not seen again until his remains were discovered in that dry lake bed, eaten away by acid. "Once we have our who," an FBI spokesman had said with great confidence, "we'll have our why."

"And," said Duke, "once we have perpetual motion, we'll be able to tell you how it works."

What a bunch of bullshit, he thought. *What a goddamned fraud.*

Investigation, hell.

He opened his eyes and looked through the window.

Look at all that smoke, he thought. *It's not just me. Everybody thinks it's bullshit. They're burning down the city just to say it's bullshit.*

Not important, anyway.

Micky Cass is dead, dead, dead.

A shame, really. Cass could write after a fashion. The fashion's in your face, purposefully offensive, but never dull. When Cass was murdered, a light was put out making the universe a little darker. It had been a bright light. It hurt the eyes, burned the skin, blistered the mind. Even those who hated Cass and everything for which he stood suspected that it had been a necessary light.

"What a bitch," Duke muttered.

It was indeed a bitch. There were many things about

Cass that he admired. There were the things for which Cass fought, how he fought for them, his passion, his hatred. Duke shared many of the same sentiments.

Duke shook his head as an old pain streaked through his soul. God, he regretted taking Micky Cass to court over the stupid color of his stupid house. What a friend Micky would've made. Sharp mind, vicious sense of humor, the guts to act out on his revenges. What a loss.

Duke shook his head slowly as he realized that he missed the nightly light show; the sight of that huge neon eyeball flashing at him out of the night. In a perverse way, it had been a compliment. That someone of Cass's literary stature would spend the time, money, and effort, not to mention changing the look of his house, just to piss off Duke Jessup. That was a compliment.

A dim memory made its way through the haze.

A moment.

There had been another moment. It had been not long after Cass had painted the cycball on his roof and had installed the strobe lights. Duke allowed the feelings to wash over him.

Anger.

Rage.

It seemed like a hundred years ago. He had stormed down the slope and shouted at Cass over the white-painted brick wall that surrounded his property. When Duke finished ranting, Cass frowned for a moment. The way Duke remembered it, Micky Cass even looked as though he felt a shade guilty.

In any event, the writer took out a notepad and wrote something down. He then tore out the page, reached across the wall, and handed it to Jessup. The slip contained Cass's name and his unlisted telephone number.

Cass had said, "Jessup, despite the overwhelming evidence, and no matter how hard you try to convince me, I cannot believe you're an absolute asshole. You might be in trouble with a chemical."

"Don't be insulting!" Duke had growled.

Micky Cass had shrugged. "If you don't have a problem with booze or some other drug, then you are in really big trouble because that means you are an asshole and there's nothing anyone can do about that. If you do have a chemical problem, though, that we can do something about. Take a look at it. If there ever comes a time when you run out of answers and want to do something about it, give me a call. I know a few people and we can sort it out." Then he went back in his house. Those were the last words Cass had ever said to Duke.

At the time he had passed off the offer as a presumptuous invasion of his private life. However, the fact was right there, staring Jessup in the face. "He wanted to help me. He tried to help me."

Duke looked down at the amber liquid in the bottle perched on his belly. Oh, yes, there was a chemical in his life and it had him by the short hairs. But there wasn't any point in trying to help Duke Jessup. He was way beyond anything like help.

But what Cass had done had been a nice gesture. An exceptionally nice gesture, considering everything that had transpired between them. It had been such a nice thing to do, Duke couldn't allow himself to trust it.

He frowned as he tried to remember what he had done with the slip of paper Micky had given him. The day Cass had given it to him had been a confusing day. Of course, every day was a confusing day. Arguments, fights, a world of problems simply too baffling to comprehend, much less solve.

That day Micky Cass and his eyeball had been one turd on the heap too many. Duke had been almost blind with rage as he stormed down through his garden. Micky Cass, his nut brown tan and his Foster Grants, that eternal smirk on his face. Duke hated smirkers. They were dishonest put-down artists attempting to build self-esteem upon the rubble of other persons' feelings, hopes, and dreams.

But Micky Cass had wanted to help.

Dead. The police, the FBI, no one had a clue who had killed Cass. Maybe the gang members down in the Chay. Maybe some nut group like the *Ahvin Rivak.* Maybe even the FBI itself. Maybe the cops did it, or the man in the moon.

Absentmindedly Duke slapped at his chest and thighs in an idle gesture attempting to check his pockets for the note. Hell, it had been months ago.

He paused, frowned, and sat up as he remembered what he had done with the note. He had thrown it on the ground. A chill went up his spine and made his skin tingle. He sent the thought away several times, physically shaking his head to deny it legitimacy. Each time, however, it came back.

"Oh, God," he said. There was a two and another two. He took them apart and put them together a hundred times, and each time the result was a gargantuan four towering above the horizon.

"I know who killed him," whispered Duke. "Micky Cass I know who killed him."

The smell in his nose caused him to remove the cigar from his mouth and look at it. The coal burned softly in the dark. He sniffed again, and the smell was not tobacco. There was a flicker of yellow against the ceiling. Shadows of smoke cutting the light from outside. He struggled to his feet and stumbled over to the window. Below, in the patio against the house, a fire was burning. The whole base of the wall was burning. "What in the . . ."

He turned, went to his desk, and picked up the telephone. Fear made its way through his haze as he realized he couldn't get a dial tone. Dropping the phone, he rushed back to the window and was startled back as a rush of flames roared by his face.

He clamped the cigar between his teeth and opened the hall door. The window wall facing Cass's house was a sheet of flame, the double-glazed glass cracking from the heat. Duke ran to the other end of the hall and stepped into his wife's immaculately appointed vestibule, all of that pure white now reflecting red and orange from the flames at all the windows.

"Why should the looters have all the fun," he muttered as he dropped his cheroot in the center of that chaste floor covering and ground it out with his foot. He turned, went to the stairs to the lower level, and stepped back as he saw flames burst in through the glass doors below. A blast of heat like the breath of Hell came up the stairs. He turned and looked through the flames that were shattering the glass at the front window. Two very familiar persons were running toward the turnoff.

"Looters, hell!" he shouted.

Suddenly all things made sense. One more small fire on the edge of a holocaust would hardly be noticed. The fire department was already overwhelmed. The grass had been dampened by the rain, so there was no threat of the hills themselves going up. It was just one house. The fire fighters were trying to put out entire city blocks. By the time they could find time for Duke's house, there'd be nothing left but the chimney, some cold ashes, and Duke Jessup's fillings. It made absolutely perfect sense.

No route of escape was left. The pair who had set the fire knew the house probably better than Duke knew it. They wouldn't have left any way out. They'd know, too, how Mrs. Jessup had refused to have anything in the house as crude, red, and garish as a fire extinguisher.

Jessup looked at the stairs going up. There wouldn't be any jumping from an upstairs window. The murderers knew him very well, knew Duke's morbid fear of heights. He backed away from the stairs until his back was against the outside wall. As his hands touched the plastered surface, they jerked back from the heat. He turned and saw the white paint blister from the surface. A crack appeared at the top of the wall, allowing a single tongue of flame to lick at the ceiling.

The smoke coming up the stairs became thick and dark, forcing Duke to his hands and knees. It was hot. So hot. He tried to moisten his lips as another wave of heat washed over him. Sparks rained out of the smoke, igniting the rug.

Lois has been had, he thought. *She paid for fireproof and got squat.* It was too hot to keep his eyes open, too hot to breathe. He didn't feel it as he fell over and landed on his side, praying only to be unconscious before the flames reached him.

CHAPTER 26

THERE WAS A large dog named Spike. Spike was taking Sylvester's head and was smacking it with an anvil.

Blam! Blam! Blam! Blam! Blam!

Sylvester knew a secret. He knew he really wasn't a puddy-tat. Deep inside, beneath the teeth, claws, and fur, beyond the thufferin' thuccotash, he knew he was really Tweety Bird.

Blam! Blam! Blam! Blam! Blam!

Spike really shouldn't be hitting him because it was always Spike and Tweety against the puddy-tat. "Hell," said Tweety. "I guess I never looked at it through the puddy-tat's eyes."

Blam! Blam! Blam! Blam! Blam!

"Jesus Christ, Spike! Let up!"

"What was that?"

Headache.

The universe throbbing.

The roar of an ancient four-cylinder engine.

Matt opened his eyes and noticed that his head was banging against something. He pulled his head away from it and saw that it was a piece of glass. A window. Homes were passing by. A pooch peeing on a palm tree.

He turned his head and saw a young Tenctonese girl driving him somewhere. Li Sinritu. Her minivan. Coldwater Canyon. She glanced at him for a moment, then returned her gaze to the road. "Are you all right, cop? I couldn't hear what you said."

"It's nothing. A dream."

"It sounded scary. Are you sure I shouldn't take you back to the hospital?"

Matt grimaced and nodded his head gently. "It was scary. Have you ever been a canary inside a cat being beat over the head by a bulldog swinging an anvil?"

"My nightmares are more about being trapped in close dark places."

"Are you kidding me?" asked Matt.

"No. I hate being confined in small places."

"Isn't that what you and the *Ahvin Rivak* want to go back to? Flying among the stars packed into a sardine can with no windows? Kid, the slaves were jammed on that ship ankle to jowl."

"Don't you lecture me on the ship, *fehn*. I was there; you weren't."

"On the ship? What do you remember? Just how old were you, Li . . . ?" At the sound of her name leaving his mouth, Matt felt himself blush once more. He turned away and rubbed his eyes.

"What's the matter, cop? I thought you wanted to fight."

"At this point I couldn't arm wrestle the Pillsbury doughboy."

"Then what is it? It was something about my name, right?"

Matt held a palm to his forehead and said, "Look, it was nothing about *your* name. It is the name Lee, though. I did a stupid thing, made myself the wrong kind of blind."

"I do that all the time. Mistakes are just mistakes."

Matt let a bitter laugh escape his lips. "Yeah. But in my case the mistake might have let a couple of killers escape. It might even get a few more people killed."

"Sikes!"

"What?"

"Look up there, Sikes! Past that hill on the left. A fire. I'm not riding into any damned riot."

"There's no rioting going on in the canyon." He leaned forward and felt a chill as he recognized the area. "Quick! As soon as you get around that hill, take the next left."

As the van wheeled around the hill, Li Sinritu made the turn, bringing Cass's house into full view. Above it on the hillside, Duke Jessup's house was surrounded by flame, the stench of gasoline heavy in the air. "Look!" commanded Matt as he pointed at the car parked next to Cass's house. "That's my partner's car. Pull up next to it and run in. Tell George to call in the fire. Leave me the keys! I'm taking the van up to see if I can get Jessup out of there!"

"How do you know anyone's in there?"

"I'll tell you what I know, Li. That fire's got no point unless it kills Jessup! Debate's over! Get going!"

Up at the turn off, Matt saw a familiar pickup truck making smoke as it raced away from the Jessup house. "Go on!" shouted Matt.

Li pulled up in front of Micky Cass's house, put the van in park, and ran into the house. Matt moaned as he slid over, put the van in gear, and squealed the tires as he turned left past Cass's house and climbed it up toward the Jessup place. The pickup truck raced away in the opposite direction. Electric green mud flaps, One Day Perot bumper sticker, and all. Take that Perot sticker off and the sticker below would be the number one slogan of every Twelve-Step program from AA to ZA: One Day at a Time. The truck even had a load of scrap metal in it.

It was either let Jessup fry or go after the Lee brothers. "Hell, I couldn't do anything even if I could catch 'em."

The downhill side of Jessup's house was a sheet of flames, as was the east side. As he pulled the van around the turn and came abreast of the front, Matt saw that there was no way in or out of the burning building.

Perhaps it was already too late.

Maybe not.

Even though he knew he wasn't thinking very clearly, Matt knew there was only one way to find out for sure if Jessup was still alive. He stood on the brakes, backed up across the street and into the driveway of the house facing Jessup's. As a wave of light-headedness passed, he said out loud, "I wouldn't be doing this except that if Jessup dies in there, it'll be my fault." He nodded once and remarked to himself, "Just so we're clear on that."

He put the van in low gear, floored the accelerator,

and aimed the van at the huge picture window beyond the flames. The wall of yellowish orange heat came closer and closer, the front wheels struck the curb and bounced up. As the front of the van struck the wall and plunged through it, Matt's head was thrown forward, his head striking the steering wheel. He lifted his head as the world spun, and noted that he had stopped in a hot dark place of pearl gray before his eyes closed and he took the boat to La La Land, saying "I thought everyone had airbags in their cars."

. . . a baton came down on his wrist, a foot stepped on his head, grinding his face into the surface of the street. A hard blow stuck his left kidney and the tears came to his eyes as, for just an instant, he looked beneath the car to see four cops on the other side bringing their batons down repeatedly on the writhing shape of Danny Mikubeh. . . .

. . . a grotesque ballet . . . As the Tenct suspect struggled to his feet and tried to defend himself, five officers, one Tenct male, one human male, and three human females, swung their batons with regulation strokes, attempting to beat the suspect into submission.

One of the officers fell, and all of them turned and drew their weapons as a hail of gunfire came from the shadows . . .

"Are you okay? Hey! Are you okay? Wake up!"

Smoke, gasoline, and the smell of whiskey. Matt struggled his eyes open and saw a grotesque mask staring back at him. A puffy face surrounded by scorched straggly hair, eyebrows singed off, two soot black tracks on the face's upper lip led into its nose.

"Jessup?"

"Yes. I'm Duke Jessup. You saved my life, friend."

"Saved your life?"

"Man, if you hadn't run that truck through the wall, I'd be a two-hundred-pound Pop Tart. Who are you?"

Matt pushed himself up on his elbows and looked around Jessup at the fire. They were on the lawn across the street from the remains of the Jessup residence. Matt could see the marks his heels had made when Jessup dragged him from the fire. A *whump* sound from inside the fire followed by a belching black cloud spelled the end of the van's gas tank. A gray car blocked off his view. As it squealed to a stop, George, Paul, and Li Sinritu leapt out, leaving the doors open.

"Mr. Jessup," said Matt, "Thanks for dragging me out of there. I guess I really messed up the carpet. I hear your wife is quite a decorator."

Jessup chuckled and sat on the grass. "Don't worry about it. The rug already had a burn in it." He held out his hand to Matt and they were both coughing, laughing, and shaking hands as the trio stopped next to them.

"Matt, are you all right?" asked George.

Paul pointed west. "Did you see who it was?"

"What about my van?" asked Li.

Matt blinked and looked at George. "I'll live."

Duke Jessup said, "It was Jimmy and Harry Lee. My gardeners."

George pointed down the hill. "The walls and shrubs around Cass's house are soaked with gasoline. Matt, you must have interrupted them before they could touch it off."

"What was it?" Paul asked Jessup. "You wanted gardenias and they wanted nasturtiums?"

Duke shook his head and looked up at the former FBI agent. "I don't know. Actually, maybe I do know. I think I can connect them to Micky Cass. I know how they got his unlisted number. Jimmy Lee knew that Micky was in NA."

"How?"

Jessup looked down with a troubled gaze. "Because I told him."

"Okay."

"On top of that, a couple of years ago Harry and Jimmy both went to a few meetings. Harry was ordered to go to some meetings after his drunk-driving episode." Duke looked down at his hands. They were black, the backs of his hands blistered and bleeding. "Jimmy and Harry must have lured Micky out of the house by telling him I was asking for help. Micky said something to me about **my problem** months ago."

George frowned. "After all the grief between you two, he'd come if you asked for help?"

Duke nodded. "I think so." He looked up at Paul and asked, "I'm certain of it."

"I believe he would," answered Paul.

"I'll call it in," said George. He turned and walked back to his car.

"They have a police band scanner in their truck," said Jessup. "It's on all the time."

George nodded. "I'll keep it in mind." He continued toward his car.

"What about my minivan?" Li Sinritu demanded. "Where is it?"

Matt noticed he had something clutched in his right

hand. He opened his fingers and looked. In the center of his palm were the keys to the van. He held them out, shrugged, and smiled. "Sorry, Li."

"Sorry? Sorry?"

He pointed toward the fire. She turned her head and looked. She caught a glimpse of the van past the flames just before it plunged through the floor of the structure into minihell.

CHAPTER 27

MT. ANDARKO'S HOSPITAL. The Tenctonese physician's assistant deposited the syringe in the hazardous medical waste container mounted on the wall and turned to face those standing around Matt's bed. "He'll be going down to surgery in about twenty minutes and he needs to relax, so start saying good-bye and making your way out of here." When he left he closed the door behind him.

Matt lifted his hand and pointed at George. "When they recover that VCR in my head, George, I want you to make sure that tape doesn't get lost. I haven't figured out yet what to do with it. Until I do, don't turn it over to anyone. Understand?"

George sat in a chair next to the bed while Dobbs and Kirk stood at the foot of the bed looking down at Matt. "I'll take care of it, Matt."

"The all-points is out," said Dobbs, "and the roadblocks have sealed the city for the past three days.

277

Nobody's leaving town without running a roadblock. We've got every place in the city either one of the Lee brothers has ever been seen staked out. Sooner or later, we'll get 'em."

Kirk shook his head. "Don't bet on it. Things are supposed to be so quiet the roadblocks might be lifted day after tomorrow."

"What?" Dobbs shook his head and folded his arms. "Man, I do not believe this. There's a war going on out there, and they think it'll just go away by saying it's over?"

"It was all there right in front of me," said Matt as he fought against the anesthetic. "From that time I visited Tian Apehna and saw their truck at the turn-off, I had it all. I just wouldn't let myself see it: the bumper sticker, the mud flaps, the metal in the bed of the truck."

"I understand where the bumper sticker fits in, but what about the mud flaps?" asked George.

"Recycle for tomorrow," said Matt. "It's the slogan for that shithole, the Sierra Environmental Center. We see the billboard every morning."

"That's where Harry Lee works," said Kirk. "So what?"

"And what does the scrap metal have to do with it?" asked Dobbs.

"Galvanized iron and steel."

"What about it?"

"Dobbs, they recover zinc from galvanized iron and steel at that fifty-acre junkyard, the Sierra Environmental Center."

Dobbs held out his hands. "And so?"

"Hydrochloric acid," answered George. "It's done with baths of hydrochloric acid You knew that, Matt?"

As his head swam, Matt shrugged and held up his hands. "Hell, yes. It's the only thing about hydrochloric acid I remembered from high school chemistry. That and you don't want to use it for gargle. I've known that since I was sixteen, yet I couldn't see it."

Matt lifted his head and looked at the fuzzy images of his fellow detectives. "You know, I never thought of myself as a racist." The room was spinning and he placed his head back on the pillow. "Jesus H. Christ. I heard about two gardeners named Lee and assumed they were Chinese-Americans."

"When I questioned them," said George, "I knew they weren't Chinese. They're from Maryland."

"I only glanced over your report," said Matt. "I'd already eliminated them in my mind."

"They aren't Chinese?" asked Dobbs, his eyebrows raised in surprise.

"They're about as Chinese as Spike Lee and Robert E. Lee." Matt rocked his head back and forth. "I made myself blind. Figured they were Chinese-American gardeners, hence, very law-abiding and incapable of doing what was done to Cass, and no motive at all. I never even looked at 'em past that. Sorry. So stupid. So blind. So sorry. Hell." He swallowed and attempted to shake his head. "I still don't know *why* they did it."

In the ensuing silence, Matt slipped into unconsciousness, still cursing the wrong kind of blindness. After a minute, Kirk turned to his partner and said, "Dobbs?"

"What?"

"You know that junkyard?"

"What about it?"

Kirk folded his arms and bit at the inside of his lower lip. He thought for a moment, nodded once, and said, "I've been there a few times getting parts for my car. There must be twenty thousand abandoned heaps in the place. It would make a great spot to lay low until the roadblocks are pulled." He raised his eyebrows at his partner. "How about it?"

"Grazer already has it staked out."

"What did Grazer do? Peel off one or two bodies? The city's still on fire and shooting the hell out of itself. A couple of blues catching Zs at the front gate aren't going to be able to cover that yard. That's fifty acres of scrap metal jungle in there and a fence with more holes in it than your head."

Dobbs pursed his lips. "Think we ought to take a run out to the Sierra Environmental Center and see if we can find a couple of bushings to shaft?"

"Just my thought."

"Remember the police scanners," George reminded. "Use a security channel."

"Good thinking," said Dobbs.

"Iniko and I'll follow along in a bit."

Kirk faced the door, and he and Dobbs left the room as Matt fought his way up from his drugged sleep. "Geor—" he mumbled. "Geor—"

"What is it, Matt?"

"I know. I know why the Lees did it. Ohmigod. His picture on the book. Tian. The balcony, George. They were on the balcony."

"Why, Matt? Why did they do it?" He shook Matt's arm. "'Matt?" His partner was in absolute elsewhere.

The physician's assistant entered the room, walked over to Matt, and said to George, "You have to go now. You can wait in the visitors' lounge if you want, but he won't be able to see anyone until much later, possibly tomorrow."

George grimaced, got to his feet, and said, "No,

thank you. I have to see a man about a bath. Did you see my companion?"

"Mr. Iniko?"

"Yes."

"He just came down from the ninth floor. I believe he's at the nurses' station."

"About the tape unit and the pictures of Matt, do everything exactly by the book. Two reliable witnesses, property bags sealed and tagged, the works. No mistakes."

"I understand, Sergeant. The photographer is standing by, and we'll take care of everything."

George took one last look at Matt, turned, and left the room.

CHAPTER 28

NERATI AVENUE, NORTH of the most devastated area of the Chay. Detective Jerry Kirk stood back and watched as Rick Dobbs talked to the two uniforms in the black-and-white. The overweight officer in the shotgun seat dribbled doughnut crumbs onto his tie and cocked his head toward the main gate of the Sierra Environmental Center. On the stylish sign flanked by rhododendrons, beneath the business name, was the slogan Recycle For Tomorrow. The place looked like a junkyard and smelled vaguely like sauerkraut.

"Nobody's gone in or out for two days," the officer said to Dobbs. "The bangers are trashin' the whole city. I guess that's why the bottom's fallen out of the junk market." The officer chuckled at his joke. His partner behind the steering wheel yawned, shook his head, covered his eyes with his cap's visor, and shuffled his ample ass into a more comfortable position.

"Enjoying the riot?" Dobbs asked the pair, the hostility radiating from his face.

Kirk turned away as he felt it again, this embarrassment, this need to explain to the uniforms that being hooked up with Dobbs hadn't been his choice.

Rasher, the fat cop with the doughnut crumbs, narrowed his eyes and squinted up at Dobbs. "As riots go, it's okay. The coffee's hot. The pastries could be a bit better, though."

"Next riot," said his partner, "Pizza Hut's promised to deliver."

Dobbs turned, poked Kirk in the shoulder, and stormed back to their car. "God damned blue frat lazy-assed bastards! A goddamned herd of dinosaurs farting through tubas could be camping out in there and they wouldn't know it. Ninety-five percent of the whole damned department ought to be run in for obstruction and as goddamned accessories!"

"Take it easy," said Kirk. "They're not bad cops. It's been a rough bunch of days, and Cass's murder is just one out of a hundred or more this week. You know how it is."

"How it is?" Dobbs stopped dead, faced his partner, and jabbed him in the chest. "How it is? No, partner. I don't know how it is. Why don't you tell me how it is."

Kirk held up his hands. "Look, Dobbs, you got that face on and there's no point in talking to you when you're like this. You're upset right now, and—"

"Upset? *Upset?* Is that some kind of word substitution for rip-shit pissed angry? Man, I am a shitstorm shot from guns! I am not upset!"

Kirk's face flushed red. "I guess what I meant to say was, those two cops are on our side, Dobbs."

"And just what in the hell is *our side* concerned with that we recruited two damned compulsive overeaters to deal with it? A movement to wipe out the doughnut?"

Kirk felt the anger rising in his chest. "Dobbs, you ever think that maybe you're just a little too sensitive?"

"Too *sensitive?*"

"Yeah. Too sensitive. Half of you people walk around just looking for something to take offense at!"

"You people? *You* people?"

"Oh, shit," answered Kirk sarcastically. "I did a Perot. How politically incorrect can I get?"

Dobbs grabbed his partner's arm, swung him around, and pointed a shaking hand south toward the black clouds on the skyline. "Look there! There! And there! You see it?"

"Yeah, I see it," Kirk answered, pulling his arm free. "The world's had its face rubbed in it for a week."

"You got a clue, partner? You have any idea what's happening out there?"

"Of course I do."

"Yeah, right. You go ask Matt what's going on now that some cop ground his face into a filthy street and stuck a rib through his lung." Dobbs lifted his arm and stabbed a finger toward the south. "That isn't just a bunch of homeboys taking advantage of an opportunity to upgrade their entertainment centers looting the local Radio Shack. That's a lot of pissed-off people who're so goddamned outraged they just don't give a shit anymore—not about the law, not about what's right, not about what makes sense, not about anything. Unless we want to spend the rest of our miserable lives watching them burn down this damned city again and again until no one wants to rebuild, somebody had better start getting sensitive, Kirk. It's one of those decision times, partner. Somebody had better start getting sensitive real quick!"

Kirk, to his great relief, saw a gray car that he recognized approaching them from the direction of Huntz Street. He pointed and nodded. "Francisco and the FBI."

Dobbs turned and wrestled down his anger as George's car pulled up beside them. Francisco and Iniko got out and walked over. George studied both Kirk's and Dobbs's faces. "Are you two all right?"

"We're goddamned terrific," answered Dobbs.

Iniko pointed his thumb back toward the black-and-white. "Didn't you call for more help?"

"Yes."

"Well, is that all the task force could spare to put on this place? Are there more units inside and on the other gates?"

"Let me be the first to welcome you back from Disneyland, Iniko." Dobbs pointed back over his shoulder with his thumb. "Nobody inside, two uniforms out front in full view zoning out on sugar. On Huntz and Gorcey there're two other chain-locked gates the Lees could've gotten a truck through if Harry has a key. If they went in on foot, there are a dozen ways they could've gotten through the fence. To contain this place properly we'd need at least thirty bodies."

"On top of that," Kirk joined in, "that yard is fifty acres of nooks and crannies: junk cars, old appliances, military surplus, shipping containers, old boxcars, heaps of scrap, sorting sheds, warehouses—"

"So," said George, "we're shorthanded."

Dobbs thrust his hands into his trouser pockets and glowered at the ground. "Man, George, I'm back in that poker game again, and the blue frat is dealing Micky Cass out."

"Jessup said they have a police-band scanner in their truck," interrupted Iniko.

"So?" said Kirk.

"If I were in the Lee brothers' shoes, and if I had a scanner, I'd keep that scanner very, very close right about now. I'd want to know where the police thought I was, and what they were planning on doing about it. I'd also want to listen to find out when the roadblocks get pulled so we can make good our escape. That's what I'd do."

Jerry Kirk thought for a moment and looked at Dobbs. "They're keeping the truck with them."

"So, if they're there, they either went in on Huntz or Gorcey. That truck's probably all they got for wheels, too. If we plug up the gates and go in, maybe we'll have 'em. We'll at least put 'em on foot."

"Not with the size of that place," answered Kirk. "They could hide out in the trunk of some old wreck for days." He frowned and pursed his lips.

"What is it?" asked Dobbs.

"Partner, what if we got in there without being noticed, first, and then put on some radio traffic that sounded like three divisions of cops descending on the yard? Think they might rabbit?"

"Like Roger on Jessica." Dobbs nodded slowly. "Well done, Kirk. Sometimes *you people* aren't a complete disgrace to the department."

"I don't know, Dobbs. If I look real hard at that, it just might be a compliment."

"Fie, fie, my boy. It's only your weeks at the master's knee beginning to pay off." He looked across the street from the junkyard. "Over there in the liquor store. If the phone lines are still open, I'll call it in to Grazer and get the okay. Then Kirk will take our unit and plug the gate on Gorcey and go in from that direction. I'll get the doughnut debs on the front to plug that gate, play along with their radio, and come in from that direction." He looked at Iniko. "Can you take George's car, plug the gate on Huntz, and work the mike while George and I go in on foot?"

"If the Lee brothers are in the habit of listening to police calls, they'll be able to pick out someone unfamiliar with the codes and slang. If whoever drives is going to need to do that One-Adam-Twelve stuff over the net, George should do it. I'm not familiar with the vernacular." He smiled at Dobbs. "If you could let me carry your shotgun for you, however, I could accompany you into the yard while George works the radio from the gate on Huntz Street."

"Of course you'd be sure not to get involved or expose yourself to any risk or danger, civilian that you are."

"Naturally."

Dobbs looked at Francisco. "That's it, then, George. As soon as I talk to the sugar twins over there and arrange everything with Grazer, you and Kirk take your units, plug those gates, and move in. Then we'll see if we can get the Lee brothers to tell us why in the hell they killed Micky Cass."

CHAPTER 29

WITHIN FIFTEEN MINUTES of Dobbs's call to Grazer, enough trash had been put on the net to convince a pine post that the entire weight of the LAPD was about to land on the junkyard. At the little-used Gorcey Street entrance on the opposite side of the yard from the main gate on Nerati, Jerry Kirk hung up the mike and stepped out of the car, leaving the door open.

He walked around the front of the car and checked the lock on the chain across the gate. The combination of the car and the heavy chain made a formidable obstacle. No one was going to drive any pickup through there any time soon. He looked around until he found a sliver of metal. He tried it in the padlock and jammed it in the keyhole. Taking a rock, he smashed the metal into the keyhole making it impossible to open the lock with anything less than a pair of bolt cutters.

He tossed the rock to the ground and stooped beneath the chain. As he straightened up on the other side, he entered the yard. On his left was the concrete bed of a weigh station, the missing glass in the windows of the tiny operator's shack shattered out years before. On his right was a mountain range of military surplus items: stacks of crates, bins and piles of ducts, cables, wheels, tank parts, electrical components, and the flotsam from almost a century of military misspending. Crooked paths and roads separated the piles, making the yard a giant maze.

Straight ahead past a dirt crossroads was a two-story structure with a conveyor belt to its left leading from its squat tower to a peak of shredded galvanized metal. Behind the shredded metal was a block-long wall of galvanized scrap. The yard was closed, nothing moving that Kirk could see save the uniformed officer who was quietly advancing toward the center of the yard from the main entrance. Kirk looked around but couldn't see Iniko, Francisco, or Dobbs. More important, there was no sign of Jimmy or Harry Lee. The uniformed officer waved at him and Kirk nodded back.

Squatting down, Kirk allowed his gaze to explore everything he could see from right to left and back again. He listened as his eyes searched. The only sounds were the eternal sirens marking the city under destruction to the south. Inside the yard there was nothing. The strategy wasn't working.

His gaze moved again to the rust-colored building with its squat tower. It was easily the tallest structure within the yard. From there, he thought, the view might be more revealing. Since they had all agreed to maintain radio silence until the quarry was spotted, he left the handy talkie attached to his belt. Instead he withdrew his weapon and ran toward the structure, taking what cover he could on the way.

As he got closer, an acid smell tickled, then burned, the insides of his nostrils. That building was the yard's facility for recovering the zinc from galvanized metal scrap. When he felt the back of his throat and his lungs burning, Kirk hid behind the fuselage of some scrapped fighter plane. "Damn, but this stink hole must be violating at least a hundred federal, state, county, and city regulations."

He thought about the possible ways he could protect himself from the fumes but could think of nothing. It was a great place for the Lee brothers to hide out. They were probably in there, wearing respirators and some sort of protective clothing. They had probably allowed a sufficient amount of the HC1 fumes to escape, thereby making it impossible for anyone not wearing protective gear to approach them. Kirk backed away from the building until he could breathe again without hurting his lungs.

The plan came into his head. It was simple but should do the trick if the Lee brothers were indeed in the building. All that was necessary was to break radio silence. If they weren't in the structure, however, his plan would give away the entire charade. It would have been so considerate for one of the brothers to drop a wrench or otherwise give themselves away. Nothing but silence, however, came from the building.

"I guess this is one of those decision times," he muttered as he removed the radio from his belt and held it to his mouth. Pressing the key he said, "Commander Dobbs, this is Kirk."

"Dobbs here," came the answer.

"I have my men in position on the west side of the

zinc-recovery facility. The Lees are inside the facility and it appears they've released some caustic fumes. We'll need the SWATs with the special protective gear after all."

"I copy, Captain Kirk," came Dobbs's answer. "They're coming in the Nerati Street entrance right now. Be careful not to spook the perps before we can get the SWATs into position. They've only got fifteen or twenty men."

Kirk, preparing to issue an authentic Broderick Crawford "Ten four" into his talkie, went speechless as he heard a very powerful engine come to life. It was a roar that came from the direction of the zinc-recovery facility, the sound echoing from the metal mountains.

"That's no Toyota," said Kirk as a crash followed by the screams of tearing metal announced an ancient surplus half-track exploding through the metal walls of the facility. The half-track was painted a dull orange and it had been modified with an earth-moving plow mounted on the front.

"They're out!" Kirk yelled into his radio. "They're driving an orange half-track toward the Gorcey Street gate."

"I'm on my way!" answered his partner.

"Dobbs, that little chain and your car aren't gonna stop 'em! Get something down here!"

Kirk could see one of the two men, Harry Lee, tearing a mask and respirator from his face. As the man looked around, he spotted Kirk, lifted a pistol, and fired a shot at him. Kirk dived for cover, and as he hit the ground he rolled and came up bringing his own weapon to bear. Harry Lee was pointing up and was screaming at his brother. Kirk looked to the top of a mountain of military surplus crates and saw Iniko just as he jumped the twenty feet down into the half-track, a shotgun at the ready. As the former FBI agent and the suspect fell to the bed of the vehicle, they disappeared from Kirk's view. He turned, noticed Dobbs and one of the uniformed officers in the distance running toward him, but the half-track would be long gone before they arrived.

"What the hell," muttered Kirk. "It worked for the FBI." He weaved between towers of crates, streaked ahead of the half-track, quickly climbed one of the towers, and waited a moment as the vehicle approached. He could see Jimmy Lee driving the thing with one hand and trying to get a clear shot at Iniko with the other. George Francisco came running from behind a pile of crates and Jimmy Lee turned in his seat and sent three quick rounds in his direction. George dived behind another pile of crates as Kirk launched himself into the air.

Just as Kirk jumped, intending to land on the driver, Jimmy Lee looked up at him, raised his gun, and fired. Kirk felt the slug strike the heel of his shoe, but he didn't realize that it had entered his own flesh and blood heel until he landed on top of the hood. His leg collapsed beneath him and the top of his head landed in Jimmy Lee's face, knocking him silly, his gun falling from his hand.

Iniko had Harry Lee face down on the bed of the track. He looked up and, just as Kirk made eye contact with Paul Iniko, he heard the half-track snap through the chain and begin its climb over the top of his and Dobbs's unit. Francisco climbed into the cab, reached between the dash and the steering wheel, and turned the key, killing the engine. Jimmy Lee awakened, shook his head, and made a grab for his weapon.

Kirk pointed his gun over the steering wheel at the

side of Jimmy Lee's head and said, "When you straighten up, Jimmy, that better be a tube of Preparation H in your hand, because, whatever it is, it's gonna get shoved straight up your ass."

Jimmy Lee froze and did not move until Iniko finished cuffing Harry and had picked up Jimmy's gun. Francisco tossed Iniko his cuffs and the former FBI agent stood Jimmy Lee up and cuffed him as Kirk sang the Miranda blues to the two gardeners. "You are under arrest. Before any questioning you must understand your rights. You have the right to remain silent . . ."

"Forget that," said Iniko, his voice deadly calm. He took Jimmy Lee's pistol from his belt and held it at the back of the man's head. As the hammer was pulled back, Jimmy's eyes went wide.

"You can't do this!" he whispered. "You're a cop!"

"No. I'm just another civilian."

Jimmy Lee was as rigid as ice. George frowned at Iniko. The former Overseer had always seemed utterly devoid of emotion. "Don't do it, Paul. Don't throw everything away over this piece of slime."

Iniko shoved the barrel of the weapon between the cords of Jimmy's neck and said, "It's happening, Jimmy. Right now, here, to you. Everything you did to Micky Cass, everything you did to this city."

"Stop him!" shouted Harry from the bed of the half-track. "Stop him! The slag's crazy!"

Kirk raised his eyebrows. "Oh, that was shrewd, Harry. Astute. Why don't you call his *binnaum* a name, while you're at it?"

"I'm sorry! I didn't mean nothin'!"

"Please!" begged Jimmy. "He didn't mean nothin'!"

"Kirk!" came Dobbs's voice. Jerry Kirk turned his

head and looked down at the ground. Dobbs was looking up at him.

"Hi, partner."

"You know you're bleeding all over the remains of our car?"

"I'll discuss it later." He looked over at George. "Hey, Francisco. Maybe you should say a little something more to your buddy."

George pulled himself between the seats and into the bed of the vehicle. "Paul? What do you think you're doing?"

The former Overseer was silent for a long moment, a tear making its way down his cheek. "Well, George, I'm trying to think of a good reason for not turning the heads of the Lee brothers into applesauce. I'm not having much success."

"Pulping them isn't going to bring back Micky Cass."

"No."

"It won't change how they lured him out—the Twelfth-Step call."

"That's right," said Jimmy. "Look, man, Cass was just another junkie. I don't get what everybody's freaked about! He was just another junkie!"

George placed a gentle hand upon Jimmy Lee's left shoulder. "Stuff a sock in it, asshole." He shifted his gaze to Paul Iniko. "That's what's really getting you, isn't it?"

"It's a great many things, George. A great many things." As his hand began shaking he brought the muzzle of the gun up, lowered the hammer, and handed the weapon to Francisco. "But I am not to judge, am I?"

CHAPTER 30

FRANCISCO. This is the third interrogation of suspect Jimmy Lee in the investigation of the death of Micky Cass. Present are Sergeant Richard Dobbs, Detective Jerry Kirk, and myself, Sergeant George Francisco. This is being recorded. Do you remember your rights, Jimmy?

J. LEE. Yeah.

FRANCISCO. Then let's get started, shall we?

J. LEE. Sure. Look, I know I got nothin' comin' to me, Sergeant, but I want to do what I can. Who could've known that the city'd come unglued. All those people dead. All those trees and buildings burned. We didn't want nothin' like that. You got to believe that. All we wanted was that damned bastard dead.

DOBBS. We've pretty much covered what you did and how you did it yesterday. What we want to talk about today is why you did it.

J. LEE. You're kidding.

DOBBS. Look into my eye, Jimmy. Do I look like I'm kidding?

J. LEE. No, I mean you really don't get it?

FRANCISCO. Get it?

J. LEE. Man, I mean for months Harry and me are out there bustin' our humps making Mr. Jessup's garden into a showplace, and there that Micky Cass was in his ugly house, just sitting there. Sitting there in full view.

DOBBS. And?

J. LEE. And what?

DOBBS. You're telling us you and Harry killed Micky Cass just because you could see him?

J. LEE. No. No, that'd be crazy. Nobody kills everybody he sees. It's just that we could see him, you know, on his balcony.

KIRK. I don't get it, Jimmy. It was because he was on his balcony? He flip you the bird or something? What was it? I don't even think you're bent enough to kill someone just for sitting on a balcony.

J. LEE. I don't believe this. You really don't get it at all.

FRANCISCO. Enlighten us.

J. LEE. It wasn't just him or him sitting on his balcony. That'd be silly. You'd have to be really sick to pull something like that.

DOBBS. Go on.

J. LEE. It was his wife.

FRANCISCO. Tian Apehna? This is because he was married to a Newcomer? You hate Newcomers so much you'd do that?

J. LEE. No. Look, I even got a Newcomer girlfriend myself. I got nothin' against Tencts. See, it wasn't him and it wasn't her. It was him and her together.

KIRK. I'm still lost, Jimmy.

J. LEE. Maybe I'm the one who doesn't get it. Is this some legal thing you cops're doin'? Tryin' to draw me out so no one can accuse you of stickin' words in my mouth?

DOBBS. No tricks, Jimmy. You and your brother have already confessed to premeditated murder. That pretty much wraps it up for the DA. You and Harry have a date with a bucket of cyanide pellets.

FRANCISCO. We're just trying to understand.

J. LEE. Jesus. I'm really going to have to spell it out for you. Okay. I didn't want to say it right out because of him.

KIRK. Who?

J. LEE. Him. Sergeant Dobbs. You know.

DOBBS. No, we don't know.

J. LEE. Okay, I'll say it flat out! Micky Cass was black and his wife was white! Is that clear enough for you? That nigger'd be up there on his balcony slobbering his thick lips all over her and laughin' at us at the same time! Damned right we nailed him, and I'd do it again.

PAUSE: 32 seconds

DOBBS. What ever made you think Micky Cass was black?

J. LEE. All you had to do was look at him. He's got some white in him like they all do, but he was black all right. He even said so in his column, talking about doing the right thing and shit like that. Hell, he was almost as dark as you, sergeant.

KIRK. Jimmy, Micky Cass's wife isn't white. She's Tenctonese.

J. LEE. I'm not into word games, Detective. I saw her, she's white, and that's that.

KIRK. Jesus Christ, Jimmy! Can't you get it

through your thick skull? She can't be white! She's not even human!

J. LEE. What's the matter with you? I've got eyes in my head. They're white. They're all white. For God's sake, don't you have eyes in your heads? Any of you. It's as plain as the nose on your face. Can't you see?

KIRK. You sorry bastard. You sick, sorry, dumb son of a bitch.

CHAPTER 31

THINGS WERE GOING back to normal in the city. The murders, burnings, and lootings had decreased to pre-riot levels, the wind from city hall came hot and meaningless, and there was just a chance that the Dodgers might make it into the playoffs. The news was still chewing over the quotes from the Lee brothers' interview as to why they had done what they had done, and a subsequent survey showed that almost half of the citizens of Los Angeles considered Tencts to be "white." This, of course, induced a veritable olympiad of academic verbal masturbation on the subject of "whiteness." Down in the Chay and everywhere else in the city, however, "us" still hated "them," and "them" still hated "us." As the queen of the Slagtown news beat, Amanda Reckonwith, put it, "The preparations for the next L.A. riot are well under way."

Elsewhere, George Francisco entered the solarium

on the ninth floor of Mt. Andarko's Hospital and paused as he looked around. Beyond the potted palms at the far end of the totally glassed-in room, facing toward the east, Matt Sikes, in pajamas and bathrobe, sat in a wheelchair looking at the still-smoldering ruins of his city. George could see the ugly purplish yellow bruises on the back of Matt's neck. The doctor had said that, besides the bruising, Matt had had four broken ribs, one of which had punctured a lung, a three-inch-long depression in his skull putting pressure on the brain, and a damaged kidney that would probably take a long time to heal completely. The doctors were convinced that if Matt hadn't been covered with Realskin and his own skin cushioned by the underlying layer of imitation Tenct blood, he probably would have died from the beating.

George walked over and came to a stop on Matt's left. "The fires are almost out," he said.

Matt glanced up at George and returned his gaze to the city. "I was just thinking they'll probably never go out. They'll smolder awhile. Five years. Ten. Then they'll erupt again. How are you doing, George?"

"The question, Matt, is how are you doing? The captain's anxious to have you back."

A slight smile touched Matt's lips as he closed his eyes and shook his head. "I'll be back, George, just as soon as I can get a few things squared away."

"I don't understand. The doctor said—"

"It's not like that. Not my health. At least, not my physical health. That'll get better."

"Matt, there's all kinds of counseling available to help you through whatever trauma you suffered from that beating."

Matt Sikes frowned and looked up at his former partner. "I'm not talking about the Seventh Street

Massacre. I have a sickness, George. A sickness of the mind that makes me useless to the department, to this city, and to myself. I'm a racist, George—"

"Matt—"

Sikes looked up at Francisco. "I'm every bit as much a racist as the Lee brothers or the officers who beat Danny Mikubeh to death."

"Matt, mistaking the Lee brothers for Chinese—"

"You mean assuming they were."

"Even so, it's only a mistake. Maybe it's even a very revealing mistake, but it's not something by which you should judge your entire life."

Matt winced as he shrugged his shoulders and looked again at the city. "Last night I talked to Kirk on the phone. Did he tell you they tracked down the Edward Lear quote?"

George nodded. "Yes. An old calendar Harry Lee picked out of the trash at the junkyard. A negative saying for every day of the year."

"Us and them," said Matt. "We see a quote we can't place and right away assume that anyone who would use it must have some kind of specialized background."

"That was a mistake we all made."

"I can only speak for myself. I've been talking to Ivo Lass again. She's entered me in a *vo,* and I'm going to learn how to change how I see things. Then maybe we'll see."

"Partner, there are millions of men, women, and children out there who are making the same mistakes every day, and most of them on purpose. It doesn't make them right; that's just the way it is. You can't change other people."

"I can change myself, George, and that's all I'm trying to do." The corner of his mouth pulled back into a wicked smile. "And once I know what I'm talking about, maybe the department will decide to send all the cops to a special *vo.*"

"Not even in your dreams, Matt. The department would never—" George frowned as he teased something out of his memory. "The videotape. The implant. What have you done with it?"

"It's been copied and put together with eyewitness testimony and the records of all of the officers, supervisors, and policymakers involved. Kirk and Dobbs helped me put it together. Two reporters, that broadcaster, Amanda Reckonwith, a few of the boys down in the Chay, and a beautiful lady named Tian Apehna. We've put together a regular dog and pony show."

"If the media got their hands on that, it could destroy the department."

Matt nodded. "Or redeem it. And we have enough media types in on it to make certain it makes a prime time splash. In any event, it'll at least cost one hell of a lot of jobs. That is, unless the chief and the mayor can see their way clear to putting in the programs I want."

"Blackmail?"

"I believe the spin doctors call it leverage." Matt looked up at his partner. "It's time for things to change, George. We—the department, the city— we can't afford any more of this 'us' and 'them' feeding frenzy." He reached up and placed his hand on Francisco's arm. "I'm coming back, partner, but right now I have to do this."

"I think I understand." George studied Matt for a moment and saw that beneath the scars and bruises his partner was right with himself. "I have to go to work."

"Thanks for dropping by, partner."

George left the solarium asking himself if Matt was

simply risking it all for nothing. What if the entire police department went through a *vo,* learned that worth comes from within, not from artificial group classifications. What if the entire city went through a *vo?* The entire country? It would still be a small drop in a very big ocean of racist insanity where people saw things that were never there and couldn't see things that had stood before them since the slime coughed up its first bit of life thousands of light-years away in a now vacant part of the universe. All one can ever change is oneself.

He punched the button for the elevator and waited for a car. There was a loud laugh that came to him from one of the hallways, and he turned his head. A voice. A very familiar voice. He walked toward it, turned down a hallway, and listened outside Room 913. There was a conversation going on. He stood square in the doorway and saw Duke Jessup in bed. His hands were bandaged, but his face was sallow and beaded with perspiration. Even so he was laughing. Seated in a chair beside him, also laughing, was Paul Iniko.

"Paul? What are you doing here? Or is that another thing you can't tell me?"

Iniko faced the doorway and said, "Hi, George."

"I thought you were going up for your hearing today to get reinstated."

"It can keep. I had something to do first."

"And?"

"He's here for me, sergeant," said Jessup. He wiped the perspiration from his upper lip and held out his wet fingers. "Going through detox. I've got a problem with a drug called alcohol. Paul has been kind enough to . . ." Duke held out his hand and looked at Iniko. "Is it okay?"

"Sure. He already knows."

"Well, Paul has been sharing his experience with me, helping me to ride this thing out." There was a hardcover book on his bed with a blue dust jacket emblazoned with the circle-enclosed diamond of Narcotics Anonymous.

George frowned and nodded. "I'm sorry for interrupting. I'm glad to see you're getting better, Mr. Jessup. Good luck."

"Thanks, sergeant."

George backed out of the room and took a few steps toward the elevator, his face still in a frown. He paused in the center of the hallway and the frown grew deeper. George Francisco had his own way to look at the universe and the beings within it. Part of that way was that he was owed by the class of Overseers. He was owed his youth, decades of freedom, and endless sufferings for the fear he had lived in since his birth. He also believed that Overseers never laughed.

He had seen Paul Iniko laugh.

He believed that Overseers were heartless in the human sense: cold, selfish, brutal, unfeeling.

He had seen Paul Iniko helping a drunk by sharing his own shame and hope.

"Some programs take longer to process than others," he muttered to no one in particular. He turned around, walked back to Jessup's room, knocked on the door, and stuck in his head.

"Yes?" Duke answered.

"I just had a question I wanted to ask Paul." He shifted his gaze and looked at the former Overseer, former FBI agent. "Would you like to come to my house tonight for dinner?"

Iniko's eyebrows went up. "I think I'd like that just fine."

"Seven o'clock. Good luck at the hearing."

"I'll be there, and thank you."

As he walked to the elevator George recognized that, despite everything, he really didn't feel any different toward Overseers. What he was doing wouldn't prevent another riot, but still he was committed to at least straightening out his own perception of the universe. Matt seemed to understand. Maybe it was that old thing about lighting a single candle rather than cursing the darkness. Or maybe it was that thing about the program he heard Bad John say at the NA meeting: "Bring your ass; your heart and mind will eventually follow."

It would be a step. Perhaps even the right thing to do.